**ELIZA**
THE MIN

ELIZABETH MARY FAIR was born in 1908 and brought up in Haigh, a small village in Lancashire, England. There her father was the land agent for Haigh Hall, then occupied by the Earl of Crawford and Balcorres, and there she and her sister were educated by a governess. After her father's death, in 1934, Miss Fair and her mother and sister removed to a small house with a large garden in the New Forest in Hampshire. From 1939 to 1944, she was an ambulance driver in the Civil Defence Corps, serving at Southampton, England; in 1944 she joined the British Red Cross and went overseas as a Welfare Officer, during which time she served in Belgium, India, and Ceylon.

Miss Fair's first novel, *Bramton Wick*, was published in 1952 and received with enthusiastic acclaim as 'perfect light reading with a dash of lemon in it ...' by *Time and Tide*. Between the years 1953 and 1960, five further novels followed: *Landscape in Sunlight*, *The Native Heath*, *Seaview House*, *A Winter Away*, and *The Mingham Air*. All are characterized by their English countryside settings and their shrewd and witty study of human nature.

Elizabeth Fair died in 1997.

# By Elizabeth Fair

# ELIZABETH FAIR

# THE MINGHAM AIR

With an introduction
by Elizabeth Crawford

DEAN STREET PRESS

*A Furrowed Middlebrow Book*
FM19

Published by Dean Street Press 2017

Copyright © 1960 Elizabeth Fair
Introduction copyright © 2017 Elizabeth Crawford

All Rights Reserved

The right of Elizabeth Fair to be identified as the
Author of the Work has been asserted by her estate in
accordance with the Copyright, Designs and Patents
Act 1988.

First published in 1960 by Macmillan and Co.

Cover by DSP
Cover illustration shows detail from
*Vicarage in the Snow* (1935) by Eric Ravilious

ISBN 978 1 911579 43 4

www.deanstreetpress.co.uk

# INTRODUCTION

'DELICIOUS' WAS John Betjeman's verdict in the *Daily Telegraph* on *Bramton Wick* (1952), the first of Elizabeth Fair's six novels of 'polite provincial society', all of which are now republished as Furrowed Middlebrow books. In her witty *Daily Express* book column (17 April 1952), Nancy Spain characterised *Bramton Wick* as 'by Trollope out of Thirkell' and in *John O'London's Weekly* Stevie Smith was another who invoked the creator of the Chronicles of Barsetshire, praising the author's 'truly Trollopian air of benign maturity', while Compton Mackenzie pleased Elizabeth Fair greatly by describing it as 'humorous in the best tradition of English Humour, and by that I mean Jane Austen's humour'. The author herself was more prosaic, writing in her diary that *Bramton Wick* 'was pretty certain of a sale to lending libraries and devotees of light novels'. She was right; but who was this novelist who, over a brief publishing life, 1952-1960, enjoyed comparison with such eminent predecessors?

Elizabeth Mary Fair (1908-1997) was born at Haigh, a village on the outskirts of Wigan, Lancashire. Although the village as she described it was 'totally unpicturesque', Elizabeth was brought up in distinctly more pleasing surroundings. For the substantial stone-built house in which she was born and in which she lived for her first twenty-six years was 'Haighlands', set within the estate of Haigh Hall, one of the several seats of Scotland's premier earl, the Earl of Crawford and Balcarres. Haigh Hall dates from the 1830s/40s and it is likely that 'Haighlands' was built during that time specifically to house the Earl's estate manager, who, from the first years of the twentieth century until his rather premature death in 1934, was Elizabeth's father, Arthur Fair. The Fair family was generally prosperous; Arthur Fair's father had been a successful stockbroker and his mother was the daughter of Edward Rigby, a silk merchant who for a time in the 1850s had lived with his family in Swinton Park, an ancient house much augmented in the 19th century with towers and battlements, set in extensive parkland in the

Yorkshire Dales. Portraits of Edward Rigby, his wife, and sister-in law were inherited by Elizabeth Fair, and, having graced her Hampshire bungalow in the 1990s, were singled out for specific mention in her will, evidence of their importance to her. While hanging on the walls of 'Haighlands' they surely stimulated an interest in the stories of past generations that helped shape the future novelist's mental landscape.

On her mother's side, Elizabeth Fair was the grand-daughter of Thomas Ratcliffe Ellis, one of Wigan's leading citizens, a solicitor, and secretary from 1892 until 1921 to the Coalowners' Association. Wigan was a coal town, the Earl of Crawford owning numerous collieries in the area, and Ratcliffe Ellis, knighted in the 1911 Coronation Honours, played an important part nationally in dealing with the disputes between coal owners and miners that were such a feature of the early 20th century. Although the Ellises were politically Conservative, they were sufficiently liberal-minded as to encourage one daughter, Beth, in her desire to study at Lady Margaret Hall, Oxford. There she took first-class honours in English Literature and went on to write *First Impressions of Burmah* (1899), dedicated to her father and described by a modern authority as 'as one of the funniest travel books ever written'. She followed this with seven rollicking tales of 17th/18th-century derring-do. One, *Madam, Will You Walk?*, was staged by Gerald du Maurier at Wyndham's Theatre in 1911 and in 1923 a silent film was based on another. Although she died in childbirth when her niece and namesake was only five years old, her presence must surely have lingered not only on the 'Haighlands' bookshelves but in family stories told by her sister, Madge Fair. Another much-discussed Ellis connection was Madge's cousin, (Elizabeth) Lily Brayton, who was one of the early- 20th century's star actresses, playing the lead role in over 2000 performances of *Chu Chin Chow*, the musical comedy written by her husband that was such a hit of the London stage during the First World War. Young Elizabeth could hardly help but be interested in the achievements of such intriguing female relations.

Beth Ellis had, in the late-nineteenth century, been a boarding pupil at a school at New Southgate on the outskirts of London, but both Elizabeth Fair and her sister Helen (1910-1989) were educated by a governess at a time when, after the end of the First World War, it was far less usual than it had been previously to educate daughters at home. Although, in a later short biographical piece, Elizabeth mentioned that she 'had abandoned her ambition to become an architect', this may only have been a daydream as there is no evidence that she embarked on any post-schoolroom training. In her novels, however, she certainly demonstrates her interest in architecture, lovingly portraying the cottages, houses, villas, rectories, manors, and mansions that not only shelter her characters from the elements but do so much to delineate their status *vis à vis* each other. This was an interest of which Nancy Spain had perceptively remarked in her review of *Bramton Wick*, writing 'Miss Fair is refreshingly more interested in English landscape and architecture and its subsequent richening effect on English character than she is in social difference of rank, politics, and intellect'. In *The Mingham Air* (1960) we feel the author shudder with Mrs Hutton at the sight of Mingham Priory, enlarged and restored, 'All purple and yellow brick, and Victorian plate-glass windows, and a conservatory stuck at one side. A truly vulgar conservatory with a pinnacle.' Hester, her heroine, had recently been engaged to an architect and, before the engagement was broken, 'had lovingly submitted to his frequent corrections of her own remarks when they looked at buildings together'. One suspects that Elizabeth Fair was perhaps as a young woman not unfamiliar with being similarly patronised.

While in *The Mingham Air* Hester's ex-fiancé plays an off-stage role, in *Seaview House* (1955) another architect, Edward Wray, is very much to the fore. It is while he is planning 'a "select" little seaside place for the well-to-do' at Caweston on the bracing East Anglian coast that he encounters the inhabitants of 'Seaview House'. We soon feel quite at home in this draughty 'private hotel', its ambience so redolent of the 1950s, where the owners, two middle-aged sisters, Miss Edith Newby and widowed Mrs Rose Barlow, might be found on an off-season evening darning guest towels underneath the gaze of the late Canon Newby, whose portrait 'looked down at his daughters with a slight sneer'. By way of contrast, life in nearby 'Crow's Orchard', the home of Edward's godfather, Walter Heritage, whose butler and cook attend to his every needs and where even the hall was 'thickly curtained, softly lighted and deliciously warm', could not have been more comfortable.

Mr Heritage is one of Elizabeth Fair's specialities, the cosseted bachelor or widower, enjoying a life not dissimilar to that of her two unmarried Ellis uncles who, after the death of their parents, continued to live, tended by numerous servants, at 'The Hollies', the imposing Wigan family home. However, not all bachelors are as confirmed as Walter Heritage, for in *The Native Heath* (1954) another, Francis Heswald, proves himself, despite an inauspicious start, to be of definitely marriageable material. He has let Heswald Hall to the County Education Authority (in 1947 Haigh Hall had been bought by Wigan Corporation) and has moved from the ancestral home into what had been his bailiff's house. This was territory very familiar to the author and the geography of this novel, the only one set in the north of England, is clearly modelled on that in which the author grew up, with Goatstock, 'the native heath' to which the heroine has returned, being a village close to a manufacturing town that is 'a by- word for ugliness, dirt and progress'. In fact *Seaview House* and *The Native Heath* are the only Elizabeth Fair novels not set in southern England, the region in which she spent the greater part of her life. For after the death of Arthur Fair his widow and daughters moved to Hampshire, closer to Madge's sister, Dolly, living first in the village of Boldre and then in Brockenhurst. *Bramton Wick, Landscape in Sunlight* (1953), *A Winter Away* (1957), and *The Mingham Air* (1960) are all set in villages in indeterminate southern counties, the topographies of which hint variously at amalgams of Hampshire, Dorset, and Devon.

Elizabeth Fair's major break from village life came in 1939 when she joined what was to become the Civil Defence Service, drove ambulances in Southampton through the Blitz, and then in March 1945 went overseas with the Red Cross, working in Belgium, Ceylon, and India. An intermittently-kept diary reveals that by now she was a keen observer of character, describing in detail the background, as she perceived it, of a fellow Red Cross worker who had lived in 'such a narrow circle, the village, the fringes of the county, nice people but all of a pattern, all thinking on the same lines, reacting in the same way to given stimuli (the evacuees, the petty discomforts of war). So there she was, inexperienced but obstinate, self-confident but stupid, unadaptable, and yet nice. A nice girl, as perhaps I was six years ago, ignorant, arrogant and capable of condescension to inferiors. Such a lot to learn, and I hope she will learn it.' Clearly Elizabeth Fair felt that her war work had opened her own mind and broadened her horizons and it is hardly surprising that when this came to an end and she returned to village life in Hampshire she felt the need of greater stimulation. It was now that she embarked on novel writing and was successful in being added to the list of Innes Rose, one of London's leading literary agents, who placed *Bramton Wick* with Hutchinson & Co. However, as Elizabeth wrote in her diary around the time of publication, 'it still rankles a little that [the Hutchinson editor] bought *Bramton Wick* outright though I think it was worth it – to me – since I needed so badly to get started.'

However, although Hutchinson may have been careful with the money they paid the author, Elizabeth Fair's diary reveals that they were generous in the amount that was spent on *Bramton Wick*'s publicity, advertising liberally and commissioning the author's portrait from Angus McBean, one of the period's most successful photographers. Witty, elegant, and slightly quizzical, the resulting photograph appeared above a short biographical piece on the dust wrappers of her Hutchinson novels. The designs for these are all charming, that of *The Native Heath* being the work of a young Shirley Hughes, now the doyenne of children's book illustrators, with Hutchinson even going to the extra expense of decorating the front cloth boards of that novel and of *Landscape in Sunlight* with an evocative vignette. Elizabeth Fair did receive royalties on her second and third Hutchinson novels and then on the three she published with Macmillan, and was thrilled when an American publisher acquired the rights to *Landscape in Sunlight* after she had 'sent Innes Rose the masterful letter urging to try [the book] in America'. She considered the result 'the sort of fact one apprehends in a dream' and relished the new opportunities that now arose for visits to London, confiding in her diary that 'All these social interludes [are] extremely entertaining, since their talk mirrors a completely new life, new characters, new outlook. How terribly in a rut one gets.' There is something of an irony in the fact that by writing her novels of 'country life, lightly done, but delicately observed' (*The Times Literary Supplement*, 1 November 1957) Elizabeth Fair was for a time able to enjoy a glimpse of London literary life. But in 1960, after the publication of *The Mingham Air*, this interlude as an author came to an end. In her diary, which included sketches for scenes never used in the novel-in-hand, Elizabeth Fair had also, most intriguingly, noted ideas for future tales but, if it was ever written, no trace survives of a seventh novel. As it was, she continued to live a quiet Hampshire life for close on another forty years, doubtless still observing and being amused by the foibles of her neighbours.

Elizabeth Crawford

# CHAPTER ONE

"COME HERE, Hester," Mrs. Hutton called. "Come and look at this miserable little picture. Of course it needs cleaning, and I don't wonder they hung it in a dark corner, but still it does give you the idea."

Other visitors to the exhibition turned their heads, and one or two moved towards the dark corner where Mrs. Hutton was telling her goddaughter Hester that this was a view of Mingham Priory, the residence of their local landed proprietor, and must have been done early in the nineteenth century before the place was enlarged and restored.

"The best thing one can say about the Priory is that it would have made a splendid ruin," she stated. "If only the Seamarks had left it alone, if only they hadn't come into all that money, it would have been one of the most picturesque things in the country."

"And so handy for you to paint," said Hester, rather admiring her godmother's single-mindedness. The Seamarks, for all she cared, could have starved in the ruin's damp cellars.

"Yes," said Mrs. Hutton with a sigh. Painting was her darling hobby, although she had little time for it and no great talent; and the kind of scenes she liked to paint, dramatic landscapes of romantic ruins, did not exist near at hand. "You should see it now," she remarked, to Hester and the other listeners. "All purple and yellow brick, and Victorian plate-glass windows, and a conservatory stuck on at one side. A truly vulgar conservatory with a pinnacle."

Hester tried to picture it, and a man standing a few feet away glanced coldly at Mrs. Hutton as if he would have liked to correct her. Hester thought he was perhaps an architect revolted by the inaccuracy of her description, for conservatories do not have pinnacles and architects are apt to be scornful of laymen's blunders; she knew this because she had been engaged to an architect, and had lovingly submitted to his frequent corrections of her own remarks when they looked at buildings together. But that was all in the past, the engagement broken off last year had become a thing she could think about without always thinking her heart was broken too; and she could discuss architecture quite calmly, though probably inaccurately, with her godmother, without feeling it to be a painful subject.

To prove this she asked whether the purple and yellow brick restoration had entirely hidden the older Priory of the drawing; and her godmother explained that it had hidden all but the side that faced the river, and *that* was spoilt by the ridiculous terraced garden which the late proprietor had constructed about twenty-five years ago, just after she and Bennet had come to live at The End House. It was the year Derek was born and she had been ill all the summer, or at least poorly, and so she had seldom visited the Priory but she could just remember how much better it had looked before the terraces were built, when the ground sloped gently to the river as nature had intended it.

"Old Mr. Seamark had no taste," she said. "None of them have. His grandfather built the brick part and they've gone on admiring it ever since. Thomas Seamark is just as bad as his ancestors. Poor thing."

Hester had only just arrived at The End House and knew nothing about Thomas Seamark, so she could not guess why he was an object of pity. But from her godmother's description of the Priory she felt that his hereditary lack of taste might rank as a crowning mercy.

"Then he won't mind about the pinnacle," she said, deliberately aiming the word at the back of the putative architect, who was still lingering within earshot while pretending to admire a case of miniatures. She fancied that the back gave a shudder, and was certain of it when Mrs. Hutton replied that Thomas Seamark would probably like to add a few turrets to the up-and-down roof along the front.

"Or should I say in-and-out? You know what I mean, Hester—the square openings for firing guns through. Though there never were any guns, of course—it's just a sham bit of mediaevalism."

"Machicolations," said Hester, her memory automatically supplying a word from a discarded vocabulary.

Mrs. Hutton at once looked solicitous, and suggested that they should have tea.

That year the county town was celebrating its six-hundredth year of being a borough, and the exhibition of pictures, old maps and documents was of local rather than national importance. Very interesting of course, but tiring, Mrs. Hutton declared, stressing her own need for refreshment in case Hester should suspect that their retreat was a flight from architecture. In the Guildhall where the exhibition was being held there was almost too much architecture, too many reminders in cornice and column and sweeping staircase of a decidedly unhappy past, and as if that were not enough she had had to make matters worse by discussing the architecture of Mingham Priory. Contrite and concerned, she would have fled to the street, to some humdrum tea-shop that could not possibly remind Hester of the architect who had jilted her; but her goddaughter pointed out that they had arranged to have tea in the Guildhall with Maggie.

Mrs. Hutton felt awkward about having forgotten it, because Maggie was her daughter.

"Oh yes, so we did," she agreed, looking about her to see if Maggie was in sight. "But she's sure to be late—I mean, the dentist probably kept her waiting—do let us go, Hester, and then we can come back afterwards and find her."

Dear as Maggie was to her, she still felt it important to remove Hester from the architectural associations; and perhaps, after tea, she could find some excuse for coming back alone to retrieve Maggie. Hester could be given some shopping to do.

"But why not have tea here as we arranged?" Hester persisted. "If Maggie is late she's sure to come and look for us in the tearoom."

"Perhaps after the dentist she won't want any tea," Mrs. Hutton said wildly.

"If we leave the building we shall have to pay to come in again."

"Don't you think we've seen enough?"

"But we shall have to come back, to meet Maggie."

Hester could be determined when she was not being politely indifferent, and Mrs. Hutton found herself descending the grand staircase, and then a not-so-grand one, to the rather dismal basement. A restaurant in the dungeons had been the town clerk's idea when the exhibition was being planned, and neither he nor the other planners would admit that the dungeons were merely cellars, and inconvenient ones at that.

The small, vaulted rooms were crowded, but they found a table in the farther one and Hester set herself to catch the eye of a waitress. While she was doing this, Mrs. Hutton was able to observe her, and to decide that her face was still much too thin, though a little less strained than it had been when she first came into their lives.

Her coming would never have occurred if Raymond had not so brutally jilted her, almost on the eve of their wedding. She had been a goddaughter Mrs. Hutton hardly knew, a contented orphan living in London, with a good job and plenty of friends and a respectable betrothed. Her mother, Mrs. Hutton's cousin, had died young, and she had been gathered up by and absorbed into her father's family, and Cecily Hutton had supposed she was a Clifford by nature as well as by name and that she would accept the Clifford way of life and become totally indistinguishable from her paternal aunts. Then her father had died; and afterwards the orphaned Hester had surprised her Clifford aunts by leaving them. It had surprised Mrs. Hutton too, when she heard of it, but she had still thought of her goddaughter as a Clifford, domiciled in London instead of in Yorkshire but placidly immune to self-mistrust or unhappiness.

"I was thinking about your aunts," she said.

Hester had ordered the tea and was looking at her questioningly, and it was imperative to say something quickly.

"Were you thinking that I look like them?" Hester asked politely.

"Oh, but you don't. Not that—well, I suppose there is a family likeness. You have the nose."

It was accepted between them that "aunts" referred to the Clifford ones, and of course it was perfectly obvious that Hester did not resemble her mother's family. The Farrimond nose, thought Cecily, had always been nondescript.

"Too long and too large," Hester said cheerfully. "But mine isn't quite as prominent as theirs."

"Dominant, dear. 'Prominent' sounds so craggy. I used to think you were like them in character too, but now I'm not quite so sure."

"Have a crumpet," said Hester, and Mrs. Hutton felt that she had blundered again, and that she was being restrained from further blunders, silenced with crumpets while her goddaughter brought the talk back to the exhibition and to the portraits of bosomy beauties that Derek had besought them not to miss. Since Derek was her son she listened patiently, though she could not help wondering whether his admiration for bosomy beauties included real-life ones.

"So we must see them," Hester continued. "They're all together in a little room beyond the two big rooms. A collection of houris."

"Hooleys?" Cecily asked, not quite catching it. "There's no one of that name living here now. It sounds Irish—"

"No, no. *Houris.* Voluptuous females. But they never did live here, they're portraits lent by Lord Warnford from Warnford Castle, and I suppose they're only here to add glamour to the exhibition. And because Warnford Castle is in the county. But they're not even his ancestresses—they're just a lot of pin-up girls of the past. A former Lord Warnford collected them."

"How interesting. Did you read all that in the catalogue?" Hester laughed.

"I knew you weren't listening. Derek was telling us last night, in the garden after supper, and you were thinking how you would paint the sunset."

A more conscientious mother might have winced but Cecily Hutton merely agreed that she had not been listening. Her conscience worked erratically, sometimes urging her to be prodigiously maternal, sometimes keeping her awake at night worrying about Derek's and Maggie's happiness; but then it would cease working and she would return to being a painter, a person in her own right.

Cecily Farrimond who had married Bennet Hutton and borne two children but who did not perpetually see herself as a wife and mother.

"I was thinking that now summer is coming I might try painting the stone bridge again," she said. "With the sunset reflected in the river."

"Do you mean the bridge near The End House?"

"No, it's the one further upstream. At the other side of the park, nearer to Monk's Mingham. I think I'll go and see Mr. Headley and ask if it's still all right for me to walk across the park. He's the agent, you know, he lives in that white house on the way to Monk's Mingham. The one Derek was telling you was haunted."

"I remember. But why do you have to ask? Why shouldn't it be still all right?"

"Because of all the new notices about trespassers being prosecuted, and the gates being locked. He had them put up last year —but he started being a recluse some time before that."

Which he, Hester wondered, but she judged that it could not be Mr. Headley, the agent. "Why don't you ask Mr. Seamark himself?" she said.

"Because I don't seem to know him as well as I used to. It's all Bennet's fault for being an invalid."

Hester felt it would be priggish to say, "He can't help that." Indeed she already suspected that Bennet Hutton had deliberately chosen invalidism as his hobby, just as his wife had chosen painting.

"But I don't see why Cousin Bennet's illness should have stopped you knowing Mr. Seamark," she said.

Because it had kept Bennet at home, Cecily explained, just at the time when he might have been some use. Of course that was his first illness, she added confusingly—the one they thought he had got over. And they had thought Thomas Seamark would get over it too but he hadn't; he had moped and moped, which wasn't good for anyone and certainly not for a comparatively young man, and then he had stopped going about, except for official things which his sense of duty drove him to, but what was the good of that . . . ?

If Bennet hadn't become an invalid he could have continued his casual visits to the Priory, the links would not have been broken and they could have gone on asking Thomas Seamark to dine, as they used to do in the past. But Bennet's illness made it impossible for him to visit the Priory, and all but impossible for his family to ask people to dinner.

Her goddaughter found this far from enlightening.

"But was he ill at the same time?" she asked, meaning Thomas Seamark.

"His first illness was just afterwards," said Cecily, meaning Bennet's. "And ever since then it has been awfully difficult to have people to dine. So dull for you, dear." She added anxiously, "But I did warn you."

Her voice trailed off; the warning had been given when she was offering Hester asylum, and might remind her of that painful occasion.

"I like dullness," Hester declared, adding illogically but politely, "not that it is dull at all. The End House is far nicer than my poky little flat, and I'm looking forward to a summer in the country."

"And there are people in the village for you to go to tea with, and Derek will be free at the weekends, someone young to talk to. . . . And there is Maggie too, of course."

"Here's Maggie coming now," Hester said.

Cecily had seen her an instant earlier; it was the sight of her that had prompted her last words. For once again she had forgotten Maggie; and this time she felt really guilty about it and spared a moment to wonder whether she was an unnatural mother, unconsciously devoured by jealousy or something even worse, the kind of mother one read about in the kind of novels the children got from the library. But there was no time to dwell on it, for Maggie had seen them and was making her way across the room. She was carrying her hat in her hand and looking decidedly tousled; but Cecily overcame the first feeling of irritation this aroused by telling herself that the poor child had come straight from the dentist.

"Did he hurt you?" she asked, with rather exaggerated sympathy.

"Not a bit," said Maggie. "He just put back that stopping that had come out, and cleaned and polished the rest."

She cast her hat down on one of the vacant chairs and herself on the other one, bumping the table and rattling the crockery and knocking the bill of fare on to the floor. "Mind the cakes!" cried Hester, but it was too late; Maggie had already put her elbow on the edge of the plate, and as it tipped up a particularly jammy cake slid towards her and adhered to her sleeve, leaving a sticky mark when it was removed. "Oh dear," said Maggie, screwing her arm round to look at it and narrowly missing the milk-jug—"still, this jacket needed cleaning anyway."

"The jacket *and* the skirt," said Cecily, who knew that Maggie was capable of having one half of a coat-and-skirt cleaned without the other.

"M'm, yes. Oh, don't bother to order more tea for me, Hester. The hot water will do."

"But there isn't another cup."

"I can use Mother's," Maggie said. "That is, if you've finished?"

"No, I haven't," Cecily said sharply.

"Then I won't bother—I'll just have a cake. This one I spoiled." Neither of her companions tried to stop her, though Hester thought it looked a horrible cake and Cecily felt sure it had hairs on it—dog hairs or perhaps cow hairs from Maggie's sleeve. Though of course she did not go to the farm in her best grey flannel coat and skirt . . . nevertheless there always were hairs on Maggie's clothes, whether she wore them to work or not. And why couldn't she have put on her hat or combed her hair—and what had happened to her gloves, which she had certainly had when they left Mingham? Looking at her daughter and at Hester, the one so untidy and the other so elegant, she felt even more strongly than before that Maggie wasn't even *trying*. Could she be backward, her mental age far below her real one? Surely at twenty-one it was not normal to be so wholly indifferent to one's appearance.

No, thought Maggie, I shall never, never make a friend of Hester, not if she stays with us forever. The most I can do is to be sorry for her because she has suffered so much. But the thought crossed her mind that Hester did not look like a sufferer; that someone who had truly loved and lost would be past bothering about her face or her clothes or the choice of a new hat. To an extremist like Maggie, Hester's elegance was, in the circumstances, a sign of insincerity; as well as being, for reasons she did not define, a bar to friendship. She regretted it, because she had hoped to find in Hester the friend she so dreadfully wanted, someone she could talk to, and who would not think her odd and clumsy and ignorant— or who would not mind if she were. But Hester was already her mother's friend, not hers; she was Derek's friend and might even come to be Papa's; and it wasn't a bit of use trying to compete with all that elegance and *savoir-faire*, she couldn't be the sort of person Hester was so it was better not to try.

Not trying, Maggie ate her cake in silence while Hester and her mother talked. She shut them out of her mind and thought about the farm, about such routine matters as the price of oil-cake and the current milk yield. Then Hester said something about the Priory, and her thoughts came circling back like homing birds— birds than never learn their mistake.

"I saw him, just now," she said.

"Saw who?"

"Walking round the exhibition. I walked round the rooms myself, you see, in case you were there. He didn't look as if he was enjoying it much."

Hester remembered she had been speaking of the Priory, "Do you mean Mr. Seamark?" she asked.

"Yes," said Maggie.

"What a pity *we* didn't see him," Cecily exclaimed. "It would have been such a good opportunity—quite easy to speak to him, meeting by chance like that . . ." She pushed back her chair. "I wonder if he's still here."

"No, he isn't. He was leaving when I came down the grand staircase. I'd seen him in the big room, and then I saw him walking across to the door."

"Oh, Maggie, why didn't you speak to him? It's so awkward, being cut off like this and feeling he doesn't want to know us any more. But it isn't that he doesn't like us, I'm sure it's just that he has cut himself off from everyone, perhaps without quite meaning to. I believe he might have welcomed the chance of getting to know us again—if only he had seen us here this afternoon."

"He wouldn't have known *me*," Maggie said brusquely. "He's hardly seen me since—since I grew up."

"He would have had no difficulty in recognising you," Cecily wanted to say. But her maternal intuition, operating in its sudden erratic way, told her Maggie would resent the implication that she still looked and behaved like a schoolgirl. And of course it was true that she had got much thinner; though somehow one had not noticed it till now and still thought of her as childishly plump.

Why, she looks even thinner than Hester, Cecily thought, comparing them again, not matching elegance against untidiness now but flesh (or the lack of it) against flesh.

In the meantime intuition was telling Hester something much less helpful, something which her godmother would consider quite disastrous. It was telling her that Thomas Seamark *had* seen them, and had not only seen but overheard them, when they were standing in front of the little picture of the Priory and Cecily was telling her about the purple and yellow restoration and the truly vulgar conservatory. She had thought he was an architect, but only because he was so annoyed by Cecily's description; and naturally he would be annoyed if it was his own house and his own family that was being so fiercely criticized.

*"Old Mr. Seamark had no taste. None of them have. . . . Thomas Seamark is just as bad as his ancestors. . . ."*

Oh dear, thought Hester. She was not a great believer in intuitions but this one felt dismally infallible, and she was surprised to find herself quite cast down by it. As if it mattered! she thought; for nothing seemed to matter much nowadays and she would certainly not have expected to take so trivial an incident to heart—to the heart that had been broken and successfully mended.

Yet it did matter. Cecily Hutton had been kind to her. Kind and vague, kind and silly, kind and mercifully forgetful; so that the kindness had been mixed with absurdity and never became unbearable. She had offered Derek and, belatedly, Maggie, as friends, assuming that Hester needed people of her own age; but the friend Hester cautiously fancied was Cecily herself, particularly when the mother and godmother were submerged in the painter of romantic landscapes, the single-minded devotee of ruins. And it was the painter, as well as the friend, who would suffer if Thomas Seamark stayed sulking behind his locked gates.

I must take action, she told herself, as she followed Maggie and Cecily out of the dungeon tea-rooms.

Taking action, solving other people's problems, had once been her talent. But it was a talent grown rusty from disuse.

# CHAPTER TWO

MINGHAM, where The End House still lived up to its name, was called Great Mingham on the map and by its Rector. But it was great only in comparison with Monk's Mingham, which was a mere hamlet without a single shop. Mingham and Monk's Mingham were separated from each other by the park and woods surrounding the Priory, and by the river which wound through the park; they were only three miles apart as the crow flies but five by the road and the stone bridge. The river was, as rivers go, a small and insignificant one, and although it undoubtedly had a name no one ever used it.

Six miles downstream, where the anonymous river joined a slightly larger one, stood the little market town of Scorling, which had a railway station as well as a cinema, several public houses, and a small factory making linoleum. There was a good bus service nowadays from Mingham to Scorling and on to the county town, but despite this link with civilisation Mingham was still quite rural and comparatively unaffected by progress. Some new council houses had been built on the Scorling road, but that was about all.

It was a long, thin village, not much more than one wide street with a lane branching off near Rudd's Garage and leading, in a roundabout way, to Monk's Mingham. The church stood at the end of the street, which was a cul-de-sac, and The End House and the rectory faced each other immediately below the church. Between the rectory and the churchyard there was a very narrow alley which was a short-cut to Monk's Mingham, but between The End House and the churchyard there was only a high brick wall, built by a former owner who disliked the sight of tombstones. The End House and the rectory both dated from the early years of the eighteenth century, and had a sisterly likeness to each other, though the rectory was considerably larger and The End House—at least in Cecily Hutton's opinion—much more beautiful.

The End House and the rectory had big gardens which set them a little apart from the rest of the village. Further down the street the houses were smaller, and Mrs. Hyde-Ridley's was a narrow box sandwiched between the post office and the equally narrow box which formed the rest of her "property." So she spoke of it, for she was proud of owning two houses and sometimes gave the impression that she owned the whole village. The two houses were attached to each other, and the one in which she lived was also attached to, and largely supported by, the post office, which was only two stories high but strongly constructed.

Her own house rose above it, and from her attic windows she had a good view of everything that went on; the front window was built out in a little bay so that she could see up and down the street, and from the back window she could study the gardens to right and left and could make sure that her tenant was keeping the adjoining one in good order.

Three weeks ago the tenant should have started mowing the lawn, it was the beginning of May and the grass was far too long, and the privet hedge needed clipping too. Her tenant was lazy and she often threatened to give her notice to quit; but a dim remembrance of difficulties in the past, with former tenants, had so far restrained her from putting the threat into effect.

She pushed open the attic window and leaned out, peering short-sightedly at the tenant's garden.

"I'll give you notice if you don't mow the lawn," she cried. No one answered, because there was no one there, so after a minute she shut the window and resumed her search for the best spare-room blankets, which had been put away since Mrs. Vandevint's last visit. That had been nearly a year ago and now she was coming again, a month before she was due. It made hospitality very difficult to assess, when one party to the game did not stick to the rules.

A little later the blankets had been carried downstairs and draped on a clothes-horse round the oil stove in the drawing-room. Mrs. Hyde-Ridley preferred oil stoves to fires, they were less trouble and also much safer, and while the blankets were airing the drawing-room would get aired as well; it had not been used through the winter and smelt a little damp. The blankets smelt of camphor and the oil stove smelt strongly of oil, and there was another smell, suggestive of dead mouse, coming from the corner behind the piano. But it could not be dead mouse because her pussies kept all the mice away, driving them next door to plague the tenant. Fresh air was the antidote to all these smells, and she edged her way round the blankets to the window, which was opened less often than the upstairs ones because it gave directly on to the street and people might peer in, or even climb in, if the lower sash were raised. The upper sash was immoveable, wedged shut by the slight tilt of the house towards its supporting post office.

The net curtains were pinned together in the middle to make them meet, and while she was taking out the rusty pins to get at the safety catch Mrs. Hyde-Ridley had a close-up view of the Rector's wife walking past. "Not like a proper rector's wife at all," she muttered crossly to herself; for she had been brought up in a day when rectors were rectors and their wives wore fine upstanding hats and were respected by everyone.

But although Mrs. Merlin fell far short of the ideal, Mrs. Hyde-Ridley always enjoyed talking to her, because in that quarter at least she could always be first with the latest news. (Which just showed; for of course a proper rector's wife would have known everything that was happening in the parish.) She tapped lightly on the window but the Rector's wife failed to hear her. However, it didn't take a moment to snatch up her hat, which was lying on a chair by the door, and pursue Mrs. Merlin down the street. She overtook her at the door of the post office.

"Have you met Miss Clifford?" she asked, as soon as the usual courtesies had been exchanged.

"I don't think so," Mrs. Merlin replied cautiously.

"But she's been here over a week! I met her the very second day. I was so interested as it turns out she's the niece of some very old friends of mine—a place up in Yorkshire—I used to know them in the old days in Italy as they used to winter at Alassio as Yorkshire is so cold in the winter as they were both rather delicate! Of course they were Cliffords too so I guessed at once as she's so like them as her father was their brother!"

Mrs. Hyde-Ridley's excited manner, her loud voice and her non-stop bursts of information, together with her enormous range of acquaintances all over England and her extensive knowledge of Abroad, never failed to make Mrs. Merlin feel slightly giddy and —much against her will—inferior.

"How nice," she said flatly. And then, battling against the sense of inferiority: "I used to know some Cliffords myself. I must go and call on her."

"But she's staying with the Huttons!" Mrs. Hyde-Ridley shrieked. "Didn't you know?"

Once again Mrs. Merlin's ignorance was exposed, her shocking ignorance of what was going on in the village. People were so secretive, she used to complain to her husband, they never got chatty no matter how often one visited them; and the Huttons, who lived just opposite and ought to have ranked as intimate friends, were as bad as the rest. Not exactly stuck-up—for they were always polite when she popped in to see them—but cagey and unresponsive. It was typical that none of them should have mentioned having Miss Clifford to stay.

"As a matter of fact I haven't seen Cecily Hutton just recently," she said, which was perfectly true. "I'm so busy you know—I just haven't the time for popping across to talk to her. But I believe I did hear they were having a visitor, though they didn't say her name."

Mrs. Hyde-Ridley was not deceived; she knew that Mrs. Merlin knew nothing about it and that she, Mrs. Hyde-Ridley, had been first with the news.

"Hester Clifford," she said. "Such an awfully nice girl! She's come for the summer as she had pneumonia so badly as I'm afraid she may be delicate like her aunts. 'You ought to have gone to Italy,' I told her, but she said she couldn't afford it as of course it's so different now as the Cliffords aren't at all well off as they had that lawsuit and lost it. She had an awfully good job in London but she had to give it up as she was ill for months as these national health doctors are no good at all! But she was able to let her flat as people will give anything for a flat in London, and Mrs. Hutton is her godmother as she was her mother's first cousin so that's why she's come here!"

Mrs. Merlin's brain reeled under this flood of information, but she endeavoured to store it away for future reference. Much as she disliked Mrs. Hyde-Ridley she had to admit that her news was generally correct; and it was poured out with a lavishness for which—in contrast with the stinginess of everyone else—she ought to have been grateful.

"Well, that's Very interesting," she declared. "I must certainly drop in and meet her." Tired of looking up at Mrs. Hyde-Ridley, who was several inches taller, she looked away and saw Miss Cardwell, the village school-teacher, crossing the street towards Rudd's Garage. "There is Miss Cardwell, and I particularly want a word with her," she said, seizing on a chance to escape.

"Of course you know she hasn't spoken to Miss Knapp for four days as they had a quarrel as Miss Knapp broke her Hoover," Mrs. Hyde-Ridley screamed after her. Mrs. Merlin was far enough away to be able to pretend not to hear, but she registered this news with satisfaction. If only Miss Cardwell and Miss Knapp would have a really good quarrel, and part company, it would save a lot of bother for everyone.

Mrs. Hyde-Ridley returned to her house, but before going in she walked into the middle of the street to get a good view of her property. She liked to admire it, to feel that it was her own, and the two tall, narrow houses could not be seen properly from the pavement. Usually she could stand in the street for as long as she liked, for there was seldom any traffic and the residents of Mingham had grown accustomed, to her behaviour, but today the pleasant interlude was quickly interrupted. The door of the left-hand house opened and her tenant, Chrysanthemum Bavington, came out.

Mrs. Hyde-Ridley would never have let her house to anyone called Chrysanthemum had she known about it in advance. But the tenant had concealed her Christian name (if one could call it that) until after she had moved in. She had been Mrs. Bavington, a widow with a grown-up son named Anthony, and Mrs. Hyde-Ridley had liked her as much as she liked any of the prospective tenants (none of them was really good enough to occupy *Firenze*), and the whole business had been settled over a cup of tea. In the beginning Mrs. Bavington had seemed a very nice woman indeed, and even the disclosure of her exotic name had not utterly damned her, but lately Mrs. Hyde-Ridley had feared she was going to turn out unreliable. Most tenants became unreliable, sooner or later, in Mrs. Hyde-Ridley's eyes; though onlookers surmised that the hazards of being a Hyde-Ridley tenant drove them to it.

"Good afternoon," Chrysanthemum called in her lilting voice. She looked very young to be the mother of a grown-up son and Mrs. Hyde-Ridley suspected that the colour of her tawny-red hair was not quite natural. But there was no fault to be found with her manners; she was always polite even when Mrs. Hyde-Ridley scolded her.

"Isn't it a perfectly heavenly day?" she said, walking out to join her landlady in the street. "Are you looking at your houses?

They look so sweet, don't they? I always wish someone would paint a picture of them."

Mrs. Hyde-Ridley relaxed. She had been expecting her tenant to suggest that the houses themselves should be painted, and not only painted but repaired. The last tenants had often tried to get her to renovate the property and to mend the leaks in the roof, and she dimly remembered having told Chrysanthemum before she moved in that the houses were to be painted the following spring; but that was a year ago, and it had not been done. She had plenty of good excuses in hand, but she was pleased that they were not required.

"They're the oldest houses in Mingham, you know," she said proudly. "All the trippers always stop to admire them as they're ever so much older than the church as they were here before the fire!"

"Yes, they're absolutely fascinating."

Chrysanthemum paid the houses the tribute of a long, admiring stare, then she turned to Mrs. Hyde-Ridley and remarked wistfully:

"I was thinking of asking you to let me paint mine outside, but I suppose you wouldn't like it."

Not like it! Mrs. Hyde-Ridley was stunned. Never before had a tenant asked to be allowed to renovate *Firenze*, and for a moment she thought she must have misunderstood.

"Paint the outside?" she echoed suspiciously.

"Oh, of course we'll do the inside too. Anthony did the bedrooms at Easter and we'll do the rest when he gets his holiday. But I had such a wonderful idea the other day—only I s'pose it mightn't appeal to you. And of course it's frightful cheek, my suggesting it."

Chrysanthemum was getting younger every minute, her pretty manner becoming bashfully childish as it always did when she was pleading for something. Mrs. Hyde-Ridley remembered how Chrysanthemum had coaxed a new sink out of her when she first arrived, and her own manner hardened.

"When Anthony gets his holiday I hope he'll put the garden in order," she said. "You know you're supposed to keep it up. The lawn—"

"I know, I know! It's perfectly dreadful of me, not cutting it before now. But there was something wrong with the mower— I had to send it to Rudd and you know how long he takes."

Mrs. Hyde-Ridley, adept at wriggling out of obligations, recognised a fellow-expert. It was this quality in Chrysanthemum which she rather admired; it lifted her out of the ruck of grumbling but browbeaten tenants and brought her nearer the level of Mrs. Vandevint, that unscrupulous, irreplaceable friend. But of course it made her potentially even less reliable than the tenants of the past.

"If Rudd doesn't send it back soon I'll have the lawn scythed," Chrysanthemum said earnestly.

"You'll have to. It will be much too long to mow."

On this firm note Mrs. Hyde-Ridley walked towards her house. As she went she gave another good look at the property, not admiring now but appraising the state of the paint. She longed to know why her tenant had made that extraordinary suggestion, but she wasn't going to ask; if Chrysanthemum was after something (and experience made this seem probable) she would raise the subject again.

The house on the left was called *Firenze* and the other was *Bonnie Appin*. Mrs. Hyde-Ridley had chosen these names when she bought the property, many years ago, to remind her of a district in Scotland and a town in Italy which she held especially dear. The inhabitants of Mingham had mastered the name of *Bonnie Appin* but they persisted in calling the other house Fur-Ends, no matter how often she corrected them. It had been a point in Chrysanthemum's favour that she knew how the name should be pronounced.

"*Firenze* would love to give you a cup of tea," she said now, as they stood at their respective front doors.

Mrs. Hyde-Ridley was tempted, because she knew there would probably be a cake as well. She had a sweet tooth, and Chrysanthemum's cakes were rich and delicious and far superior to any that could be bought locally. But she guessed that the invitation was a prelude to more coaxing and she shook her head.

"I'm afraid I can't spare the time today as I've any amount to do," she said quickly. "I'm expecting my friend Mrs. Vandevint to stay and I must get on with the spring-cleaning as these women are no good as they grumble all the time and don't do their work properly."

Every daily obliger in the village had worked for Mrs. Hyde-Ridley at one time or another, but none of them had lasted long. (They complained that she was always grumbling and that they couldn't do the work properly because the rooms were cluttered up.) At present she was dependent on occasional help from an obliger who lived in Scorling and was thought to be half-witted.

"Yes, it's awfully difficult," Chrysanthemum said sympathetically. "When is Mrs. Vandevint arriving?"

"Soon," Mrs. Hyde-Ridley replied, walking into her own house and shutting the door behind her.

She felt quite exhilarated. Not only had she had the pleasure of telling Mrs. Merlin about Hester Clifford and exposing her shocking ignorance, but she had learned that her tenant was up to something which needed her co-operation. She was in a strong position, she would be able to get quite a lot out of her tenant in return for whatever it was she wanted. The lawn would be mown and the garden tidied, there would be no more washing on the line —now she came to think of it, there hadn't been any for a week— the house would be painted and she could count on getting the rent promptly. And there would be gifts of cakes and luscious fruit tarts, such as Chrysanthemum had occasionally brought her in the past; but they would be more plentiful now, and would come in very useful for feeding Mrs. Vandevint, whose sweet tooth equalled her own.

But I mustn't let her get me alone, she thought; for she meant to postpone learning what Chrysanthemum wanted for as long as possible, so that the bribes and placatory actions might continue unchecked. Mrs. Vandevint's premature visit now seemed quite providential, since it would provide her with a constant companion. The sooner she came the better.

Mrs. Hyde-Ridley sat down at her desk and took out a postcard. She always used them because they were cheaper than letters and she believed they went quicker.

V. glad to get your letter! [She wrote in her emphatic postcard style.] V. glad to have you but come as *soon* as *possible* as it will suit me better as am thinking of having house painted later. What about Fri. or Sat.? Mon. at latest. Did you see Connie Williams had died in The Times last week? Only 67!!! Beautiful weather here and the Mingham air will do you good! Looking forward v. much to seeing you *soon*.

# CHAPTER THREE

THE END HOUSE and the rectory face each other across the village street; but it is a very wide street and the gardens are well screened by trees, so we are not in the least overlooked. I haven't seen the Rector yet, as we didn't go to church last Sunday, but his wife came in to inspect me last night. She has beady eyes and an inquisitive nose, and seemed to take it as a grievance that she hadn't been told of my arrival. She'd heard about it from Mrs. Hyde-Ridley, whom I mentioned in my last letter —the tattered old crow who claims to have known you in Italy.

So Hester wrote, to the Clifford aunts who had brought her up, and about whom she was feeling slightly guilty. She knew how gladly they would have had her back, how fervently they would have sympathized, how scornfully they would have denounced the man who had jilted a Clifford; but for these reasons a retreat to Yorkshire had been unthinkable. Still, it must have hurt them that she had gone elsewhere; and a long letter, a regular series of letters, was the only balm she could apply. But it was difficult to know what to write about, when the aunts were interested only in their family, their parish church, and foreign missions.

The opening of her bedroom door came as a welcome interruption, but when she turned round there was no one there. That had happened before, on several occasions, and to a non-believer in ghosts it seemed probable that there was something wrong with the latch. Hester walked across the room to examine it, and from across the landing Maggie called out to her:

"You must remember to put the weight."

"What weight?"

"Didn't Mother tell you? The latch doesn't work properly," Maggie explained. "So you must put the weight against the door, when you're inside, to keep it from bursting open. It generally bursts open if people run upstairs in a hurry—as I did just now."

Hester wondered why the latch couldn't be mended. She looked round for the weight.

"It's there, by the fireplace," Maggie said helpfully. She had come across from her own room and now stood in the doorway, looking particularly tousled and untidy because she had just returned from the farm and was still in her working clothes.

"Just stand it against the door, and it won't even rattle," she said. "Look—I'll show you."

Advancing to the fireplace she picked up a large, brass, urn-shaped object, which Hester had thought to be an immovable fixture, carried it back, slammed the door shut, set the weight down with a thud, and stood back for Hester to see.

"Mother ought to have told you, but I suppose she forgot. It's ages since we last had someone to stay."

"I'll remember. Thank you for showing me."

Evidently the broken latch was a permanancy, Hester thought. It had been accepted as one of life's awkwardnesses and nothing was going to be done about it.

Then she remembered the other awkwardness, the awkwardness of Cecily's having alienated Thomas Seamark by publicly criticizing his house and his family. Nothing had been done about that either, and it was a shock to realize that the episode had taken place several days ago. She wondered whether the slothful Huttons were unconsciously corrupting her.

"You ought to sleep in this room yourself," she said to Maggie. "It's much too nice to be kept for occasional visitors."

"Is it?" Maggie looked round in surprise. "I suppose it's all right," she acknowledged, "but, you see, I've had *my* bedroom all my life."

"That's no reason for not changing to this one," said Hester.

It was a very good reason, Maggie thought, her Hutton inertia reinforced by antagonism. Hester was much too managing, she had already started to reform Derek and one could see she had her eye on Mrs. Pilgrim. If she was like this in convalescence what on earth would she be like when fully restored to health?

"And this room has such a wonderful view," Hester continued. "Come and look at it."

Half against her will Maggie walked across to the window. She was of course familiar with the view, though she could not see it from her own bedroom. If she slept in this room she would have it spread out in front of her all the time; the view across the park and the river to the distant, wooded hills. On this May evening it was all green and gold, the great oak trees just breaking into bronze leaf and the nearer water-meadows lush and vivid in the late sunlight. It was beautiful; she could not deny that it was better than the view from her own bedroom, which looked over the village street to the rectory chestnut trees. But she would not want it spread out in front of her all the time.

"Where is the Priory?" Hester asked.

"You can't see it. It's down by the river, beyond that high ground on the right. The river runs through quite a deep valley in the woods, before it gets to the water-meadows."

"The Priory must be rather shut in."

"Oh no, it isn't. It stands on a high bank and there are terraced gardens in front, going down to the river. And quite a nice outlook —well, I suppose it is a bit *enclosed*," said Maggie, as if that was different from being shut in, "but you can see the river, and the woods on the other side. In winter, when the trees are leafless, you can see Monk's Mingham."

Hester thought it sounded rather gloomy, but perhaps she was influenced by Cecily's description. "What is Mr. Seamark like? Nice?" she asked casually.

"We hardly know him. You see, he's turning into a recluse."

"Yes, your mother said so. But you used to know him. Can't you stop it—if he's nice?"

"It's been coming on for a long time. Ever since his wife died."

"Oh," said Hester.

She had not expected to run into tragedy. She had been thinking of Thomas Seamark as a shy eccentric, but Maggie's solemn voice suggested that he was the victim of a broken heart. How tiresome, she thought, shying away from a situation that too nearly resembled her own last winter, which she had no wish to recall.

"She was very beautiful," Maggie said sadly.

"Oh. Did you—was she a great friend of yours?"

Maggie shook her head "Of course not. I told you, she died quite a long time ago. I was still at school."

Not last winter then, Hester thought; it must be at least three years since Maggie left school. Her discomfort changed to annoyance, partly with herself for being so easily discomforted, but partly with Mr. Seamark for being—though unwittingly—the cause of it.

"Then the sooner he's stopped from turning into a recluse the better," she said briskly. "We—I mean you—must stop it."

"That's the gong!" Maggie said. "And I haven't even washed my face."

She rushed from the room, pausing only to move the weight that kept the door shut. Crashing the weight down on the floor and slamming the door relieved her feelings, they were ways of saying what could not be said in words—"Hester is much too managing." But Hester did not guess that these extra-loud noises had any special meaning, because the gong was still booming through the house and reducing all rival sounds to comparative insignificance.

It was a gong that could be heard all over the village, Bennet Hutton had said, if it were struck really forcefully. It had come out of a bishop's palace. He had told her this on the night of her arrival, when Derek's evening performance on the gong had brought her hurrying downstairs wondering if the house was on fire; for she had not expected so ceremonious a summons to a meal humbly described as "cold scraps." Cousin Bennet had been quite talkative that first evening, but since then she had scarcely seen him. A malaise, vaguely defined as "not being so good today," had kept him in bed or at least in his own room.

This evening he was back at the end of the table. It was a long table and he looked rather far away, but perhaps that was what he preferred, since he did not seem inclined for conversation. The cold scraps were served by Cecily, and Derek was sent back to the kitchen to fetch the things that had been forgotten; the bread, then the bread knife, and finally the bottle of yellow salad cream which Hester so much despised. When she had been here a little longer she was going to ask Cecily to let her make a real French dressing, which they would surely prefer once they had tasted it.

"I ought to have bought some more cooked ham, but I forgot," Cecily said apologetically. "Still, there's plenty of cheese."

"Mousetrap cheese," Derek said softly.

"Do you mean it's rather dry?"

"Well, Mama, just look at it. All those cracks."

"This kind of cheese always has cracks in it," Cecily declared.

"Then couldn't we have some other kind?"

No one answered him. Maggie, who had come in late, was hurriedly eating her meagre share of the ham and Cecily was obviously not feeling maternal. Hester was debarred from agreeing because she was Cecily's guest and it would have been a criticism of her hospitality. But she was pleased to learn that at least one of the Huttons could distinguish good food from bad. Leaving out Cousin Bennet, who appeared to live on some patent mixture out of a packet and hot milk, she had thought that none of them knew or cared anything about food except as a means of sustaining life.

Derek was rather sweet. He had a nice, pink, innocent face, and yellow, hair like Maggie's—though unlike Maggie's it was well cut and neatly brushed. He was a little older than Maggie and a little younger than Hester, but somehow he seemed the youngest; no one could say he was pampered, but he had the air of being the baby of a large family. Hester thought of him as a younger brother, and found him much easier to get on with than Maggie, whom she could not think of as a younger sister. But she knew this was probably because she had always wanted brothers to play with, in her rather lonely childhood in York-shire, and had never invented imaginary sisters.

When the cracked cheese had been eaten, Maggie fetched the coffee. This was the moment Hester had been waiting for, the right time for discussing problems and preparing to solve them. She leaned forward and addressed Cecily.

"Maggie was telling me about Mr. Seamark," she began. "We were admiring that wonderful view from my bedroom window. It reminded me of what you were saying the other day—about asking Mr. Headley whether you could still walk across the park. Have you seen him yet?"

"No, I haven't. One never meets him when one wants to. I shall have to go to the estate office."

"Why bother?" Derek asked. "You always used to walk across the park. We used to go picnics there."

"But we haven't been for a long time," Maggie said.

"That's just it. One feels awkward about starting again, with the notices about trespassers, and the locked gates . . ."

"But, Mama, they're a defence against the masses. Lots of people drive out to Mingham in the summer—far more than used to come when we were young." Derek spoke as if this were several decades ago, which Hester found rather endearing. "The notices are for us."

"You don't understand. It's because he has become a recluse. He doesn't want *anyone*."

"But that's all rot, Maggie. Chaps oughtn't to turn into re-cluses. Not at his age."

Hester was delighted to hear him say it. "I think so too," she exclaimed impulsively. "And Thomas Seamark didn't look the type either. I mean, he looked much too young and—"

"How do you know? You've never seen him."

Hester was disconcerted. She had not meant to tell them about her intuition but now she was forced to; it was of course her own fault for giving herself away, but she felt rather vexed with Maggie for pouncing on her so swiftly.

"I saw him at the exhibition," she retorted.

"But how do you *know*? You don't know what he looks like." There was nothing to be done but tell them the whole story; for if the intuition was to be justified it must be supported by the facts.

"I bet you're right," Derek said when she had finished. "It sounds like him, and what more natural than that he should be lurking near the picture of his Priory? Chap must have had a nasty shock when he heard Mama denouncing all the restorations."

"Oh, Mother, how could you be so tactless!"

"No use venturing into the park now, Mama. You'd be flung out like the trippers."

"Oh dear, what shall I do?" Cecily cried. Ignoring Maggie's reproaches and Derek's mockery, she instinctively turned to Hester. "What *can* I do? If only I hadn't spoken so loudly—if only I'd known he was there!"

"It is no good being wise after the event," Bennet Hutton said suddenly.

It was the first time he had spoken and it gave Hester quite a shock, for she had almost forgotten his presence. But she turned round at once, pleased by the crisp little intervention, and by having aroused his interest. He hadn't, after all, been dozing.

"Then let's be wise about the future," she said. "What shall we do now?"

He looked surprised, and she guessed that he was not accustomed to being consulted. He was an invalid; it was for other people to take responsibility and deal with difficulties; he had made the rules to suit himself and they had gradually grown into a hedge which restricted as well as protected him.

Over this hedge he peered at her cautiously, ready to swerve aside if she came too close. He looked rather like a Joshua Reynolds cherub grown elderly and temperamental, with plump cheeks and bright eyes and silky brown hair fluffed out over his temples, as he sat there tugging at the ends of his shawl. The shawl lay across his shoulders to keep out draughts, and he sat in an easy chair on two cushions to bring him up to the level of the table.

"We must get to know him again," he said, after an interval for thought. "Re-establish the relationship, and remind him that we're part of his past. Then he will realize that Cecily was speaking in the character of a very old friend."

"Well, yes," said Hester. "I see what you mean. But wouldn't it be better if *you* got to know him again, on your own, without her? So that he would be reminded of the more distant past first, and not straightway of last week?"

"My dear, you have the cunning of the serpent," Cousin Bennet assured her.

There was a hint of mockery in his voice, but Hester ignored it.

"The question is—how?" she said, fixing him with an appealing gaze and willing the others not to interrupt. But they were dumbstruck, Derek said afterwards, dumbstruck by Papa's sudden participation in a family conclave. They sat as still as Hester, waiting to hear what he would say next.

"How?" he echoed, giving the word a pathetic quaver to show that he was still an invalid.

"Yes. How?"

Cousin Bennet was perhaps flattered by the respectful silence of his audience; it must be a long time, Hester thought, since anyone had hung on his words. He pondered, tugging the shawl more closely around him, and then, symbolically, he threw it back across his chair.

"Quite a warm evening. Summer at last. Must wait till June for my thin vests. But you might air them, Cecily." He spoke in staccato chirrups, like a bird getting ready to sing. "Warm enough for an outing. To the Priory!"

"That's an excellent idea," Hester said. She wondered how he would get there.

"The electric chair," Cousin Bennet chirrupped, as if he could read her thoughts. "But the battery will need charging."

"We'll get that done," his wife said quickly. "And Derek will oil the right bits and pump up the tires."

"And Hester will walk behind you," Derek said, "to rescue you if the chair breaks down. She can lurk in the rhododendrons while you're doing the actual calling."

Maggie said nothing. But at least she did not raise objections, and after supper she went out with Derek to unearth the electric chair—which sounded lethal but was merely electrically propelled —from its home in the old stable, where it had stood idle for quite a long time.

"We got it when Bennet lost the use of his legs," Cecily told Hester. "But that was just a temporary symptom and he can walk quite well now, if he wants to. Though not, of course, as far as the Priory."

She went on to thank Hester warmly for persuading Bennet to go to the Priory; for putting the idea into his head and encouraging him to act on it. Her goddaughter protested that she had done nothing, but then she remembered his look of surprise when his advice was asked, and his ready response, and she began to think she had done something after all. His wife and children neglected him a little, she decided, or at least they had allowed the hedge to grow up without trying to prune it.

"But I'd better not go with him," she said. "Because I should remind Thomas Seamark of the incident at the exhibition."

"Oh no, dear—it was I who offended him. I don't suppose he noticed you."

Hester saw that this was meant to be reassuring but she could not help feeling a little cast down.

"Perhaps he didn't," she agreed meekly.

"Bennet will enjoy having you with him. It will give him confidence—because that chair *is* rather unreliable. And then, as Derek said, you can wait in the shrubbery while he pays his call. You will be quite hidden, as the rhododendrons grow right up to the house on the north side and they're extremely thick."

To be left hidden in a shrubbery, while a social event was taking place, struck Hester as even more of a come-down than not being noticed at the exhibition.

# CHAPTER FOUR

THE ONLY THING wrong with The End House, apart from minor inconveniences due to its age, was its proximity to the church and the rectory, which made one feel one must attend morning service occasionally so as to please the Rector.

Not that he was fussy, Cecily added, but she would feel awkward about meeting him in the street if she never went to church at all.

"But even if you lived at the other end of the village he would still notice if you didn't come to church," Hester argued.

"I dare say, but I shouldn't feel so awkward about it if I didn't live opposite him. Whenever I meet him I always feel awkward about the empty pew."

"I don't quite see—"

"Of course Maggie goes quite regularly, but she will go to the early service. I can't think why. If she would only go to matins the pew wouldn't look so empty."

"Well, it won't look empty this morning," Hester said soothingly.

"Are you sure you don't mind coming, dear? There's no need for you to come if you don't agree with it."

"But I do agree. I mean, I go to church quite often. I was brought up to it," said Hester, wondering how her Clifford aunts would have reacted to the idea that one went to church to fill up the pew and please the Rector.

"I'm so glad. It will make all the difference. Derek practically never comes, and of course poor Bennet can't."

With an envious glance at poor Bennet, Cecily went upstairs to get ready, and to ask Derek to put the joint in the oven at half-past eleven. When Hester followed her she found them both on the landing, looking out of the big south window and discussing Maggie's career.

"Don't fuss so," Derek was saying. "If Maggie likes working at the farm, what's the harm in it? They're frightfully respectable, and she seems perfectly happy."

"There's the son," Cecily said anxiously.

"Oh, Mama, don't get notions! He's got his own farm anyway, over on the other side of Scorling. Maggie hardly ever sees him."

"How do you know? Does she talk about him?"

Hester walked on to her bedroom, feeling that Maggie's career was not her concern. But a little later, while they waited for the church bells to break into the hurry-up rhythm of the last five minutes (for Cecily did not intend to get to church any sooner than was absolutely necessary), she found herself being asked for advice.

"Do you think Maggie ought to have a different job, Hester? In an office, or—well, you know what I mean. Somewhere where she would meet more people."

"And not ruin her hands" hung in the air between them.

"I don't suppose she'd want it, if she likes farming," Hester replied. "But I don't even know exactly what her job is."

"She's supposed to do the accounts and keep records and fill in all the forms and things. It's a big farm on the way to Scorling . . . not our sort of people, but I believe they're very nice," Cecily said hurriedly, skating over the thin ice of social differences. "But I know she does all sorts of things—making herself useful, she calls it—and I'm so afraid she will get weather-beaten and muscular, and perhaps even rather *odd*, and be lonely in her old age. If she doesn't . . ."

She broke off, but Hester guessed that the feared alternative would be for Maggie to marry the socially ineligible son. She laughed. "Maggie is only twenty-one," she said. "You don't have to start worrying about her old age just yet."

"I know, but—And then there's Derek. He's even more of a problem than Maggie."

"Oh, but why?"

"He is so irresponsible. And when I try to talk to him he only laughs and says I'm nagging. But it's serious, Hester. He is just the opposite of Maggie; she *will* stick to this job, which is unsuitable for her, and Derek won't stick to *any* job. Since he finished his National Service he has had seven. And I'm afraid he may be getting engaged to someone quite wrong for him."

Hester realized that her godmother was in her maternal mood, the mood which came but seldom and made up for it by its intensity.

"That must be very worrying," she said sympathetically. "But why don't you like her? I mean, why is she wrong for him?"

"Oh, there isn't a 'she' that I know of, it's just that I feel there might be. Of Course I wouldn't mind at all, if they were the *right* kind of girls—but Derek is so irresponsible. He has been engaged twice before and broken it off each time."

Hardly had Cecily spoken than she remembered Hester's own broken engagement, and she racked her brains for a tactful way of changing the subject. But Hester spoke first, and quite calmly. "Weren't they the right kind of girls either?"

"I never saw them. One was in Germany and one was in Aldershot. . . . There's the bell hurry-upping at last."

The church, like much of the village, had been re-built after the great fire at the end of the seventeenth century. It was rather large, as if the builders had expected Mingham to grow into a town, and its appearance suggested that the architect had admired the churches of Sir Christopher Wren and had done his best to imitate one or several of them. It was severely classical, with a handsome portico facing the length of the village street and a spire reminiscent of St. Bride's on a smaller scale. The interior still retained much of its original cream and gold splendour (though the pitch-pine pews, installed in 1863, looked sadly incongruous), and the sunlight still streamed in through large, clear windows, which the renovators in 1863 had wished to replace by stained glass, but which had been mercifully preserved from this fate by a shortage of money.

"Not a bit like a village church, is it?" Cecily whispered complacently.

She led the way down the aisle. Then she stood aside, motioning Hester to enter the pew on the left, and at the same time indicating by a slight frown that things were not quite as they should be. Her goddaughter saw that the pew was already occupied by two women. But as it could easily have held six she did not think this mattered.

Cecily, however, was put out. Although all the pews were now 'free,' and although she seldom came to church, she liked to think of this pew as hers, or rather, as belonging to The End House. And the two strangers were sitting at the far end, where she liked to sit herself because it was a less exposed position and she could relax and close her eyes during the Rector's dreadfully dull sermon. Moreover they had got the best hassocks as well as the best places; the two plump, solid hassocks which were so much more comfortable for kneeling on than the new foam-rubber ones. Worst of all, their presence made her own unnecessary; the pew would not have looked empty this Sunday even if she had stayed at home.

The intrusion of these strangers continued to vex her, and prevented her from achieving the resigned, half-awake state which she called peaceful contemplation; the proper state of mind for enduring the dull sermons and the erratic behaviour of the organ. The organist was Mrs. Merlin, but the organ's occasional whoops and groans were not her fault, for it had an incurable ailment which made it very difficult to control. Cecily wished she had warned Hester about the organ before they entered the church. Still, Hester was accustomed to church-going, and perhaps other organs were subject to the same failings. One didn't know; one knew so little about Hester . . . or about organs. . . .

Jerking herself awake (for it would not do to fall fast asleep in this conspicuous seat at the aisle end of the pew), Cecily began to think about Hester. How nice she was, and how brave. Few people would have guessed she was suffering from a broken heart. Of course it had been last year, yes, nearly a whole year ago now, but broken hearts did not mend easily; she knew that, because she had once had one herself.

It might have been wiser, she thought, for Hester to have given way to her grief, instead of ignoring it and trying to carry on, as she had done all the autumn and winter, and getting colds and bronchitis and finally pneumonia and ending up in hospital. Such a horrid hospital too, so gloomy and depressing . . .

how did they expect the sick to recover, when they nursed them in places like that?

Cecily knew what the hospital was like because she had visited Hester there, in response in an undemanding, uninformative letter which she had correctly interpreted as a cry for help. Well, of course it was; the mere fact of her writing it, to a godmother she hardly kept up with, had shown how badly she needed help. The excuses about not wanting to worry her fussy aunts had not deceived Cecily, who perfectly understood why Hester did not want to retreat to Yorkshire. The great thing about Mingham was not its good country air but its remoteness from everything connected with Raymond.

So here she was; and no one, looking at her, would guess what she had suffered . . . I've thought that before, Cecily told herself, fighting off sleep and a tendency to think in circles. But the sermon must be nearly over, the Rector had raised his voice as he always did towards its end (perhaps with the kindly intention of rousing the sleepers), and the organ had given a small, stifled groan as if it were preparing itself for the offertory hymn. Cecily turned and looked along the pew, and managed to identify the intruders as Miss Cardwell, the school-teacher, and her friend Miss . . . something like carpet. Hester was sitting back, they were drooping slightly forward, and she realized it was only their unfamiliar Sunday hats that had made them appear total strangers. But why did they come and sit in this pew when they had never done so before?

Miss Carpet was feeling faint, she thought, she looked like a waxwork melting in the heat and Miss Cardwell was half supporting her. The interest of wondering whether Miss Carpet would last out to the end got Cecily through the remainder of the sermon, and as soon as the service was over and the choir had disappeared into the vestry she nudged Hester and rose to her feet.

"Help them out quickly," she whispered. "The little door at this side."

Miss Cardwell's tottering friend was escorted out through the little door, Hester and Miss Cardwell supporting her and

Cecily following with a mixed collection of prayer-books, hand-bags and gloves. Outside the door stood a massive tombstone like a solid table, and on this convenient surface the patient was laid down to recover. Miss Cardwell fanned her with a prayer-book, and Cecily officiously removed her scarf and laid it under her head for a pillow.

"Let me introduce my goddaughter," she said chattily to Miss Cardwell. "Miss Clifford—Miss Cardwell and Miss—er . . ."

She indicated the sufferer, whose name she could not re-member; but then no one would expect her to make a formal introduction to a green-faced, semi-conscious figure lying flat on a tombstone. "Knapp," said Miss Cardwell, who did expect it.

"Of course," Cecily said quickly. "Is she all right?"

"Water," Hester said briskly. "Is there a tap anywhere near?"

"Water," said Miss Cardwell, approving of the suggestion. "No, but I'll get some here."

She looked round, walked over to a grave where there was a bunch of flowers in a green tin vase, lifted the flowers out and returned with the vase. Hester thought it showed presence of mind but Cecily thought it was dreadfully unhygienic. A mere sprinkling, however, brought Miss Knapp to her senses. She blinked and sighed deeply and lifted her arms to ward off fur-ther remedies, then she slowly sat up and began to apologise for giving so much trouble.

"It's because we were sitting in the middle of the church," Miss Cardwell declared. "Where we used to sit, just by the vestry door, was much cooler."

"Then why don't you go on sitting there?"

"Because it's been turned into a Bishop's Corner."

Before they could find out what this meant they were joined by Mrs. Hyde-Ridley, who had seen their departure by the side door and had come round from the main one to find out what was happening. The delay in her arrival was due to her having to say good morning to all her acquaintances and collect any news that was going—a pleasurable duty which she faithfully performed every Sunday morning.

"Only a faint!" Mrs. Hyde-Ridley cried. "I thought you must be really *ill* as they had to take you out by the little door, as everyone knows it's never used now and it was just lucky it wasn't locked. Fainting's just nerves, you know, and what you should have done was to put your head right down on your knees the minute you began to feel dizzy. When I was a V.A.D. we always made people put their heads right down if they thought they felt faint!"

Hester rather agreed with this speech, for she thought Cecily and Miss Cardwell were making far too much fuss about the faint and that fresh air alone would have cured it. Miss Cardwell on the other hand resented the implication that her friend had given in too easily.

"Miss Knapp is delicate, as you very well know," she said. "If I'd had my way she wouldn't have been in church this morning, for I could see she wasn't fit for it. But she isn't one to make a fuss about herself. That's never been her habit."

This speech told Mrs. Hyde-Ridley what she wanted to know: that Miss Cardwell and Miss Knapp had been reconciled and were now bosom friends again.

"It was frightfully stuffy in church this morning," Cecily said tactfully. "I wish Mr. Merlin would have more windows open, but I suppose he feels the cold."

"He's so thin," said Mrs. Hyde-Ridley. "He fasts too much, as that's a good thing of course but not if you over-do it!"

"If you feel all right, Myrtle, we'll be getting along now," Miss Cardwell said to Miss Knapp.

"Oh, she'll be perfectly all right now she's out in the open air," Mrs. Hyde-Ridley declared. "I dare say she's anaemic as vegetarians so often are as it isn't a natural diet whatever they say."

"We are not vegetarians," Miss Cardwell retorted sharply.

Mrs. Hyde-Ridley had already heard a rumour that they had abandoned vegetarianism, but she was glad to have it confirmed. The reform must have taken place since Christmas, because she knew for a fact that their Christmas dinner had been a nut duck and a pudding made without beef suet, and that the latter had been a dire failure.

Of course Bennet Hutton knew what a Bishop's Corner was. He never went to church, but he was keenly interested in church affairs and had even contributed to the expense of this minor alteration. The last three pews in the north aisle, he explained, had been removed to make a small space, in the corner by the vestry door, where the Bishop could put on his robes of office, on the very rare occasions when he visited Mingham. The space had been screened off by curtains (like a cubicle in a dormitory) to give the Bishop privacy. Naturally one couldn't expect a Bishop to squash into the vestry with the choir and the Rector; he was entitled to a corner of his own.

Maggie, too, knew all about it; but she had never thought of telling them. Cecily spoke about this after lunch, when Hester was helping her to wash up. "Maggie never tells me anything," she complained.

"Oh well," said Hester, "I suppose she didn't think it would interest you."

"But of course it does—especially if they're going to sit in our pew."

"What a beautiful church it is. Much too large for a village, though."

"Maggie can be very difficult," said Cecily.

Hester made a sympathetic reply, but went on talking about the church. Much as she liked Cecily, there was something a little awkward about the situation; it was as though she was being forced to take sides, and to side with her elders against her contemporaries.

"Let us hope this weather lasts," said Cecily. "I think you're looking better already, Hester. Better from pneumonia, I mean," she added anxiously; for she was always careful not to remind Hester of the past and she did not want her to think that her appearance was a kind of gauge to the state of her heart.

The pretence about pneumonia did not deceive Hester, but it reminded her of all the kindness Cecily had shown. And of the horrible hospital as well, and the miseries of last winter; but that was not Cecily's fault, because it was touchingly obvious that she was trying to be tactful.

"Of course I'm better," she said. "I'm quite recovered, really. If I hadn't let the flat I could go back to London and look for another job."

"Oh no, dear—not back to London. It's much too soon. And you know I want you here for at least the rest of the summer."

It *was* too soon, Hester reflected wryly; though she hadn't thought so until Cecily mentioned it.

"Anyway, I've let the flat," she said.

"Such a good thing," Cecily said, with a significant look that at once reminded Hester of how hateful the flat had been all last winter. "I shouldn't go back there, if I were you. Couldn't you find another flat? I mean, I don't think Chelsea is healthy for you, so near the river . . . low-lying, and all those fogs. Perhaps somewhere in Hampstead . . ."

Hester put the last coffee-cup back on its hook and shut the cupboard door with a slam.

"That's the lot," she said. "And now I'd better go and write to my aunts. I write them a joint letter, you know, which is perhaps rather lazy of me but they both read all my letters anyhow, so there's really no point in writing separate ones. . . . Oh, I don't think Hampstead, Cecily, it's too far out and not a place I've ever wanted to live in."

Cecily hoped these objections to Hampstead didn't mean that Raymond had lived there. How stupid of her not to have thought of that; no wonder Hester had changed the subject and gone rushing upstairs to write to her aunts.

But if Hampstead was a blunder, she had at least managed to avoid worse blunders; she had mentioned pneumonia and avoided mentioning broken engagements; she had skillfully drawn attention to the low-lying, foggy nature of Chelsea, as an excuse for not returning to the flat.

It was so important, Cecily thought, that Hester should not be reminded of the past.

# CHAPTER FIVE

DEREK HUTTON and the proprietor of Rudd's Garage were alike in thinking that one day was as good as another, and it was not until the following week that the electric chair's battery had been charged and its tires pumped up ready for action. In the interval of waiting, Bennet Hutton changed his mind about going to call on Thomas Seamark, but as time went on he changed it back again. It just showed, said Derek, that a good long delay was better than a brief one.

The entrance to the park was only a short distance from The End House, along the road which led to Monk's Mingham, but from the imposing gates a flinty drive went curling away through the park for nearly a mile. At first it ran gently uphill towards a low ridge, with a pretty view of the fine old oaks on the lower ground and the water-meadows beyond. But over the ridge the scene changed; the woods closed in and the drive ran between banks of rhododendrons, zigzagging steeply down the side of the valley towards the hidden Priory. The rhododendrons were old, and grew thickly, towering high above the drive and shutting out the light, but many of them were in flower and the verges were bright with bluebells, so that the general effect was not sombre at all. Cousin Bennet had described it as a tunnel of dripping evergreens, but he must have been thinking of a wet day in winter.

Following the electric chair as it bowled briskly downhill, Hester was glad she had come. She had come as an escort, to assist Cousin Bennet if the chair got stuck in a rut or broke down, but it seemed unlikely he would need any help; the chair was going beautifully and he drove it with considerable skill, avoiding the ruts and pot holes and negotiating the bends of the zigzag with ease. Sometimes he went so fast that she had to run to keep up with him, but usually a quick walk sufficed. She walked behind, to give him more room to manoeuvre round the pot-holes, and this had made conversation a little difficult to begin with, but in the sheltered quietness of the rhododendron tunnel they could hear each other clearly.

"A fine afternoon like this, he's sure to be out," he called cheerfully.

"But you want him to be in. You won't be able to start getting to know him again, if he's not at home."

"Not sure I do want to get to know him again. Probably all a waste of time."

"But it's important, for Cecily's sake. She feels so dreadful about having insulted him."

(For some reason it was quite all right to speak of Cecily *tout court* but impossible to drop the formal title of "Cousin" for Bennet. His dignity seemed to demand it.)

"Do him good," said Cousin Bennet. "Do her good too. A useful lesson."

He was being perverse and difficult, but that was just his way. The chair continued to advance and she felt sure he was looking forward to the task he professed to dislike. It would be, after all, a new beginning for him as well as for Thomas Seamark, an escape from the routine of invalidism—which he had perhaps adopted as an escape from something else but which he now found tedious. It was pleasant to feel that she had helped to rescue him.

"Useful lessons are all very well," she said, "but it would be a shame if Cecily was refused permission to come and paint. I can see that she feels the need of a—a particular sort of scene. The picturesque, I suppose."

"There'll probably be nothing left of the picturesque, once he gets going."

"What do you mean?"

"He'll begin making improvements," Cousin Bennet predicted. "All the Seamarks do, sooner or later. He'll pull down that old ruin of a mill and fell the tottering oaks and clean out the river and re-build the home farm. That for a start."

"But why should he start now?"

"It's overdue. He came into the place when he was fifteen, you know—inherited it from his uncle who left all the money tied up in a trust so that Thomas couldn't get at it. A life interest to the wife, I believe—and she went off to the south coast in a huff and lived another twelve years."

"Whose wife?"

"His uncle's, of course. Don't be stupid—Thomas wasn't married then. He was only a boy, to begin with, then there was the war and he was in the army. Then, when his old aunt died in nineteen-fifty or thereabouts, he could have started making improvements but he didn't. I've often wondered why."

"He got married instead," she suggested.

"Not till a couple of years afterwards." Cousin Bennet let the chair slow down while he brooded on the problem. "He had two years to make improvements in and he didn't. Very odd, considering he's a Seamark."

"I don't see why—"

"You don't know them. Of course it's easy to see why he hasn't done anything since. Getting married and losing his wife and all that."

". . . There's a morbid streak in them, too."

"What happened to her?"

"Killed in a car smash abroad."

"How sad. But it was—how long ago?"

"Must be four years. That's what I mean. Any day now we shall find he's got over it and is beginning to plan improvements. It is, as I said, overdue."

Evidently there were two schools of thought about Thomas Seamark. Cecily and Maggie saw him as a figure of tragedy, an inconsolable recluse; Cousin Bennet saw him as a man with an inherited zeal for improving his property, which circumstances had hitherto thwarted but which was bound to break out soon. On the whole Hester preferred Cousin Bennet's view to the other, although she hoped he was exaggerating the scope and nature of the improvements. A model farm, a river without its picturesque tottering oaks and ruined water-mill, would hold no inspiration for Cecily.

"Here we are," said Cousin Bennet. "Well, almost."

Giving the chair its head he drew rapidly away from her, for the drive had levelled out again and was better surfaced than on the hill.

"You wait here," he called as he went.

Hester still did not see why she should be a mere bath-chair attendant, left to lurk in the shrubbery while Cousin Bennet paid his call. She had meant to coax him into letting her accompany him, but his sudden departure took her by surprise; she had not realised the Priory was so near. She walked on slowly. At the end of the straight stretch the drive turned at a right angle and she could see that it opened out into a gravelled forecourt. But the Priory itself was still hidden behind trees and rhododendrons. She had been told to wait out of sight, but she did not intend to come away without getting a glimpse of the building whose re-markable ugliness had started all the trouble. Strictly speaking, it was Cecily's description of it that had started the trouble, but one would like to know whether she was right.

A narrow path led into the rhododendron thicket on her left, and she guessed that it was—or had once been—a way through to the forecourt. It was badly overgrown but she edged her way along, following its windings with difficulty, until she found her-self standing on the edge of the forecourt, nicely screened by an azalea bush. Or so she hoped, because there was more activity there than she had expected.

The exterior of the Priory was being painted and repaired. The east front, which faced her, was partly covered by scaffold-ing and there were ladders everywhere. In the forecourt stood a lorry and a small van, several workmen were unloading the lorry, and others were at work on the house. There were noises of hammering and chipping and scraping, they were re-pointing the brickwork and painting the windows, and high up behind the parapet they were doing something pretty drastic to the roof.

"But it doesn't need it," was her first thought. Her second was that Cousin Bennet was a better judge of character than Cecily and Maggie.

The Priory looked impressively hideous and practically inde-structible. It had been built, or at least enlarged, in glazed purple and yellow brick which neither time nor weather could mellow; and of course no ivy or creeper had been allowed to hide the pattern, bands and lozenges of purple against a yellow background, which Thomas Seamark's grandfather had chosen for his fine new facade. There were a great many plate-glass windows, some of them jutting out in heavy, square bays, and an imposing flight of white steps leading up to the door, and more white stone at the top—the in-and-out parapet Cecily had mentioned—and cast-iron ornamentation crowning the protruding bays. Brick and stone, cast iron and plate-glass, all looked enormously solid and durable, the very best quality, aggressively capable of surviving anything.

"Golly," Hester said aloud. And, inescapably, she wondered what Raymond would have said if he had been with her.

But the Priory was too dominant, too overpoweringly visible, to leave room for phantoms or silence for a remembered voice. It shouted, it glared, it monopolized the attention. She had not even noticed the absence of Cousin Bennet's electric chair, which she might have expected to see parked at the foot of the white steps. But at this moment it came nimbly round the corner of the house, with Cousin Bennet in it and Thomas Seamark walking alongside.

It was the corner nearest to her and they saw her at once, the azalea being rather thin on that side. Bennet said something explanatory to his host and then he waved, commanding her to come forward. Since Hester had never mastered his reasons for abandoning her she did not feel she was committing a social blunder by joining him now; but she wished she had been with him from the start. It was a little awkward to be discovered lurking in a shrubbery.

"How do you do?" Mr. Seamark said formally. Her presence in his shrubbery did not appear to surprise him, and he showed no sign of remembering that he had seen her before. Perhaps Cecily was right, and he had not noticed her.

"Thomas was just going out, when I arrived," Cousin Bennet said chattily. "I spotted him disappearing round the corner of the house, so I went after him." (I was right, Hester thought, he's been looking forward to this tremendously.) "Pity not to see you, Thomas, when I've come all the way for the pleasure of renewing our acquaintance."

"It is good news that you are able to get about again," Mr. Seamark replied politely. "Won't you come into the house?"

He led the way. At the foot of the white steps he showed, for the first time, a touch of genuine interest and surprise, when Cousin Bennet deftly extricated himself from the chair and walked unaided up to the door. "You really *are* better," he commented; and Hester wondered whether he was comparing Cousin Bennet's recovery with his own.

"I have my good days, and my bad ones. It was a germ, you know. An insidious germ."

Hester was interested to hear Cousin Bennet's own explanation of his mysterious malady, but she wasn't sure she believed it.

The great hall was full of trophies of the chase and brass ornaments of an oriental nature. She noticed that the brass was highly polished and the antlers free from dust, so evidently Mr. Seamark had an efficient domestic staff. But it was all rather grand and ugly, in keeping with the exterior, and she was pleasantly surprised by the library to which he conducted them, on the other side of the house. For this room looked lived in and comfortable, and bore hardly any traces of the hereditary Seamark bad taste.

The three long windows opened on to a formal terraced garden, from which steps led down to a lower terrace and then to the river. The river was overshadowed by the trees on the far bank, but the terraced garden lay in full sunshine and the library itself was dazzlingly bright after the cold, dark hall. It was really quite charming.

"What a pretty view," she said, thinking that it wasn't nearly so "enclosed" as Cecily and Maggie had led her to expect.

"I see you're having the house painted," Cousin Bennet chimed in quickly.

"It's very picturesque . . . with the river and the woods in the background," said Hester.

"Maintenance is an expensive business these days. Especially with a house this size," Cousin Bennet.

"Yes . . . yes," said Mr. Seamark, trying to deal with both conversations at once.

"I like that steep bluff on the other side, and the way the cliff overhangs the river at the bend. It's so unexpected, compared with the rather flat country the other side of Mingham."

"Paint doesn't seem to last as it used to."

"Won't you sit down?"

Cousin Bennet sat down. Hester continued to stand at the window, making her point about the scenery being picturesque and unusual. (For so it was, and she realized now why Cecily needed the freedom of the park.) It was a point which could quite easily be made by a stranger, seeing the view for the first time, and she wasn't going to be deflected from making it.

It took her another minute to realize that neither of them was listening. Thomas Seamark, despairing of listening on two fronts, had plumped for the subject that interested him. Cousin Bennet was telling him about the shockingly ruinous state of Mrs. Hyde-Ridley's property and the intriguing rumour that it was going to be painted at last.

"But haven't you looked at those houses, Thomas?" he piped. "Don't you ever drive through the village?"

"Sometimes. But I don't stop."

"You should. You should. I don't know how they continue to stand up. She can't have spent a penny on them since she bought them."

Mr. Seamark looked suitably appalled. "I'll stop next time," he said.

"Do. And come and see us while you're about it."

Unnoticed, Hester sat down. Cousin Bennet hadn't lingered over the invitation, he'd thrown it out and then returned to the rumour. She wondered how he heard these rumours, then she remembered Mrs. Pilgrim, the daily obliger.

"The rumour is that the tenant is going to put them in order," Cousin Bennet was saying. "But that can't be right, can it?"

"No tenant would be so altruistic," said Thomas Seamark, in the gloomy voice of a landed proprietor. "Unless of course, the tenant is negotiating to buy the property. Suppose that was the real truth behind your rumour—"

"I'm sure it isn't," Hester interrupted. "Mrs. Hyde-Ridley is very, very proud of owning property. I'm sure she wouldn't want to sell it."

Her certainty was hardly justified, since she had met Mrs. Hyde-Ridley only twice, but she felt it was time she said something.

Just to remind them she was there.

Mr. Seamark responded politely, as if he were conscious of having neglected her and wanted to make amends. But Cousin Bennet turned sulky, contradicted her twice, and then said it was time to go.

"You must stay for tea," said his host.

He walked towards the fireplace, beside which Hester observed an old-fashioned brass bell-handle set in the wall. She waited with interest for him to ring it—not since the days of her childhood had she seen anyone ring a bell to summon a servant—but Cousin Bennet scrambled to his feet.

"No, Thomas, not today. Mustn't be out too long. Doctor's orders."

Hester could have smacked him. No doctor had given orders to Bennet Hutton, she thought; he had invented the doctor just as he had invented the illness. He wanted all the limelight for himself, he had sulked like a child the minute she diverted Thomas Seamark's attention, and now he was dragging her away, just as she had begun to lead up to the subject of landscape painting.

She was not given a chance to continue. Cousin Bennet, who had entered the house unassisted, required a supporter on each side to get him out of it, and as he shuffled along between them he talked without stopping. When he had been helped into the electric chair he commanded Hester to walk beside it, falsely asserting that it needed a guiding hand for the sharp turn into the drive, and he barely gave her time to say good-bye before setting the chair in motion. As they proceeded rapidly across the forecourt she looked back and saw Mr. Seamark standing at the foot of the steps, watching their departure with an air of faint surprise, not unmixed—or so she hoped—with regret.

"Don't forget—stop and have a look at *Firenze*!" Cousin Bennet called as they turned the corner. The rhododendrons engulfed them, the Priory and its owner were hidden, and Hester took her pseudo-guiding-hand off the chair and dropped a pace behind. He ought to have reminded Thomas Seamark to look in at The End House as well, she thought—it would have been a good moment to stress the invitation. But she said nothing. Cousin Bennet had annoyed her so much that she did not want to talk to him.

The steep climb to the top of the ridge taxed the chair's powers severely. It crawled up at a snail's pace, with Cousin Bennet uttering encouraging chirrups to it on the worst gradients—and never giving a backward look at his silent escort. This behaviour had its effect; Hester's quick temper cooled and she began to suspect that she, too, was sulking, and to remember that Bennet had seemed, not so long ago, a man deserving of rescue. And even a *malade imaginaire*, she reflected, might be genuinely tired by his first outing after months of seclusion.

When they reached the top of the hill she quickened her pace and drew level with him.

"I think that can be counted a real success," she said in a friendly voice.

"Choo, choo!" said Cousin Bennet, presumably to his chair.

"And you were quite right about his hereditary passion for improvements being due to break out. I suppose having the Priory painted is just the first stage!"

"Choo, choo!"

He was being difficult again. But Hester, when she wasn't in a temper, prided herself on being able to cope with the difficult.

"He's a bit *farouche*, isn't he?" she went on, with a sympathetic smile for Thomas Seamark's near neighbour. "But I suspect that it's only a pose. He thawed so quickly. I'm sure he really wanted us to stay for tea—he was glad to see us. From his point of view, as well as ours, we came at the right moment."

"I did," said Cousin Bennet. "Not you."

"Difficult" seemed an understatement, but Hester remained calm. "Do you mean he didn't like me?" she asked patiently. "I thought we were getting on quite well, but—"

"Who cares whether he liked you or not? You should not have been there. I told you to stay in the shrubbery. I foresaw that you would be a hindrance to me, even—at that stage—a *fatal* hindrance," Cousin Bennet declared shrilly. "And I was right."

"But how—"

"Chatter, chatter, chatter! 'What a pretty peep through this window—what a picturesque park—is that a ruined water-mill I see in the distance?' Pah! If I hadn't put a stop to it I believe you'd have talked about sketching expeditions."

"And why not?"

"So crude, so obvious," said Cousin Bennet, muttering away to himself like an angry hen. "And fatal—absolutely fatal. He hasn't forgiven Cecily for insulting his home and his family. He would have Seen what you were after, and forbidden it. Don't you realize, my dear child, that it will be twice as difficult to get him to say Yes, if we once allow him to say No?"

Belatedly, Hester recognized in Cousin Bennet a serpent more cunning than herself. By his standards, indeed, she hadn't been cunning at all. (So crude, so obvious.) She saw it now, and wondered why on earth she hadn't seen it sooner. She no longer wanted to smack her mentor, but naturally she found it hard to apologize to him.

"I suppose you're right," she said reluctantly. Then, meeting his twinkling glance, she laughed and added, "Of course you are. I went in with both feet, didn't I? I should have stayed in the shrubbery."

"Not at all, not at all. I should have taken you with me and briefed you first. No harm done, anyway."

Thanks to my superior judgment, said his twinkling eyes. But he could afford to be generous; Hester had admitted her error and they were friends again, and he had enjoyed himself enormously and could look forward to more enjoyment. To other excursions, with the summer coming on; to purposeful diplomacy, now that she was here to encourage it.

They had reached the lane now, where the surface was smoother and he could increase his speed. The wasted years—years of failure and discontent—seemed to stretch behind him like the stony drive. He was riding away from them.

# CHAPTER SIX

"SEEMS AS THOUGH you've brought the fine weather with you," Mrs. Pilgrim told Hester. But though she said it quite often she did not sound very pleased about it. Soon she took to adding, "We could do with some rain," as if she held the visitor responsible for the lack of it.

"I don't think Mrs. Pilgrim likes Hester," Cecily confided to Bennet. "I can't think why, because Hester isn't a bit of trouble— she dusts her own room and helps with the washing-up and so on— and she's as nice and friendly as possible."

"But critical. You can see it in her eye. Mrs. P. is conscious of being criticized. Naturally, she resents it."

"But Hester *doesn't* criticize her. I'm sure she would never dream of doing such a thing."

"Her manners are irreproachable. But she notices things, and Mrs. P. notices that she notices, and being far more sensitive than her Anglo-Saxon exterior suggests she feels hurt, therefore hostile. It's understandable, isn't it? No one likes being faintly despised." Cecily did not dispute it, but she was far from convinced. Bennet always made things sound more complicated than they were and it did not do to take his imaginative flights seriously. Hester wasn't critical and contemptuous; and even if she had been, Mrs. Pilgrim was certainly not sensitive enough to notice mere nuances of behaviour. She gave her husband an indulgent smile— the smile that made allowances for ill-health and a fanciful nature —and then cast her eye over the objects on the bedside table, the things that had to be there, each in its proper place, before he could settle down for the night. The clock just beneath the lamp, the glass of water to the right of the clock, the lump of rock sulphur in one corner, the biscuit diagonally opposite . . .

"Ask her and see," Bennet said crossly.

"Ask who what? You haven't got your patience cards, they must be in the other room—"

"Ask Hester what she thinks of Mrs. P.'s cooking. Or her dusting, come to that. No, don't. Just wait, and she'll soon tell you."

"I don't want them."

"Don't want them?" she echoed. She was so startled by this departure from routine that she forgot what he had said first. "And the board isn't here either," she cried, looking down at where the patience board ought to have been propped against the table leg.

"If I don't want the cards it follows that I don't need the board."

"But, darling, you always like to have them there."

"Can't I change my mind? I've given up patience."

He sounded exasperated; the words could have had a double meaning. But his wife did not look for double meanings where one would suffice, and her only fear was that Bennet might be running a temperature. She bent over him and felt his forehead.

No, it felt quite cool. But the departure from routine troubled her and she lingered a moment longer, waiting for him to change his mind back again—which in an invalid was tolerated—or to say something else.

"It's going to rain," he said.

"Is it?"

"Don't *humour* me, Cecily. If I say it's going to rain, say 'No it isn't' or something!"

After being married to Bennet for more than twenty-five years Cecily knew how to deal with this sort of remark. It was quite easy; one simply ignored it.

"Good night," she said placidly, bending forward again to bestow the wifely peck on his cheek which was part of the routine.

"Good night," he replied. He looked away from her and appeared to be addressing the wardrobe. But that, too, was routine.

"It's going to rain," said Maggie, in a knowledgeable way.

"The forecast didn't say so," Derek retorted.

"I don't trust those forecasts."

"You sound like a crusty old farmer. 'Never did trust them chaps up in Lunnon.' No, seriously, Maggie, you mustn't turn into a cocksure local barometer. It's the first downward step."

"What on earth do you mean?"

"Leading to handwoven tweeds, dancing round the maypole, brewing nettle beer—the lot. Back-to-the-land-ery!"

Maggie laughed. "I don't do any of those things," she protested.

"Not yet. I'm just warning you."

Being warned by Derek was different from being criticized by her mother; she could argue with him and yet admit to herself that his warning was justified. She could even admit it to him.

"I suppose I *am* getting rather rustic and weather-beaten," she said.

"Not exactly weather-beaten. But you do look rather a scarecrow, sometimes."

They were in her bedroom and she leant forward to stare at her reflection in the looking-glass. "I don't seem able to look like other people," she muttered.

"Oh, rot! You're not at all bad, really. Better than a lot of girls," he said hurriedly. "Well—what about this picnic on Saturday?"

Maggie scowled at her reflection and then turned away from it, wondering why she had been tempted to confide in Derek. He had only come in to discuss his picnic, she thought, and he only wanted a picnic because Hester was staying with them. It was to be an entertainment for Hester, because she was pretty and elegant, the kind of girl who could count on people doing their best to amuse her.

"Oh well, I suppose we could have a picnic," she conceded. "If it doesn't rain."

"The three of us, I thought. Hester can borrow Mama's bicycle."

Maggie wondered whether Hester would like that. Then she thought of something else.

"Not a picnic in the park," she said.

"I don't see why not. We always used to, and now Papa and Hester have re-established our claim."

"I don't think they have," said Maggie. "I should feel like a trespasser, if we went there without asking Thomas—after all this time, I mean. But I don't see why I have to come, anyway. You and Hester don't need a chaperone."

"It would be better if you came," Derek said, rather unexpectedly. "More fun," he added coaxingly.

"Oh, all right. But it's going to rain."

"No, it isn't. We shall have a beautiful hot summer, going on and on. It hasn't rained for ages, so why should it start now, just when I want a picnic?"

Mrs. Hyde-Ridley could have told him why. Her friend Mrs. Vandevint was notoriously unlucky with the weather, and Mrs. Vandevint was arriving on Friday afternoon.

It was characteristic of their friendship that a plea to come sooner had been countered by a decision to come later; for each of them was stubbornly determined not to let the other dominate her. Mrs. Hyde-Ridley's urgent postcard had been answered by a letter in which Mrs. Vandevint gave six excellent reasons for not being able to leave home at once, or even next week. And now she was coming on a Friday, in spite of her old friend's advice never to travel on a Friday, or because of it; and that meant, almost certainly, that they were in for a wet weekend.

Mrs. Hyde-Ridley was a natural optimist and she always hoped that Mrs. Vandevint's bad luck would change. On Friday her optimism seemed justified, it was a fine, sunny afternoon and the glass as steady as a rock. She tapped it before she went to meet Mrs. Vandevint, and again when they entered the house together, and again before they went to bed. It did not waver.

"It doesn't move because it can't," said Mrs. Vandevint, watching her critically. "All that tapping is very bad for them, you know. It prevents them behaving naturally."

Mrs. Hyde-Ridley scoffed at the idea that her glass wasn't behaving naturally. She tapped it every morning and evening and it had never gone wrong. That was what glasses were for.

But in the small hours she was woken by a familiar, unwelcome sound, the drip of water in several tin basins in the attic overhead. It must be raining hard if the water was coming in already. She got up and climbed the stair to the attic, to make sure that all the leaks had basins underneath them, and then she went down to the kitchen to put towels along the window-sill where driving rain came under the rotting sash-bar. She counted the pussies and there was one missing, so she could not shut the window in the scullery by which they went in and out, but she fetched the back-door mat and laid it on the floor to absorb the rain. Then she shut the kitchen door on the pussies and went back to bed, angry with the weather but feeling at the same time that the weather couldn't help itself. It was bound to rain when Dulcie came to stay.

Neither of them believed in early rising, and it was ten o'clock before Mrs. Vandevint came down. She edged her way into the tiny dining-room and at once began to complain.

"Violet, what *were* you doing? You woke me up in the middle of the night and I didn't get a wink of sleep afterwards. And then a very nasty thing happened—a big, wet *cat* came in at the window and tried to get into my bed!"

"Oh, naughty pussy!"

"Don't say it was one of yours," Mrs. Vandevint cried in disgust.

Mrs. Hyde-Ridley had already said so; her cats were known to her as pussies, while other people's were merely cats. Remembering, however, that Dulcie disliked cats, or pretended to, she deftly changed the subject.

"I had to get up as it was simply pouring as I knew the attic window was open," she said rapidly.

"But then you went downstairs! I heard you. You were bumping about in the kitchen for ages."

"Have some toast."

Mrs. Vandevint eyed the toast balefully, for it was burnt, but she said nothing because she was just as bad a cook as Mrs. Hyde-Ridley and she knew that if she criticized the toast Violet would in due course criticize hers. They were very lenient about each other's cooking, they had to be; even the direst failures—blackened chops, curdled custard, bullet-like potatoes—were eaten if it was humanly possible to swallow them. Luckily both the ladies had cast-iron digestions.

But their leniency was only for the cooking; about everything else they were ruthlessly firm. Over the years their friendship had turned into a game played according to strict rules, and each was determined to see that the other kept them. They were rules for hospitality, based on memories of their Edwardian youth, of rounds of visits and a full, social life at home, of big houses and big families, of a world where there was always "something going on," and in which hospitality was generously given and as generously returned. They had not known each other when they were young but their memories were very similar; though each suspected the other, with some justification, of exaggerating the glories of her past.

"Not a very nice morning," Mrs. Vandevint remarked. She pushed her plate aside and stooped for her handbag, the battered twin of Mrs. Hyde-Ridley's, bulging with old letters, newspaper cuttings, prescriptions, address-books, crumbs and dust. But unlike Mrs. Hyde-Ridley's bag, hers had also to hold a cigarette case and matches and her reading spectacles, and could seldom be persuaded to stay shut. She lit a cigarette, and gave her friend a look that said, "How are you going to entertain me today?"

Mrs. Hyde-Ridley staved it off. "Oh, this endless smoking!" she shrieked, jumping up to open the window. "I really don't know how you *can*, Dulcie, as everyone knows it's awfully bad for you as you inhale as *all* the doctors say you shouldn't!"

Mrs. Vandevint puffed away steadily, her eyes as unblinking as agates.

"That woman ought to be here by now!" Mrs. Hyde-Ridley grumbled. "I *told* her she was to come on the early bus while you were staying with me. And she promised she would but I suppose she's missed it. I'd better clear the table."

Mrs. Vandevint, who knew Violet to be an inspired liar, doubted the woman's existence or alternatively the existence of an early bus. She too found it difficult to get a reliable daily; but the absence of one did not affect the rules.

"Sit down while I finish my cigarette," she said. "You shouldn't go jigging about just after a meal—you'll get high blood-pressure. *My* doctor tells me it's very common nowadays, simply because people won't learn to sit still and relax."

Medical opinion was frequently quoted by both of them, to score a point or clinch an argument, as if it were Holy Writ. Mrs. Vandevint always said *"my doctor,"* with the air of one who owned a private oracle, but Mrs. Hyde-Ridley fought back by invoking doctors in the plural.

"I'm not dead yet," she retorted. "It's just nonsense, all this talk about sitting still and relaxing, as everyone knows it makes you old before your time! Still, if you want to, Dulcie, you can do it."

Mrs. Vandevint saw the danger just in time, the danger that she would find herself anchored in the drawing-room for the day, her only entertainment some dull book, on the excuse that it was what she had wanted. How cunning Violet was, taking advantage of a casual remark like that! Her heart warmed towards her wily friend, and her spirits rose, as she hastened to thwart her.

"Just half an hour after meals, that's what *my* doctor says—not all day. I quite agree with you, Violet, we don't want to grow old before our time."

"Not all day—no, of course not!" said Mrs. Hyde-Ridley, as though she would never have dreamed of suggesting it. "You must get all the fresh air you can while you're here as the Mingham air is so good even if it is raining, but I'm sure it's going to clear."

She peered out hopefully at the sodden garden. If it stopped raining before lunch she could take Dulcie a short walk in the afternoon, towards Monk's Mingham and back by the path through the woods, and then they could have tea in the garden—their own private picnic—and that would be quite enough entertainment for the first day. At least, it would do. But if the rain continued she would have to provide a wet-day entertainment. This meant a tea-party (but it was too late to organize one) or a bus-journey to Scorling and a cinema or tea in a cafe. Wet-day entertainments cost money, and she grudged spending money on Dulcie the very first day; also, the supply of wet-day entertainments was limited so they must be saved up for really bad weather.

"There she is at last!" she cried in triumph, hearing the slam of the back door and the clatter that always followed it, which was caused by her stupid obliger falling over the pussies' tin plate. "Now I'll just have a word with her and then we'll go out and do the shopping. Just to the post office and the butcher and baker, it won't take long but it will be a breath of fresh air."

"Fresh air—yes," said Mrs. Vandevint, giving it her qualified blessing. She waited. Mrs. Hyde-Ridley thought rapidly, peered once more at the rain, and then regretfully abandoned her plan for a nice country walk. Even if it cleared, the path through the woods would be much too muddy and the trees would drip on their hats. (Poor Dulcie, anyone could see she was town bred . . . such a fuss last year about the shortcut through Bogwash Meadow.) But the clouds looked higher, and it would be a fearful waste to use up a Scorling entertainment on an afternoon that might be fine. . . .

"This afternoon I thought we might pay some calls," she said, giving look for look. "Only in the village, as I tried to get Rudd's car but it's hopeless on a Saturday as he's always booked for a wedding. I'll take you to call on the Langleys and the Wrights sometime next week, but this afternoon we'll call on the rectory and the Huttons and perhaps the Headleys. I haven't paid any calls for ages as I've been so busy with the spring-cleaning! And then afterwards if it's fine we'll have tea in the garden—just like a picnic—or perhaps some of them will ask us to tea as they're all old friends except the Merlins, but that counts just the same because it's the rectory!"

"That will be very nice," said Mrs. Vandevint, nodding her approval. "And now, while you are seeing your woman, I'll write a line to my sister-in-law. Very high blood-pressure, poor thing, and a kind of stroke last year, so I always let them have my address when I'm away from home. Just in case."

As an entertainment it would do, she decided; but how typical of Violet to start off with something that didn't cost a penny. (When she stayed with me I took her to watch the *thé-dansant* at the Majestic the first day, *and* we had eclairs.) Oh well, it was better than nothing—and if she didn't keep Violet up to the mark she would find herself sitting in the garden all day long, or even being expected to weed it. (Must remind her about the shilling she borrowed in the bus yesterday.)

She sat down at the desk, delved in her bag for her fountain pen, and then paused to ask herself how long she would be staying here. A month, certainly; for Violet had stayed a month last autumn and the rule was that each visit must be equal in length. But this time she wanted to stay longer than a month, and naturally she was prepared to have Violet back for longer in return. Perhaps she had better say a month, to begin with, just in case . . .

She always wrote proper letters, which were sacrosanct, but her sister-in-law, like Violet, generally used postcards, which could be read by anyone because it wasn't dishonourable to read other people's postcards. It would be awkward if Violet learned from Sybil's reply that her friend was staying all the summer, before the facts had been explained to her. And one had to choose the right moment, with Violet.

Surely that voice in the hall wasn't the woman's. (It was a waste of time to memorise their names, since they never lasted long enough to be there at the next visit.) Abandoning the letter, Mrs. Vandevint dived for her bag and rummaged through it for her compact. A dab of purplish powder on her nose and a smoothing of her grey fringe and she felt tidy—though not at her best, because she was wearing the old mauve cardigan and baggy skirt which did not appear in public.

The door opened and Violet brought in a stranger whom Mrs. Vandevint instantly distrusted. "This is my tenant, Mrs. Bavington," she cried. "Oh, but of course you've met before, haven't you? Chrysanthemum was in *Firenze* last year when you were here, Dulcie, as I remember introducing you to her in the post office."

She remembered also that there had been some difficulty with Chrysanthemum at the time, not exactly a quarrel, but a coldness, which had kept them out of each other's houses. The encounter in the post office had been brief and formal.

Perhaps Chrysanthemum remembered it too. "It was just before I went to stay with my sister," she said, smiling ingratiatingly at Mrs. Vandevint. "That's why I never asked you to tea or anything —'cos I was just about to take wing. But I hope you'll come this time. I've heard so much about you from Mrs. Hyde-Ridley—it's almost like meeting an old friend."

Mrs. Vandevint could look very like a toad, and she looked it now. She sat perfectly still, fixing Chrysanthemum with her unblinking gaze, silently rejecting the proffered status of old friend. After an uncomfortable pause she said:

"Yes, I remember now that we met once before. I thought you were a stranger when you came in."

If Chrysanthemum felt the rebuff she did not show it. "I hope I shan't be a stranger any longer," she said, laughing merrily. "But I won't stay chatting now, 'cos I know what it is, all the chores and dusting to do—I wouldn't have come in at all, only Mrs. Hyde-Ridley caught me. I was just going to leave my little offering and speed away."

Underestimating Mrs. Vandevint, she waited for her to show some interest. But it was Mrs. Hyde-Ridley who broke the silence, and her matter-of-fact voice did less than justice to her tenant's generosity.

"Chrysanthemum has brought us a cake," she said.

"Oo—just a little one," its donor protested prettily. "A little cake with pink icing."

"Most neighbourly," Mrs. Vandevint remarked.

Chrysanthemum sped away rather sooner than she had intended. They weren't very forthcoming, those old ladies, they weren't as friendly or as grateful as people ought to be. But she had seen the gleam in Mrs. Vandevint's eye when she mentioned the pink icing, and she knew the little offering had been well-chosen and well-timed. It would make a good impression—specially when they tasted it, and specially on greedy old ladies who had never learned to cook.

# CHAPTER SEVEN

HAVING AGREED rather against her will to go for a picnic, Maggie was illogically as disappointed as anybody when the day proved wet. The idea of a picnic had become more agreeable, and she had looked forward to seeing the Monk's Mingham woods again and even to showing them to Hester. Hester had been looking forward to the picnic so much; she had not been—as Maggie rather oddly expected—blasé or merely polite, but gaily enthusiastic. For the first time a younger, livelier, even a sillier, Hester had been visible, a girl not much older than Maggie herself. Maggie had cautiously begun to think that a picnic with this Hester might be fun.

It was this Hester who insisted on cutting sandwiches and hard-boiling eggs before lunch, when the rain seemed to be lessening. "I'm sure it's going to clear," she said; and Maggie, the weather-wise, encouraged her, although the view from the kitchen window showed more clouds looming up above the roof of the stables, and Mrs. Pilgrim's face looked as black as any of them.

"I shan't be in your way here, shall I?" Hester asked, taking possession of one end of the kitchen table.

"Not at all, thank you, miss."

Mrs. Pilgrim had been with the Huttons for years and they all knew she was extra-polite when extra-annoyed, but Maggie ignored the danger signals and naturally Hester did not recognise them.

Maggie spilt sardine oil on the newly mopped floor. Hester moved the pan of potatoes to another part of the stove, to make room for the eggs. Presently Mrs. Pilgrim collected her rags and the tin of brass polish and went out into the hall, where Cecily found her cleaning the brasses with rather ominous zeal. She paused in surprise, because it is not the day for the brasses and anyway it was after half-past twelve and Mrs. Pilgrim always liked to leave early on Saturdays.

"Seems I'm in the way, in there," Mrs. Pilgrim said, jerking her head towards the kitchen door.

"Oh dear—are they in your way?" her employer asked, correctly interpreting this as a complaint.

"Well, madam, it's impossible to get your lunch started when they're all over the place with their tea."

Not for years had Cecily been addressed as "madam," and it alarmed her very much.

"They should have waited till afterwards," she said. "But don't worry, Mrs. Pilgrim—I'll see to the lunch myself. You'd better go home now, it's after half-past twelve."

"I did manage to get the potatoes on, but Miss Clifford she went and shoved them to the back of the stove. Don't blame me, madam, if they're not done in time."

"Of course I won't. How—how thoughtless of her."

"A picnic for the ducks, it'll be," Mrs. Pilgrim said sardonically. "There's the gooseberry pie I left on the kitchen table for you, but where it is now I couldn't say I'm sure."

Her sortie into the hall had been successful, she had managed to attract her employer's attention and work off her annoyance. She felt better for it; but Cecily felt worse. She had already been anxious about Mrs. Pilgrim's attitude to Hester and now her fears were proved true. Mrs. Pilgrim did not like Hester.

"Couldn't you have waited till after lunch?" she said, entering the kitchen after a five-minute interval to give Mrs. Pilgrim time to depart.

"But we want to start early—if it clears," Maggie explained. "It's not going to clear—it's raining harder than ever. What shall we do with all these sandwiches—and the hard-boiled eggs?"

"Eat them. Derek will eat them for tea, even if we can't have the picnic."

"And I'll use up the hard-boiled eggs in a casserole for supper," Hester said helpfully. "I'd love to do some cooking, if you'll let me."

"So you see they won't be wasted, Mother."

"You should have waited all the same. You upset Mrs. Pilgrim."

Cecily felt that she sounded nagging, querulous, but the thought of an upset Mrs. Pilgrim drove her on.

"You know she doesn't like people in the kitchen when she's cooking," she continued, addressing Maggie but intending Hester to listen. "And she's always in a hurry on Saturdays, trying to get our lunch before she leaves at half-past twelve. Saturday is really her busiest morning."

"Oh, well—she'll get over it," Maggie said.

"I wonder whether she'd like me to do the cooking on Saturdays. You share the cooking with her, don't you, Cecily?—so I don't suppose she'd mind if I did some too. I could be your Saturday cook."

Of course Hester meant to be helpful, kind, considerate; she could not have the least idea how much Mrs. Pilgrim would mind. Checking the horrified veto that rose to her lips Cecily said instead that they would have to think about it. Mrs. Pilgrim, she heard herself explaining, was rather sensitive.

Afterwards she remembered that this was what Bennet had said. She must unconsciously have been quoting him—speaking without thinking as people do in moments of panic. Because it was absurd to say that Mrs. Pilgrim was sensitive; she wasn't the type to be, and only Bennet would invent such far-fetched explanations, crediting other people with complicated—and complicating—emotions which they did not possess.

For Cecily it was all quite simple. Some people did not like other people. One could not like everybody, and she herself, though not claiming to be sensitive or hypercritical, definitely disliked— well, the Rector's wife, and to a lesser degree the woman in the post office. And Mrs. Pilgrim, unfortunately disliked Hester. A perfectly straightforward antipathy.

It was unfortunate because Mrs. Pilgrim was a treasure. Every housewife who has employed a treasure knows the supreme importance of not upsetting the treasure; and the longer the treasure has been there, the worse is the loss. Mrs. Pilgrim had been treasure to The End House for over ten years, and Cecily could not think —could not bear to think—what she would do without her.

I must make it quite clear to her that Hester will only be here for the summer, she thought. Then she remembered how she had begged Hester to stay for as long as she liked, and wondered uneasily what would happen if Hester should decide to settle down with them. It was unlikely, of course, but just supposing she did?

"Maggie and I will wash up," Hester said after lunch. "You sit down and have a rest."

"I don't want a rest."

But they overruled her. "We want something to do," Maggie said, "while we're waiting for the rain to stop. Derek can come too."

Cecily had her rest in the drawing-room. Bennet had taken *The Times* into his study, someone else had taken her library book, and the children's library books were, as usual, all about very strange people analysing one another's behaviour; such a waste of time and not at all like real life. The rain drummed against the windows and the drawing-room looked dull and faded and reminded her of her middle-aged self. For like her it had faded through the years; it had become cluttered up with family possessions, a mere dumping-ground and resting-place, untidy and useful, a room so taken for granted that none of them ever looked at it —except, as now, when the tide of family life had temporarily receded. It must be years since she had consciously looked at the picture near the door, painted by herself in that summer when the first evacuees had left and the Salchester dispersion was still to come.

It's good, she thought. What's gone wrong with me since then?

Five minutes later she was on her way upstairs to the attic that used to be her studio. In recent years she had done nothing but sketch out-of-doors ("a ladylike amateur," she thought), and the attic-studio was deep in dust and cobwebs, and full of unfinished and long-neglected work and all the paraphernalia she had collected round her. The rain drummed on this window too, but she did not notice it. Time passed, and she did not notice that either.

"It isn't raining quite so hard," Derek said. "But still too wet, I'm afraid, for bicycling. What a pity we can't go in the car."

"In the what?" Hester demanded.

"In the car."

"But you haven't got a car!"

Maggie and Derek looked at her in surprise.

"But of course we have. Out there." Derek pointed towards the stable block on the other side of the yard. "Perhaps you haven t seen it yet, but it's there. It lives in the old carriage-house."

"We very seldom use it," Maggie admitted.

"Well, really!"

"What is so odd about us having a car, Hester?"

"I walked," Hester said softly. "I walked all the way to the Priory and back, escorting your father who went trundling along that very bumpy drive in an electric chair. And we've been to Scorling, and even to Salchester, by bus. And you were proposing that we should bicycle to Monk's Mingham for our picnic, lending me your mother's bicycle which hasn't got any brakes. And now you say you've got a car. Well, in Heaven's name!"

"You don't understand. Our car is not like other cars."

Your family is not like other families, Hester thought. "Is it perhaps an heirloom?" she asked.

"Not exactly, though it's pretty antique. It belongs to Papa. And now he has given up driving it."

"But I could have driven it," Hester said. "I could have driven him to the Priory."

Maggie and Derek both explained that this would have been impossible; their father distrusted all other drivers and never allowed himself to be driven anywhere. Their mother could drive, but she hated doing so and much preferred to travel by bus. Derek could drive, but . . .

They looked at each other, their duet dying away into an awkward silence. Derek grinned. Maggie looked sympathetic.

"I bumped into something," Derek said. "A dreadful accident. So now I'm not allowed to drive it."

"Was anyone badly hurt?" Hester asked.

"Oh, dear me, no. No one was hurt at all—the accident took place here in the yard when I was getting the car out. *It* was hurt. I dented the wing and scratched the hub-cap. That was all."

"And the side-light," Maggie said.

"Oh yes, I forgot—the side-light got broken. Of course it's all been mended now. But our car is very precious."

"Even if you were allowed to drive it, Hester, it couldn't go out today. The weather is much too wet."

"Yes," said Derek. "I was forgetting that."

"I don't understand you," Hester said. "Why do you keep a car if no one drives it? Is it licensed and insured?"

"Yes, indeed. It's all ready to take the road. We keep it, you see, for an emergency—or for very special occasions. Suppose one of us had to be rushed to hospital, or—or we had to go to a wedding in some rather remote church, in our best clothes, on a wet afternoon like this? That's not very probable," Maggie added thoughtfully. "But it's just to give you an idea of the kind of things the car is used for."

"*Might* be used for, if we could nerve ourselves to take it out." Hester stared at them. "But why do you put up with it? It's nonsense to own a car and go everywhere by bus or bicycle."

"It doesn't seem so to us," Maggie replied calmly. "I suppose we're used to it."

That was the Hutton inertia, Hester thought—the lazy acceptance of a ridiculously inconvenient situation that should never have been allowed to develop. Seeing them as the victims of heredity she felt quite sorry for them; more especially for Derek, whose alleged irresponsibility was probably a feeble effort at rebellion, an attempt to break out of the family mould.

Derek must be encouraged to stand up for himself. Maggie, too, of course; but, in the matter of the car, it seemed easier to begin with Derek.

"Show me this car," she said to him. "Or can it not be looked at by strangers?"

"You're not a stranger, Hester. Our own second cousin."

"The key of the carriage-house is on the hook," Maggie said. Derek went off to wherever the hook was; Maggie said she would get tea. It was rather early for tea but they might as well have it, she added; perhaps the rain would stop and then they could go for a walk.

"Or for a drive," said Hester, jokingly. But she perceived that the notion of taking the precious car out in the rain, merely to alleviate the boredom of a wet afternoon, was not considered funny.

"Very different from the old days," Mrs. Hyde-Ridley muttered as they left the rectory. "Fancy her having a bath in the middle of the afternoon!"

The call at the rectory had been a failure. The door had been opened by the Rector himself, after a long delay which was accounted for by his having been in his study and not hearing the bell, and his wife upstairs in her bath, hearing it but unable to answer it. "She had to stamp several times," Mr. Merlin explained, "and naturally I went upstairs first, fearing she was in some difficulty. The stamping, you will apprehend, did not convey to me the knowledge that it was the front door-bell."

His hearers had apprehended it from the start; but it was typical of Mr. Merlin to pile one explanation on another, obscuring the point of his sermon and keeping callers standing out in the rain. He had not realised at first that they wished to enter the house, and when they had got inside he did not seem to know what to do with them. They had supposed that Mrs. Merlin would soon descend from her ill-timed bath and that the call would then proceed on conventional lines. But they had been wrong.

"He should have gone and fetched her," Mrs. Hyde-Ridley declared angrily.

"But she knew it was callers. I heard the bathroom door open and shut while we were talking in the hall."

Yes, Mrs. Hyde-Ridley had also heard it. What a very strange woman for a Rector's wife; as everyone knew that rectors' wives were there to run the social life in the parish as that was *the thing* about having married clergymen and not celibates. But Mrs. Merlin spent all her time trying to start country dancing and wanting to teach people the flute (or the lute or something), which no one had time for in Mingham.

Muttering indignantly, the two ladies put up their umbrellas and crossed the street. It never occurred to them that the paying of formal calls was a lapsed custom, though they sometimes wondered why so few people returned their calls. But this could be attributed to the sloth and bad manners of the defaulters.

"They're sure to be at home on a wet afternoon like this," Mrs. Hyde-Ridley said, as they advanced on The End House. "And they're sure to offer us tea," she went on hopefully.

Mrs. Vandevint gave a sceptical grunt, because it was too early for tea; at the same time she made a firm resolve that she would not walk through the rain to call on the Headleys in the hope of getting tea there. Nor was she going to have tea in Violet's damp garden, even if the rain stopped. She would not pander to Violet by accepting this minimal form of picnic and pretending that it "counted."

Mrs. Hyde-Ridley was well aware that Dulcie was both sceptical and cross, and this added considerably to her triumph when Maggie led them into the drawing-room and she saw that they would get tea after all. For it was there, at least the food was, and plenty of it—chiefly piles of sandwiches, but some cake as well. It almost looked as though the Huttons had been expecting them

"You must stay to tea," Maggie said—as she was bound to, with so much tea in evidence. "Do sit down, and I'll find Mother." While they waited the ladies kept glancing from plate to plate in pleasant anticipation. After an inadequate lunch both of them were ready to do full justice to this bounteous spread, even if it did look rather like a feast for hungry schoolboys.

After some time Maggie returned. "I can't find Mother any-where," she said, "but Hester is making the tea now, and Father will be here in a moment."

"I thought he was an invalid," Mrs. Vandevint whispered, when Maggie had gone to fetch the tea-tray.

"He can just manage to drag himself about the house but they don't expect him to last long as it was one of these tropical germs and it's quite incurable!" Mrs. Hyde-Ridley responded rapidly.

The door opened and Bennet Hutton walked in. He did not stride or bound in but no one could have said he was dragging himself. He greeted Mrs. Hyde-Ridley genially and seemed pleased to make the acquaintance of her friend. True, he was wearing a white Shetland shawl on top of his other clothes, but although this looked rather odd it did not suggest that he was a dying man. Mrs. Vandevint looked forward to twitting Violet on the falseness of her information.

Hester and Maggie came in, presently followed by Derek. Hester was introduced to Mrs. Vandevint, tea was poured out, sandwiches were greedily eaten. Mrs. Hyde-Ridley talked to Hester about her aunts, while Mrs. Vandevint talked to Bennet Hutton about a number of subjects, ranging from Folkestone, where she lived, to the curious behaviour of Mrs. Merlin. Mr. Hutton agreed with her that the afternoon was no time for a bath, but charitably suggested that the Merlins were at the mer-cy of their erratic hot-water system. Sometimes the water would not get hot for days, so it was probably wise of them to bathe when they could.

Mrs. Vandevint was not impressed. "They should put in an immersion heater," she said. "I have one in Folkestone. I have often told Mrs. Hyde-Ridley that she ought to get one."

Something in her manner suggested that *Bonnie Appin*'s hot-water system was no better than the rectory's. Bennet Hut-ton leaned forward, chirruping sympathy, and quite soon he was being told, in a hushed voice, about the discomfort of staying in a house that was falling to bits.

He enjoyed the tea-party very much; it was as good as Mrs. Pilgrim on her most expansive days. "We ought to entertain more," he said when the callers had left. "See more people. Go out a bit. I must speak to your mother—where is she, by the way?—about the silver. That tea-pot's a disgrace, not been cleaned for a month. We could ask someone to dinner."

His children were temporarily speechless; for whose sake had visitors been discouraged, dinner parties abandoned, noise and excitement forbidden? But Hester was quick to seize her chance.

"You should go out more," she said, smiling encouragement at the convalescent. "It would do you good, Cousin Bennet—I'm sure it would. And meeting people, too, now that you feel strong enough. Look, why don't you go out in the car? You could drive out and call on all your old friends. I'm sure they'd be delighted to see you out and about again."

"Your sympathy, my dear, does you credit. Unfortunately I have no old friends. Friends of my youth—all dead," he explained, huddling the shawl round his elderly shoulders. "In any case I cannot drive the car. Dr. Jamieson has absolutely forbidden it." Hester knew better than to query the doctor's orders or argue about the deceased friends. "What a pity," she said. "Still, you can go for drives. I'll drive you, Cousin Bennet. Do let me. It will do us both good."

"I don't think—"

"Oh, do let me! I'll be very careful. And it would be such fun."

"Well . . ."

It was as good as Yes; at any rate, it wasn't No. Hastily, in case he changed his mind, Hester began to talk about the other amusements suitable for a convalescent. Seeing more people. Asking someone to dinner.

# CHAPTER EIGHT

"So much seems to have happened since you arrived," Cecily said to her goddaughter. "It's as if you were a—a—What is the word I want?"

"A bad influence?"

"No, no. Just one word. A rather impressive one."

"I'm glad I am not a bad influence."

Privately, Hester thought she was a very good one. The Huttons had got into a rut and her coming had jolted them out of it, she was rescuing Cousin Bennet from hypochondria and Cecily from lazy stagnation and Derek from spoilt babyhood. She was not yet sure whether Maggie needed rescuing, but she was prepared to rescue her if necessary. She did not agree that much had already happened, but the breath of change was in the air; and probably that was what Cecily meant.

"It is very strange that Bennet should want someone to dinner," Cecily said.

She sounded rather displeased, and Hester guessed why; the threat of a dinner party had upset Mrs. Pilgrim. For Mrs. Pilgrim, too, was in a rut. Hester felt no urge to assist Mrs. Pilgrim, but her being upset was a nuisance. The Huttons were still at a stage when they would happily slip back into their own ruts if any excuse offered.

"Cousin Bennet is a convalescent, and they are always bored," she said. "I was dreadfully bored myself, until you asked me here."

"Oh, but it was different for you, dear. You were—Well, what was I saying? About having someone to dinner . . ."

How kind she is, Hester thought; for she could not but be grateful to her godmother for avoiding the subject, for not reminding her of what she was trying to forget.

Yet somehow, in spite of meaning so well, Cecily often did contrive to remind her of the past, and in a way that made it seem worse. It had become unmentionable, too sad and humiliating to be discussed, but her very avoidance, her tactful haste to change the subject, gave it importance and kept it alive. Like an over-zealous amateur nurse, forever applying fresh bandages and antiseptics, she never gave the wound a chance to heal.

It was different with Derek. He did not apply fresh bandages, he simply tore them off; and oddly enough the unorthodox treatment did Hester a lot of good.

"You *were* engaged, weren't you?" Derek began, on an evening when Hester was assisting him to pump up the tyres of the precious car. "Mama said so, but she's not very reliable. I mean, she doesn't always distinguish between being properly engaged and just—well, *you* know—attached but uncommitted."

Hester wondered whether Derek himself had been properly engaged. She only had Cecily's word for it.

"Yes, I was," she said.

"And what happened?"

"It was broken off."

"Did you quarrel with him?"

"Yes," she said shortly. Conditioned to tactful avoidances, she found his curiosity disagreeable.

"Oh, come off it, Hester. I really want to know."

"And I really don't want to talk about it. It's over and done with."

"Meaning you're still pining for him?"

"No."

"I suppose that means you are."

"No," Hester said loudly. "No, no, no! Can't you understand No when you hear it?"

Hateful Huttons, she thought, giving Derek an annihilating look that would have included the rest of his family if they had been present. She did not know which was worse, the unspoken pity and too obvious tact of the others, so humbling to her pride, or this prying curiosity.

"Actions speak louder than words," said Derek. "That's what my governess used to say. Though she might have changed her mind if she'd heard *you* speaking, when you're enraged."

"I had to shout to get it into your thick head."

"Quite so, Hester, quite so. And now you've shouted no doubt you'll feel better. You'll feel better still if you'll tell me what happened to your romance. And of course I shall feel better too, because I shan't lie awake at night wondering just what did happen." There was something awfully nice about Derek; a disarming candour and friendliness that made her regret having shouted at him. After all, she thought, his curiosity was quite natural; she would have been equally inquisitive herself. Suddenly it seemed quite reasonable to talk about the past, to satisfy

Derek's curiosity and to correct his wrong impressions. For she knew that her angry denials—which were prompted by sheer irritation—had made him think she was still pining for Raymond.

"All right, I'll tell you what happened," she said. "We were engaged and we were going to be married quite soon. And then Raymond cried off, very much at the last moment. I supposed I ought to have seen it coming, but I didn't know—I didn't know—"

"How horrid of him," Derek, in his most precise, elderly-baby voice.

"Oh, Derek!"

If he hadn't made her laugh she would have cried; and the relief of being able to dissolve into laughter was so great that she felt quite dizzy, as if after months of being shut up in one room she had suddenly emerged into wind and sunlight.

"Horrid," she echoed. "Absolutely horrid."

She leant against the car, still laughing, and saw Derek looking at her with what seemed like anxiety.

"It's all right. I'm not having hysterics."

"I was thinking of the paint."

"The paint," said Hester. "Oh yes, the precious paint. Your precious car."

She sat down on the running board—for the car possessed these obsolete attachments—and Derek sat down beside her.

"And you languished and fell into a decline," he observed.

"I suppose I did. This thing—being jilted—happened last year. I seemed to be getting over it—and then I wasn't. I got pneumonia instead. Not till this spring, but I suppose it was because I was so depressed."

"And not eating proper meals or bothering to change your wet feet. Living in dreary squalor."

Hester's laugh sounded more natural this time. "Oh, no—at least, I hope not," she protested. "I did cook things. I despise women who live on sardines and bread-and-butter."

Derek nodded approvingly and patted her shoulder in a brotherly way. She was back to thinking of him as a young brother now—and a nicer one than he had seemed at first. She felt nearer to him and to everyone else, as though a curtain had lifted which she had not known to be there.

"Tell me about Raymond," he said.

"There's nothing special to tell. He was an architect—a partner in a London firm. Rather a good architect, I think. He'd been married before and it hadn't worked out. He lived in Islington, in a house he'd converted, with a very amusing bathroom and an enormous hi-fi for Bach and Monteverdi. He dressed just a little bit arty, but it suited him."

"But this is quite irrelevant. I meant . . . tell me why he jilted you."

It was a word Hester had often said aloud, to hear how it sounded, but it sounded much worse when someone else used it.

"I don't know," she answered, clinging to the last shred of a bandage.

"Oh rot, Hester. You must know," said Derek, tearing it off.

"He said I was far too managing. Bossy. He couldn't stand being married to someone who thought she knew best about everything. It had been growing on him for weeks, this feeling, but he'd ignored it because he knew I was—fond of him. Finally, he realized that affection wasn't enough."

"Oh dear—how frightful for you. I know just what he was like, now. Well-meaning and no guts but a very strong instinct for self-preservation."

Hester stood up. "He isn't a bit like that!" she said hotly.

Then she realized that this would confirm Derek's belief that she was still pining for Raymond, and she managed to speak more calmly.

"You've got it all wrong, Derek. But it doesn't matter, because the whole thing is finished now, and I really have got over it. It's so stupid to go on chewing over the past. I only do it, I think, because I had that long spell of illness . . . when there was nothing else to do."

"Well, yes, of course. Illness is very demoralising. And I'm sure you will feel much better now that you've told me about it."

How absurd he was, and yet how sincere; how infuriating, and how oddly likeable. He had made her laugh, against very long odds, and she certainly felt better for that.

"Perhaps I shall," she said, restraining the impulse to laugh again in case it should hurt his feelings.

Across the yard a bell clanged loudly. This was the bell that hung outside the back door, formerly used to summon a gardener or coachman and nowadays as a reminder of approaching mealtimes. Hester glanced at her watch in surprise; Derek picked up a neglected pump and set to work on a rear tyre.

The yard was at the side of the house, cut off from the village street by a high wall and solid wooden gates, and from the big garden behind it by the stable block itself and the wall between the stables and the house. There was a door in this wall, and a few minutes later Maggie came through it, obeying the bell's summons. She turned towards the old stable where the gardening tools were kept (and the electric chair and the broken mangle and a hundred other things), and Hester called out to her as she went past.

"Are we having supper early tonight, Maggie?"

"Mother didn't say so. At least, I haven't seen her yet—I went straight into the garden when I got home."

"Perhaps my watch is slow."

"Mine doesn't go at all," said Maggie. She walked on, put away the hoe and the weeding basket, and returned to the carriage-house. "Are you really going to be allowed to drive the car?" she asked.

"I don't know yet. I hope so."

The bell rang again, quite a lively jangle. "Mama sounds impatient," said Derek, strolling out to join them.

But no one moved towards the house. Punctuality was not a virtue for the Huttons; and the kind of supper they had, cold snacks and cheese and left-overs, wouldn't suffer by being kept waiting. It was a fine, warm evening, the first after a wet week. Hester looked at Maggie and Derek and felt full of loving plans for their rescue and improvement. Hitherto she had been prompted by energy rather than affection; their rescue had presented itself as a way of passing the time and keeping her mind off other matters. But tonight a curtain had lifted.

The bell rang again.

"Could there be a flap?" Derek asked calmly.

"Perhaps we'd better go and see."

The back door of the house was flanked by an old wash-house so that it could not be seen from the stable block. The bell hung in a wooden bracket on the wash-house wall and was rung by pulling a rope in the kitchen, an ingenious arrangement which saved the summoner quite a long walk, because there was a big scullery and a stone-flagged passage between the kitchen and the back door. Cecily was to be imagined in the kitchen, tugging impatiently at the rope; but as they crossed the cobbled yard she came hurrying round the corner of the wash-house, almost before the bell had stopped ringing. They realized instantly that this was a crisis of the first order.

At the sight of them she cried out in vexation.

"You must have heard the bell! I rang and rang—I thought you were all at the end of the garden. Why didn't you come?"

"Coming now, Mama."

"Maggie, you'll have to change. Why don't you change when you get back from the farm? Those clothes aren't fit to be seen!"

"But they are the clothes I always wear," Maggie said in surprise.

Cecily took no notice; indeed it was clear that Maggie's clothes were only a last straw breaking the back of an already overburdened camel. Maggie's hair looked no more untidy than usual, but Cecily's grey curls were standing on end as though she had run distraught hands through them. When she spoke to Hester, her dear godchild, she sounded as cross as when she had spoken to Maggie. "You're always wanting to cook so now would be your chance. Only there's nothing to cook!"

"But what's up, Mama? Tell us what has happened."

"Your father," said Cecily, gazing accusingly at Derek and Maggie.

Hester had noticed that Bennet was always "your father," not "my husband," when things were being difficult. But never before had she heard him quite so indignantly repudiated.

"Friday evening," Cecily rushed on, "He knows it's the end of the week. The most awkward night possible. But he'll do it. I'm sure he will. I feel it in my bones."

"Do *what*?"

"Thomas Seamark. He'll ask him to dinner. Thomas is here now—with your father—and I know he'll ask him, I looked out of the little window on the landing and saw his car outside, and I rushed down to catch Bennet and remind him there was nothing in the house. But I was too late—Thomas was in the study with Bennet. I could hear them talking."

"Didn't you go in?" Hester asked.

"No, I didn't. That's another thing—the awkwardness about the exhibition. I feel so awkward about meeting him again. I'd planned the first time quite differently."

"Perhaps the two things will cancel out," Derek suggested. "He'll be so annoyed with you that he won't want to stay to dinner."

"Oh, he'll stay. People always do when it's inconvenient. Your father will persuade him."

"Poor Thomas," Maggie said sadly.

Maggie was sorry for Thomas, Cecily was pitying herself, and Derek (Hester felt sure) was hungrily contemplating cold scraps that had to serve six people instead of five. But none of them was prepared to deal with the crisis; they just stood there, waiting for it to overwhelm them. Until Hester gave her orders and spurred them into action.

'Derek, you start scraping potatoes at once. They're in a box in the larder. Maggie, you go and change as quickly as possible and then come down and help me. I suppose you'll want to change too, Cecily '—she meant that Cecily would need to comb her hair— "but first come and show me all the food there is. Surely you have some tins somewhere."

"You can't make dinner out of nothing."

"Yes, I can. Well, I can make a meal of sorts, if there is any-thing in the store cupboard. I regard it as a challenge."

Maggie and Derek looked at her with respect. She did not notice that Cecily was giving her a very ambiguous look, as if new hopes of retrieving the situation had got mixed up with past prophecies coming true.

Nearly an hour later Bennet Hutton began to think it was time he warned his family. He had expected one of them to turn up before now. He had been waiting to say, quite casually, that he'd persuaded Thomas to stay and take potluck with them; which would have given Maggie or Hester time to slip away and organise a meal. But the minutes went by and nobody came; and then he remembered it was Friday. He looked at the clock, won-dering how long it would take to organise a meal on a Friday.

Since Bennet dined on milk and his patent digestive food he didn't pay much attention to what the rest of the family ate; but it came to him that on Friday nights the scraps were even scrappier than usual, and the cheese sometimes a mere sliver. Of course there must be food in the house—he thought vaguely of a joint sitting in the larder, of soup simmering on the stove and perhaps some fish in the refrigerator—but it would not get cooked unless he warned them.

He would not admit that the impulsive invitation had been a mistake. Instead, he blamed his family, particularly Cecily who ought to have looked in before now to see that he was all right.

Or one of the children should have come, or Hester. Even Hester neglects me he thought, getting up from his chair and shuffling, in a neglected manner, to the door.

"I'll just find out where they've all got to—tell them you're here," he said to Thomas Seamark. He shut the door behind him and shuffled across the hall to the drawing-room. It was empty. As he walked down the passage to the kitchen he did not shuffle at all. Anxiety made him walk quite briskly.

Maggie had been laying the table and as she came out of the dining-room she saw him hurrying kitchen-wards. She heard the kitchen door open, and the burst of voices. They were all in there, but dinner was nearly ready; he would not be a nuisance.

She turned the other way, back across the hall to the room he had left.

"Hullo," she said to Thomas Seamark. And then, as he did not instantly respond: "Have you forgotten me? I'm Maggie."

But that was a silly thing to say, because they knew each other quite well. They lived in the same place, and sometimes Thomas Seamark, driving his car, met or overtook Maggie on her bicycle. Sometimes she waved to him, though she was never certain whether he waved back, because he was a fast driver and the car would be past her before she could see the wave—if there was one. Still, he must know who she was, meeting her here in The End House. And of course they had met on Salchester station rather more than a year ago, and more recently at the exhibition. No, that didn't count, because he certainly had not seen her then. She had seen him. Perhaps he *had* seen her at the exhibition when she wasn't looking, and not known who she was. Perhaps he never knew who it was waving to him from a bicycle as he went by. Perhaps he thought it was some shameless total stranger.

"Hullo, Maggie," said Thomas Seamark, putting a timely end to these agitating speculations.

He hadn't changed at all since the last time she had seen him close to, on Salchester station. (At the exhibition he had been rather a long way off.) Having assured herself by the briefest possible scrutiny that he did not appear mortally ill and destined for an early death, Maggie ceased to look at him. She stared past him, out of the window, wondering whether to tell him that she would be twenty-one next month.

Thomas Seamark was working it out for himself, starting from Maggie s tenth birthday which he remembered vividly because it had been his first summer back at Mingham after the war and he had driven the Hutton children and two others and Cecily to the sea for a picnic and on the way back they had run into a cow, or rather, they had run into a bank while trying to avoid the cow, which was only slightly grazed but tremendously indignant. And Cecily had been indignant too, and the children had screamed and Derek had been sick, and the front axle had got bent . . . no, he would never forget that picnic. 'Forty-seven, 'fifty-seven; she must be nearly twenty-one. He still thought of her as about sixteen and only at home for the holidays.

"What are you doing with yourself these days?" he asked, logically pursuing the line of thought.

"I work for Mr. Enderby at Scorling Gate Farm."

(And a total stranger she must have seemed to Thomas as he swept past her on the Scorling road.)

"Oh, *there*," he said. "I've sometimes seen you on that road. I used to wonder what you were doing in Scorling."

A warm glow of relief replaced the bitterness of being a total stranger; he had recognized her after all.

"I thought you were going to school," Thomas Seamark continued. Looking at her stricken face, he very quickly added: "Or to art classes, or something."

"I never went to school in Scorling! I was at a boarding school. And I left it three—nearly four—years ago."

"I'm sorry, Maggie. It was very stupid of me. Yes, it was that year . . . But I was away, you know. It was the year that Beatrice died."

"You've been at home since," Maggie cried furiously.

The next instant she was covered in confusion. How could she have said such a thing—why had she not shown him, by word or look, that she knew what he had suffered and did not blame him for becoming a recluse, for letting the years go by unheeded?

"Yes, I've been at home since," Thomas Seamark agreed. "Part of the time, anyway. Quite long enough to—I mean, it was my mistake . . ."

A ridiculous mistake. He looked at her, seeing her, as he now felt, for the first time; or at any rate seeing her quite differently. The schoolgirl had gone forever, he was looking at Maggie grown up.

"Very stupid of me," he repeated. "I simply wasn't thinking . . ."

"I'm sorry, Thomas. I spoke without thinking, too."

The door opened and Cecily made a dignified entrance, which looked as if it had been rehearsed outside.

"Maggie!" she exclaimed. "We couldn't think where you were. You'd left the glasses in the pantry but it's all right, Derek has taken them in. Why—Thomas—how nice to see you again."

The opening speech had been rehearsed as well; a defensive apology, contrite but brief, which Thomas could hardly have refused to accept when he was standing in her own house. But the surprise of finding Maggie there had driven it clean out of her head.

# CHAPTER NINE

ALL CECILY's best ideas came to her at unexpected times and in unexpected places. Not in the bath, where everyone got them, but in places such as this. She looked round Mrs. Bavington's room, whose four walls were each papered with a different pattern, and even while she was considering its oddity (could they have bought remnants of wallpaper in a sale, as one buys remnants of dress material?) the idea flashed into her head. Meeting Hester's eye she hurriedly glanced away, feeling guilty but at the same time exultant. It was like the wonderful moment of inspiration when one "saw" the subject of the next painting in all its golden perfection.

"Of *course*," she said to herself. "Why did I never think of it till now?"

For the idea, like the picture seen in the mind's eye, had the simplicity and balance of a true masterpiece.

"When Anthony comes we must have a real party," Mrs. Bavington was saying. "He'll be so thrilled to meet you. Of course, he simply adores the country—that's really why we moved out here —but I'm afraid he does sometimes get a bit bored with his old Mum."

Her laugh said "That's me!" and Hester laughed too, and so did Cecily, after a moment's delay while she wrenched her mind away from the idea. It wasn't quite enough for Chrysanthemum, who craved for verbal assurances that she looked absurdly young, but she had to be content with it. Having them to tea was, after all, a triumph in its own way; she had stolen a march on Mrs. Hyde-Ridley and the other neighbours, and she knew that none of the teas they might eat subsequently would compare with hers. Her cooking, like her appearance, was something she was rightfully proud of.

"'Smatter of fact, Anthony is going to be kept frightfully busy," she told Hester. "He's going to paint the outside of the house."

He would also have to mow the lawn and mend the fence and do one or two odd jobs for Mrs. Hyde-Ridley, who had not yet agreed to Chrysanthemum's plan. The whole thing was supposed to be a secret while it was still under discussion, as Mrs. Hyde-Ridley didn't want it to get out till she had made up her mind.

"But I know you won't breathe a word," Chrysanthemum said earnestly. It was a mere formula; she did not wait for their assent, but plunged into the story she was dying to tell.

Hester listened attentively and asked the right questions, but Cecily went back to her idea. At intervals she made sounds expressive of interest, but it was clear to Hester—perhaps also to her hostess —that her mind was on other matters.

She is absorbed in her painting, Hester thought, admiring Cecily for her ability to ignore other people and concentrate on her real interest.

She is the very person, Cecily thought, admiring Hester for her self-possession, her *savoir-faire*, even for her Clifford nose. The right age, the right temperament, the right background. And, with her own sad experience behind her, well able to understand what Thomas Seamark had been through. The two disasters, his and hers, were a kind of meeting-ground; and a meeting-ground was just what was needed. They would be ideal for each other. She couldn't imagine why it had not struck her sooner.

"We shall have to have another dinner party," she said.

Everyone—even Bennet—looked surprised. They had just sat down to supper, and as Hester had cooked it the meal was better than usual. Association of ideas, Bennet thought, with an envious glance at the cheese soufflé, which custom forbade him to eat. That was the way his wife's mind worked, simply and directly.

"We've just had one," Hester replied. "If you count Thomas Seamark as a dinner party."

"He was as much bother as a Lord Mayor's banquet," Derek retorted.

"Only because we weren't expecting him," said Maggie.

Bennet got his word in first, before they could start the fuss again. Even his invalidism had not protected him from reproaches. (A fuss about nothing; as if a houseful of women couldn't be expected to produce a simple meal without a week's notice.) He leaned forward, demanding their attention.

"I saw Merlin this morning. He told me his wife is giving a display, on Pooley's Piece, in aid of the church beetle."

"Who is going to pay to see Mrs. Merlin?" Cecily asked rhetorically.

"I suppose that depends, Mama, on what she's going to display."

"Country dancing," Bennet said crossly. He did not like the joke being taken out of his hands, snatched away and vulgarized and ruined. "A display of country dancing. We must go and watch it," he said. If it wasn't his joke it mustn't be anyone's; the subject must be treated seriously.

Derek made a face, Maggie muttered that she simply loathed country dancing; but Hester turned towards him and asked where Pooley's Piece was.

"It's that bit of open ground at the other end of the village," said Derek, before his father could answer. "It's a sort of common. It belongs to the village."

"Nothing of the kind," said Bennet. "It belonged to Jacob Pooley, who held this living at the end of the eighteenth century, and he left it to the church and directed that it be preserved as an open space for the benefit of the villagers. He was distressed by the Enclosure Act and wanted to compensate the people for the loss of their common, which—"

"That's what I said. It's a sort of common."

"*No.* It is not a common at all. You don't listen."

He looked a very cross cherub indeed, and Hester judged it time to tell the news she had been saving up for him.

"It's perfectly true that Mrs. Bavington is going to paint the outside of *Firenze,*" she said.

"Choo, choo! I heard that a month ago."

"But guess why! She is going to sell cakes there, and serve teas to tourists."

This news produced a sensation, surprising even Cecily who had heard it before. "I thought she said a tea-shop in Scorling," she protested, "Surely Mrs. Hyde-Ridley would never let her have one here?"

"Mrs, Hyde Ridley has almost but not quite consented. Till she does, it's supposed to be a secret."

"A secret," Cousin Rennet echoed ironically. He chuckled to himself, savouring the news, comparing it with what he had already gleaned. "Back-door bribery," he said softly. "Cakes and promises. Oh yes, Cecily—of course Mrs. Hyde-Ridley will consent. She will get the property repaired, and no doubt a bigger rent. She'll get everything she can, before she consents. She is more than a match for the Bavington."

"But we don't want a tea-shop in the village."

"Why not, Mama? We have other shops."

"I don't see why not," Maggie said. "Thomas will be pleased anyway, if those houses are repaired. He said they were an eyesore."

"Thomas is a very good landlord," Cecily said, "He has such high standards."

She glanced at Hester, for whose ear this praise was intended. But Hester was looking the other way.

"How do you know about the back-door bribery?" she was asking Bennet.

"Oh guessing, just guessing. It is reported that the Bavington is very good to her landlady, always slipping across with little offerings and studying to please her."

He knew everything. But he was always glad to have the rumours confirmed or explained; and the reason for Chrysanthemum Bavington's unnatural generosity to her landlady was now apparent. He sat back in silence, fitting the pieces of the jigsaw together, while his family argued about the merits of a tea-shop in the village.

"She makes delicious cakes." Hester said, "I dare say it will be a great success."

"I suppose Anthony will live at home and help," said Maggie. "What does he do at present?"

"He cooks," said Derek. "It must run in the family."

"We don't know that he's a chef, but we suspect it," Maggie explained. "He has a job in the County Hotel in Salchester—that's the grand one on the river—and somehow it's easy to imagine him in a chef's cap. He has the right kind of face."

"Not the real chef, of course—not at his age," said Derek.

"Perhaps he has just been gaining experience while they saved up to start their tea-shop."

"It will be a restaurant before they've finished," Hester said. "They'll buy out Mrs. Hyde-Ridley and turn the two houses into one. They'll make their fortunes."

"Bonnie Firenze Appin. Not a name to forget."

"I think it's a dreadful idea," Cecily cried. "Not funny at all. Even a tea-shop would be a mistake, here in Mingham. It would spoil everything."

"Oh no, it wouldn't, Mother. It would be *more* picturesque, not less. Olde Englishe and cosy."

"That isn't the point. It would commercialise the village. Why, we should get *charabancs* coming!"

Her children reminded her that these were now called coaches. Hester said soothingly that she did not believe coaches would visit Mingham just to let their passengers taste Chrysanthemum's cakes. Maggie said Mrs. Hyde-Ridley would never sell *Bonnie Appin* and Derek backed her up and added that Mrs. Hyde-Ridley would probably live to be a hundred. By their united efforts—for they could see she was really annoyed—Cecily was calmed down and persuaded that little was likely to come of Chrysanthemum's plans, certainly not a restaurant called Bonne Firenze Appin.

Hester had been soothing and kind; but to begin with she had been an enthusiast for the tea-shop. It was her restless vitality, Cecily thought, that made her welcome such plans. Change and action, clean sweeps and new enterprises, seemed to her good in themselves, because she felt the need for an outlet for her own abundant energy.

It was delightful, of course, to have her here to talk to; her presence was both stimulating and agreeable. But it was also, in a way Cecily had never foreseen, a disturbing threat to everything she cherished most. The peace, the fixed framework, that left her with plenty of time to dabble and potter and live her own life.

"I must ask Jamieson about my diet," Bennet said at bedtime.

Cecily made sounds of wifely agreement, not paying much attention because Dr. Jamieson was never difficult about diet; he always encouraged Bennet to eat whatever proprietary patent food he fancied would suit him. But a moment later she realized that he was proposing to abandon all the patent foods and take to what he called "a proper supper." And the proper supper was to be the kind of meal they had been having since Hester had volunteered to cook it.

"Surely not cheese soufflés at night, darling," she protested quickly.

"Why not? I'm out of the wood now."

"Cheese gives you bad dreams."

"It's all in the cooking. Properly cooked cheese is perfectly digestible."

It was Cecily who had the bad dreams, dreams of becoming a household drudge, a slave to a new routine of elaborate suppers and other meals. In the dream kitchen she toiled alone; Hester, having raised the standard of living, had returned to London, and Mrs. Pilgrim had long since taken umbrage and left. It was a relief to wake and remember that Mrs. Pilgrim was still with them. But in the bleak light of early dawn the dream looked fearfully portentous, and she lay awake recalling the number of times Hester had managed, quite unintentionally, to upset The End House's treasure.

Maggie and Derek left the house early, Maggie bound for the farm and Derek for the bus which would take him to Scorling and the bank. He disliked the bank almost as much as he disliked Uncle Malcolm, who had found him the job. Uncle Malcolm lived in London and exercised some authority in the bank's head office, and one was supposed to be grateful to him for using his influence.

Sometimes Derek thought of leaving the bank and trying something else. But what? His earlier experiences had at least taught him that he wasn't cut out for the law, or for selling insurance, or for —well, there were a number of things he wasn't cut out for. And it would be very awkward if he left the bank, where Uncle Malcolm had put him, and then could not find any better alternative.

On the way to the bank from the bus-depot there was an antique shop, and he nearly always stopped to look at its window as he went past. It was quite a small shop and it did not look very prosperous, but on the other hand it had been there as long as he could remember, so the chap that owned it must be able to make a living. A shop like that would just suit him, he thought; there would be the interest of handling old furniture and china and glass, and the thrill of going to sales and perhaps spotting some rare treasure, and the human contact with customers in the shop. To own an antique shop was his favourite dream, he felt he had a vocation for it, and he used to plan what he would do with the window of this one; pretending, for a few minutes, that it was his to arrange.

All the junk would come out, of course, and the moth-eaten red curtain at the back would be replaced by something semi-transparent, giving glimpses of other treasures in the shop, and the cardboard boxes with their tatty assortment of cameos and bric-à-brac would be exchanged for a flat velvet cushion on which the best of the stuff would be laid out so that it could be properly seen. And right in the front . . .

Right in the front, this morning, was a small card bearing an inky notice. It said: "Assistant wanted. Apply within."

Derek stared at it for several minutes.

There was still time to get to the bank without being late, but he would have to hurry. He might come back in his lunch hour, just to see what the prospects were. Perhaps the notice would be gone by then; perhaps someone else, with no sense of vocation but quicker off the mark, would have got the job.

He opened the door and went in.

The proprietor of the antique shop was an elderly man with a limp and an asthmatic cough. He wasn't a good advertisement for the business, Derek thought; he did not look successful, or intelligent, or enthusiastic. And the interior of the shop looked much less beguiling than the window, for it was dark and dreadfully overcrowded, and sadly in need of dusting. Just a junk-shop, really, and surely too small to support an assistant as well as the proprietor.

"Are you after the job?" the proprietor asked.

He had come out of a room behind the shop, and through the open door Derek glimpsed even worse confusion. He thought of pretending he just wanted to buy something, but another part of him briskly answered:

"Yes."

"Why?" the proprietor asked despondently.

"It is a job I should like," said the other Derek, while the rational part adjured him not to be impulsive.

"What are you doing at present?"

"I work in a bank."

He named it. The proprietor coughed and stared at him and coughed again. "I need someone trustworthy," he said.

"I am utterly trustworthy."

"What's your name?"

His own name was Frost. Edgar Frost, son of Ernest Frost, and nephew of Mrs Minnie Wildgoose who had founded the business but who had been dead these twenty years. He had come to help her after the first war, in which he had been gassed and wounded. Aunt Minnie had offered him a home, and eventually his sister had joined them, and after Aunt Minnie's death they had run the business together.

But three months ago, with no warning, his sister had gone off and got married—at her age!—and left him single-handed. He had to have someone to look after the shop when he went to sales, and someone to do the accounts which had always been done by his sister. Aunt Minnie had taught him a lot about antiques but she had never been able to teach him book-keeping.

All this was revealed to Derek in the lunch hour; for after staking his claim he had had to hasten off to the bank, where he had arrived late and done no work to speak of. But it did not matter, because he knew he had found his true *métier*; already he knew that Mr. Frost would employ him if he chose to come, and he did so choose. The preliminary interview, the enquiries about references and past experience, were only a convention. He and old Frost had realized almost from the start that they would suit each other very well.

When his future employer remarked that he had a lot to learn, Derek replied that it was the kind of stuff he could learn with ease, and both of them believed it. Confidences were exchanged; Mr. Frost admitted that the business had suffered since his sister's departure, and Derek confessed that his family thought him irresponsible because he had had too many jobs already.

"But I'll stick to this one," he said.

"I hope so, my boy. Why didn't you stick to the other?"

"They were soul-destroying."

"You mean they were not your own choice."

"Well, I had to do something."

"Quite so. The antique trade is frequently exasperating, but you will not find it, er, soul-destroying."

They parted friends; and Mr. Frost agreed that it would be unnecessary for Derek to tell his people that he was leaving the bank. It was not as though he were going to be out of work, was it?

"I shan't tell them for ages," Derek said. "It'll come easier when I can say I'm settled in a job I'm really fitted for. Save them from worrying."

Halfway home, he remembered Uncle Malcolm. It would be awkward if Uncle Malcolm heard about his leaving the bank and wrote a nasty letter to Mama, forestalling his own confession. Thinking it over, however, he decided there was no immediate danger from that quarter; Uncle Malcolm was too remote, and had nothing to do with the staff of provincial branches; it would be weeks or months before the news reached him. Probably not till the end of the year, when he might ask for some kind of progress report on his nominee. But by then the family would know all about it.

In the sequence of Derek's thoughts, as he travelled home in the bus, there was a single gap, where he carefully avoided thinking of the day when he would tell the family. But the thoughts preceding the gap, and following it, were bright and cheerful.

# CHAPTER TEN

JUNE WAS A depressing month, it rained every weekend and most of the other days as well. The Saturday picnic was put off again and again, and everyone but Hester agreed that it was far too wet to think of taking the precious car out of its carriage-house. Ben net had a slight relapse and retired to bed for the wettest of the June weeks, and Maggie could talk of nothing but the bad outlook for the hay.

Just as Hester had begun to think that even Yorkshire and her aunts would be preferable to claustrophobia in The End House, the weather cleared up. It was the new moon, said Mrs. Pilgrim; other people said that Mrs. Hyde-Ridley's unlucky friend must be leaving. Mrs. Merlin, who had been rehearsing her country-dancing team under great difficulties in the rectory drawing-room, came across to ask for the use of the Hutton lawn.

"Our own is all cut up with flower beds," she explained. "And anyway it's very soft and will take ages to get dry after all this rain. Yours looks quite hard already."

"Not hard enough to stand a lot of people thumping up and down on it," Bennet said quickly.

"Oh, but they don't thump. Country dancing should be light, light!"

Mrs. Merlin skipped about the room, demonstrating the lightness of her art. Bennet found it highly entertaining, and encouraged her to demonstrate other steps and to play some tunes on the recorder she had brought with her as a kind of warrant card. After showing so much interest it was impossible for him to refuse her request, and in fact he did not want to. The thought of watching Miss Cardwell and Miss Knapp and the other devotees prancing lightly, lightly on his lawn had become irresistible.

"Your father has been most co-operative," said Mrs. Merlin, meeting Maggie on her way back to the rectory. "And he is looking so much better, isn't he? Really almost his old self."

"Yes, he does seem to be getting better."

"Why don't you join our country-dancing group? You're just the type," said Mrs. Merlin, peering at her like a kind earwig. Or perhaps not a kind one but merely determined; for it was not the first time she had attempted to enrol the younger Huttons. Maggie shuddered inwardly, and explained with outward politeness that country dancing did not appeal to her and that she got plenty of exercise as it was.

"That's what they all say in the village. Such a pity—they would love it if they tried it, and so would you. People are frightfully apathetic in Mingham, they need someone to give them a lead. At Wrightley, where we were before, things were quite different. They were really keen."

Mrs. Merlin sighed, as she often did when recalling the keenness of Wrightley. Maggie shuddered again, thinking how ghastly it would be to live in a suburb where the parishioners were so enthusiastically old-English and spent all their time practising obsolete rural pursuits.

"I was wondering about Mr. Seamark," Mrs. Merlin continued.

For a moment Maggie imagined that Thomas was going to be invited to join the country-dancing group, and she found it hard not to laugh. But then she realized her mistake. He was, of course, an important local figure, and it was as a patron, not a performer, that he was needed.

"I was wondering whether he would let us hold the display in the park, instead of in Pooley's Piece," Mrs. Merlin was saying. "Pooley's Piece isn't really suitable—and naturally a lot more people would come if it was in the park. And I could get a county team down, to give really good value. What do you think?"

"Well, you could write and ask him."

"That would be no good. My husband wrote about another matter and it was simply passed on to the estate office—and of course Mr. Headley doesn't co-operate in anything. I believe Mr. Seamark was away at the time, but that's not to say it wouldn't happen again, it is?" said Mrs. Merlin, with a cunning look.

"I really don't know."

Maggie turned her bicycle towards her own gate. They were standing in the middle of the street, where she had dismounted to speak to Mrs. Merlin, and she could see a car approaching from the other end of the village. It had already passed the crossroads so it must be coming to The End House or the rectory—unless it was heading for the lane between the church and the rectory, which led back to the Monk's Mingham road but was so narrow and twisting that cars seldom used it.

"There's a car coming," she called to Mrs. Merlin, who had her back to it.

The Rector's wife gave a squawk of dismay and started to run to her own side of the street. Then she changed her mind and ran back towards Maggie. The car was quite close by now, but fortunately it was going slowly and the driver was able to stop. Mrs. Merlin looked back at the danger she had so narrowly escaped and gave another squawk—but this time of startled delight.

"How truly providential," she exclaimed "Just when we were speaking about you!"

Maggie had already recognised the car and its driver. Providence was like that, she thought—generous in one way and grudging in another. For it had kindly arranged for the Rector's wife to behave like a flustered hen and force Thomas Seamark to stop, but now it wouldn't lift a finger to remove her from the scene.

Thomas wished them both good evening and asked Maggie what they had been saying about him.

"We were discussing an appeal to your good nature," Mrs. Merlin answered quickly. "My country-dancing group, you know, is to give a display—so important to get people interested, such apathy in the village about everything—and we were wondering if you would let us have it in the park. Such an attraction, if we hold it there—so much more suitable than Pooley's Piece! Maggie said we should write to you about it, but / said it would be better if we asked you. And now in the very nick of time you appear!" She was nervous, but determined. She was cunning, but not really deceitful. Well, surely not, thought Maggie, whose respect for the Church extended to the wives of its rectors. Only, without meaning to deceive, she was giving Thomas quite the wrong impression, making it appear that both of them wanted the country dancing to take place in his park, and that both considered it a justifiable intrusion on his cherished privacy.

"A small entrance charge, I thought—or perhaps a silver collection," Mrs. Merlin continued rapidly. "It will be for the beetle, of course—and that's a good cause in itself, isn't it?"

Maggie could not see Thomas because Mrs. Merlin was standing at the door of the car, but she heard him say coldly that he could think of better causes.

"Oh, but it's such a beautiful church," Mrs. Merlin replied, confident that everyone would understand that the death-watch beetle was to be destroyed, not subsidised. "But quite apart from that, the dancing itself is important, because it's a communal activity, a way of getting together. And as we were saying before you arrived, a display in the park would attract a much larger audience. We do hope, Mr. Seamark, that you will consider it."

Again, that misleading "we." Maggie had propped her bicycle against the garden wall, and now she moved forward with a wild idea of shouting over Mrs. Merlin's shoulder a firm denial of her own support for any scheme that might annoy him. But how could she put it? She had to content herself with making a warning face at Thomas, whom she glimpsed for a moment as Mrs. Merlin shifted her position. The next instant he was hidden again, and she doubted whether there had been time for him to realize that she was conveying regret, sympathy, and a disavowal of any personal interest in communal activities.

She heard him say he would consider it and let Mrs. Merlin know. Yes, he realized she would have to get the posters out. Yes, but these things could not be settled off-hand; there was, for instance, the question of a suitable site. Yes, he supposed she would be a good judge of that . . . all right, he would be at home on Monday afternoon and would expect her at half-past three.

He sounded crosser and crosser; Maggie felt very sorry for him and even sorrier for herself. When Mrs. Merlin at last stepped back from the car she moved too, making what she hoped was an inconspicuous retreat. But he observed it.

"Maggie—wait a moment," he called.

Maggie waited where she stood. Mrs. Merlin waited too, midway between them.

"Have you time to drive up to the lodge with me now?" Thomas said, opening the door of the car. "I wanted to ask you about something. I'll bring you back," he added rather angrily, as though someone had voiced a protest against abduction or a long walk home.

Maggie got into the car. Thomas drove off, accelerating with unnecessary force and taking the sharp corner into the lane at much too fast a speed. But once between its high banks, out of sight of church and rectory, he let the car slow down.

"What did you want to ask me about?" she began, in a calm social voice that was an echo of competent Hester's.

"Those extraordinary faces."

"What?"

"Those extraordinary faces you were making, the only moment I could see you. What's happened? Something wrong at home?" Maggie's social voice refused to work. Misunderstanding her silence, Thomas stopped the car and turned towards her. "Is there anything I can do?" he went on. "Or were you just warning me not to come in?"

"Oh, no."

"I was going to call in—that's why I came back this way— but then I thought better not. I thought something had gone wrong, but that you didn't want to talk about it in front of that woman. So I made an excuse to—to detach you."

"It was very kind of you, Thomas. But there's nothing wrong at home, nothing at all. Oh, it was kind of you to bother—"

"Not at all. We're supposed to be old friends, aren't we?"

He did not sound like an old friend just then. He sounded as angry as he had been with Mrs. Merlin. But Maggie knew what it felt like to offer kindness and sympathy and find they were not required. One felt a fool, and naturally feeling a fool did not come easily to anyone as brilliant as Thomas.

"I *was* trying to warn you," she said. "But not about that. I was trying to show you that I didn't agree and that it wasn't my idea and I didn't mind about it anyway—and that you weren't to think so—and that I was sorry about your having to have the country dancing in the park when I knew you wouldn't want it. And I couldn't say so, because there wasn't time and Mrs. Merlin wouldn't stop talking. But she was giving you the wrong impression, saying 'we' and bringing me into it. So I made a face to try and explain."

"I see," said Thomas. He looked at her, not angrily, but thoughtfully. "No wonder you frightened me, making a face to say all that."

"I'm sorry. I was acting for the best—and it's always a mistake, isn't it?"

"Not always, but it can be misleading."

"Well, I'm sorry," she repeated. "And now I've explained properly I might as well get out here and walk home. It's no distance, and it will save you having to bring me back."

"Nonsense," said Thomas, setting the car in motion. "We're half-way to the main road already and you won't get home any quicker by walking."

Maggie felt she had somehow contrived to mislead him again, for it was his time, not her own, that she had offered to save; the car could not be turned in the narrow lane and now he would have to do the journey twice over. But she did not argue, partly because Thomas was in no mood for argument and partly because even the shortest journey in his company was a memorable pleasure.

The lane joined the main road at the corner of the park, just short of the entrance gates with their deserted lodge. Thomas turned left, towards the gates, instead of right as Maggie had expected.

"You've got time for a drink, haven't you?" he asked.

"Well, yes. Thank you."

It was quite a long way through the park to the house, which gave her time to think that he must have repented of his anger and that this was his way of making amends. He had been angry with Mrs. Merlin as well, but amends would be made to her on Monday; he was practically committed to having the country-dancing display in the park and that would repay the Rector's wife for any amount of ill temper.

They drove down the rhododendron tunnel and into the forecourt. The east front of the Priory, in all the glory of its dazzling new paint and patterned brickwork, burst on Maggie like a vision.

"A long time since you've been here," Thomas said.

"Yes, isn't it? I'd forgotten how beautiful it looks."

He gave her a sceptical glance but she did not notice it; she was gazing at the house with genuine admiration.

"It's just been painted, hasn't it?" she said, following him across the hall to the library. "Are you having the inside done as well?"

"When I can afford it."

"It must cost a lot—I know what it cost to paint all the farm buildings last year. I mean Mr. Enderby's farm, where I work. And of course that was nothing, compared to this. But it looks wonderful now it's done."

Maggie chatted nervously, while Thomas mixed the drinks. It was certainly a long time since she had been inside the Priory; and the first time, as far as she could remember, that she had been the only guest. And now, to her dismay, he was looking cross again, as if he had suddenly decided that she did not deserve compensation. Her chatter died away into an uneasy silence.

"That's not what your mother thinks," he said abruptly.

"What isn't?"

"Though perhaps you are 'acting for the best.' But don't overdo it, because there's a limit to the amount of flattery I can stand. . . . And you don't need to pay for your drink."

For an instant Maggie wondered whether grief had unbalanced Thomas, because these remarks simply did not make sense.

"What are you talking about?" she asked anxiously.

"My house. You needn't bother to praise it to the skies. Your mother says it's vulgar and hideous, and I dare say you think the same when you're at home. So don't let us have an unreal conversation without a word of truth in it. Let's start again."

His voice wasn't angry, only mildly reproachful. He was reproaching her, she thought, as if she were still a child.

"No," she retorted. "Why should I start again? Why do you think me insincere because I admire your house? You admire it yourself, don't you? It's awfully unfair of you to scold me because of something Mother said, which you weren't meant to hear anyway."

Thomas looked considerably taken aback, but her indignation enabled her to ignore it.

"You overheard her at the exhibition, didn't you?" she went on. "Hester noticed you standing near by, but then she didn't know who you were. She told us about it afterwards, and then we guessed it was you, and I was—we were—very sorry, because it must have been a cruel shock to you. But naturally Mother didn't mean to be unkind—and anyway, it was she who said it, not me."

"Yes," said Thomas. "Yes, I realize that, now. I'm sorry. Only I thought—"

"And I must say Thomas, that it's wrong of you to take it so much to heart and go on brooding over it all this time."

"I wasn't brooding over it. Only I thought—when you started praising the house—"

"But you *know* Mother," Maggie said impatiently. "You know she only admires the kind of houses she likes to paint, and they're always tumbling down and covered with ivy, or else fantastically Gothic. She isn't at all practical, you see. That's why it was rather silly of you to mind so much what she thought about the Priory."

"I suppose it was. But she's not the only one. Other people —well, Beatrice—thought the Priory was pretty well the end."

"Oh dear," said Maggie.

Once again she was checked by the shadow of the past. She did not know what to say; for although she was shocked to learn that Beatrice had not liked the Priory she felt that the opinions of a beloved dead wife were beyond criticism. Moreover, she had said far too much already.

"Oh dear," she repeated awkwardly, searching for a crumb of comfort. "But still—you mustn't regret it too much, Thomas. I—I dare say Beatrice would have grown to like the Priory better, when she got older. It's just part of the dreadful sadness of her dying so young."

He looked at her for a moment without speaking, and she felt an odd certainty that he was about to take her into his confidence, to talk to her about his lost love.

But it would not do. Sorry though she was for poor Thomas, she did not want him to tell her about Beatrice. Her eloquence had deserted her, like the indignation that had inspired it, and she could only ward off the confidences by a desperate plunge into trite, bright irrelevancy, to put an end to the silence which had lasted too long.

"Hester told us the Priory was being painted," she said quickly. "They were working on the east front when she came here with Father."

Thomas accepted the desperate new start with an expression she couldn't fathom. If he were laughing, it wasn't at her.

"They've still got this side to do," he replied. "The paint's in a bad state—it ought to have been done long before now."

That single, oblique reference seemed to dispose of the past. They talked about other things, until Maggie noticed the time and pictured Hester ringing up Scorling Gate farm to find out why she hadn't come home. Thomas demurred at this picture, but she explained that no one but Hester would think of telephoning the Enderbys, or even notice that she was later than usual.

"Not that Hester worries, exactly," she said. "But she is very practical. She thinks of everything. She is gradually taking control of our home and getting it into apple-pie order. Until she came we never realized so much was wrong with it."

Then it occurred to her that she was being rather unjust to Hester, and as soon as they were in the car she started again.

"She is really very agreeable, and we like having her," she explained. "And I don't mean that she looks down her nose at us for being so incompetent—only she is so efficient herself that she can't help spreading efficiency around her wherever she is. It's as natural as light from the sun."

Thomas laughed.

"The paragon of all the virtues," he said teasingly. "And good-looking in spite of it. She's remarkably pretty, your cousin Hester." For the first time Maggie thought about being in her working clothes, and wished she weren't.

"Oh, yes. Hester is pretty," she loyally agreed.

## CHAPTER ELEVEN

HESTER HAD NOT actually rung up the Enderbys, but she admitted she had thought of doing so.

"Only it seemed a bit presumptuous," she explained, "when you had a family on the spot."

"But they'd never have dreamt of it," said Maggie. "You see, we're none of us very practical. And it was a good thing you didn't, Hester, because if you'd found out that I'd left the farm, and not come home, you would have had all the bother of searching for me. They wouldn't have been very helpful in that way, either."

"Surely Derek—"

"Well, perhaps he would have assisted you. But Derek isn't any more practical than the rest of us. He wouldn't be any good on a desert island, for instance, would he?"

"Perhaps not," said Hester. She hesitated and then added, "But that doesn't mean he's no good at anything. He only seems childish because you all treat him as a child."

"I'm very fond of him," his sister protested.

Hester did not reply. Maggie glanced sideways at her, wondering what she was thinking. The buzz of the mower grew louder, then diminished again as Derek turned and retreated to the other end of the lawn. A part of Hester's thoughts somehow communicated itself to Maggie.

"Yes—he's older than I am and yet I often think of him as younger," she said.

"That's what I meant. He's rather like the spoilt baby of a large family."

"M'm yes, perhaps he is."

Of course Hester could not rest content with a diagnosis; she had to discuss the remedy. Derek was not irremediably spoilt, she said; he would soon become adult and responsible if he left home. What he needed, she said judicially, was to get right away from his family.

At this point the subject of the discussion returned, on the last lap of the mowing, and halted the mower beside them. He switched off the engine and flung himself down on the grass by Hester's deck chair.

It crossed Maggie's mind that Hester was being unusually managing, even for her. Getting the house into apple-pie order was one thing; a calm suggestion that one of its inhabitants should go and live somewhere else was quite another. But she had grown used to Hester's managing ways, and she no longer resented them as she had done in the beginning. She had grown used to Hester, she supposed. It occurred to her now that she had even grown fond of her.

"Picnic tomorrow," Derek said confidently.

It was a Friday evening and he was looking forward to the weekend even more than usual, for tomorrow he would say goodbye to the bank forever. On Monday he would start his new career with Mr. Frost; never again would Mondays be darkened by the misery of returning to the bank. He lay on his back in the sunlight, full of happy thoughts about the future, which he wished he could tell to Hester and Maggie. Or at any rate to Hester. But it would be disheartening if she sided with his family and reproached him for changing his job; it would be much more disheartening, somehow, than the ordinary family reactions.

"Where shall we go for the picnic?" Hester asked.

"In the park," said Maggie.

Derek sat up. "But you said you wouldn't, last time!"

"Oh, but it's all right now. I asked Thomas about it the other night and he said of course it was all right."

No one could imagine what Thomas and Maggie had found to talk about. Hester was surprised to learn that Maggie had had the sense to ask him about going in the park, because her lame account of the occasion suggested that they had only exchanged a few remarks about the weather and its effect on the hay. And that seemed quite probable, since neither of them valued the polite art of conversation and they had no interests in common. Hester had wished that she, not Maggie, had been standing outside The End House when Mrs. Merlin crossed the road and forced Thomas Seamark to stop. Not that she envied Maggie a visit to the Priory, but she felt she would have made much better use of the occasion; it would have been a chance to prove to Cousin Bennet that her diplomacy was not always "crude and obvious."

"If we're going to the park we'd better take Mama with us," Derek said. "Then she can have a nice afternoon painting."

"We'd better take your father as well," said Hester.

"But why? Picnics aren't his thing."

"If we take him he will probably let us take him in the car. I can't believe he really likes trundling about in that electric chair."

"How cunning you are, Hester. Our car will be quite worn out before you've done with it."

Maggie said tolerantly that it would do the parents good to be taken for a picnic. And she told herself, even more tolerantly, that it would do Hester good if she drove the car into a ditch. But this was just a private joke; for her common sense told her that it would do the precious car no good at all.

Cecily and Bennet never thought of themselves as that composite article, "the parents," and they would have been dismayed to know that they were being asked to the picnic in that role, to do them good. Even lacking this knowledge, they did not welcome the invitation.

Cecily mystified everyone by saying that sketching in the park would be rather a waste of time and she had plenty of work to do in her studio.

Bennet said he did not want to miss the country-dancing team, who would be rehearsing on the lawn that afternoon.

These ungrateful refusals had the effect of making Derek, Maggie and Hester obstinately determined to take the parents with them whether they liked it or not. (True, they were not Hester's parents, but in this tussle she felt as though they were; she sided with her contemporaries and was as obstinate and indignant as they.) Faced by a united opposition, Cecily and Bennet gave in without quite knowing why. It was perhaps the first time they had had to do battle as parents.

Cousin Bennet seemed almost subdued, Hester thought. He made no difficulties about taking the car, except for stipulating that it should be pushed, not driven, out of the carriage-house, and through the yard doors on to the road. They had to push him as well, so that he could steer it, and then there was a slight delay while he transferred himself to the front passenger seat and showed Hester the gears and cautioned her about the car's idiosyncrasies. Cecily, Derek and Maggie wedged themselves into the back, together with all the things for which there was no room in the boot, and Hester carefully set the precious car in motion.

To her surprise it seemed to go quite well. It creaked and rattled a lot, as though it found movement painful after its prolonged inactivity, but there was nothing wrong with the engine. She congratulated Cousin Bennet on having so reliable a car, and it seemed to cheer him up a little.

"Hoot here," he said at intervals, and she obediently pressed the horn, and obediently changed down for the little dip in the road beyond Mr. Headley's house. They did not enter the park by the lodge gates but followed the road to Monk's Mingham until they reached the second drive; an inferior one, said Derek, for the inferior persons approaching the Priory from Monk's Mingham. But they turned off this drive before they reached the Priory and drove down a very steep track through the woods (which Hester was made to negotiate in bottom gear) to the ruined water-mill beside the river.

It was very pretty, a charming spot for a picnic and eminently paintable. But Hester was disappointed that they had not come past the Priory. Mr. Seamark might have been outside and could have been asked to join the party, or she might have suggested stopping at the Priory to invite him. It seemed to her that the Hutton-Seamark *entente* was making very slow progress, and that picnicking in his park would do nothing to stop him becoming a recluse if he did not even know they were there.

Cecily, who had scorned sketching as a waste of time, at once carried her paraphernalia to a spot twenty yards down the bank and set to work furiously. Cousin Bennet demanded that rugs and cushions should be carried in the opposite direction and up the low cliff where the river emerged from its miniature gorge. This was the right place for tea, he said, and they gave in to him because after all parents must be humoured. A fine view, said Cousin Bennet, looking round him appreciatively. Hester, still humouring him, agreed, but she privately thought the view would have been finer if it had not included the Priory, which from this higher ground was all too evident. It stood foursquare above the terraced garden, dominating the scene.

Cecily, of course, had her back to it, and in any case the Priory was not so aggressively visible from the river bank below the cliff, being obscured by the woods. Hester was pleased to see Cecily so absorbed in her painting; as she said to Maggie, it showed they had been right to insist on her coming.

"Well, I suppose so," Maggie replied. "But still, she would have been just as happy painting at home."

"Creative artists are always happy in a sense," Hester admitted.

"They do seem so—if you mean Mother. Let's go and see what she's painting."

"No," said Hester. "Leave her alone. She'd hate to be interrupted now. She's really serious about this, you know, and one ought to respect it."

She steered Maggie back to the old mill, and then round to the other side of it where they would not be in Cecily's way.

"Well, I dunno," Maggie said cheerfully, when the reason for the second move had been explained to her. "I don't *mind* Mother's painting, of course, but I don't see why we should respect her for doing just what she likes doing."

Neither Derek nor Maggie was a creative artist; nor was Hester.

Hester had lived in a world where self-expression was commended and encouraged and where the arts were taken seriously.

She had been taught, by Raymond and his friends, to value creative artists above other mortals—always provided that they were "serious." It would have been difficult to define this term, but she knew exactly what it meant.

Perhaps it was against the background of Mingham, so wholly rural and uncultured, that Cecily stood out, by contrast, as a creative artist. Certainly Hester had very little to go on. But she had accepted from the start that her godmother was "serious"; and it followed that she must be admired and respected and encouraged to pursue her vocation. Her present predilection for Gothic ruins and dramatic landscapes was a sort of hangover, Hester thought, some kind of psychological thing that would work itself out in time; look at Picasso going through the pink and blue periods. And look at that picture in the corner of your drawing-room, she told Maggie. Anyone could see with half an eye that the painter of that picture had *something*.

Maggie listened amiably, looking blank at the mention of Picasso and dubious when it came to the picture in the drawing room. "It isn't very like," she objected. "But of course you haven't seen the place it's a picture of."

A little later, she said, "Yes, Hester, I do see, in a way. But there's nothing to worry about, is there? Mother may have been frustrated in the past, but she isn't any longer. She's painting like mad, up in that attic she calls her studio. And we rather dragged her to this picnic but she's painting like mad now. If that's what you call the good life, she's certainly leading it. It's Derek and me you ought to worry about, really."

"Why?" Hester asked in surprise.

"No creative talent—no means of self-expression! And a mother who is so busy expressing herself that she can only be— well, a sort of imitation of a real mother. In fits and starts, you know—when her conscience smites her."

Maggie wasn't speaking seriously; she hadn't any sort of a grievance. But she was speaking as a daughter, and her words made a deeper impression on Hester than she realized at the time. They were words spoken between contemporaries, criticising though without rancour—a parent, and they strengthened the bond that had been forged that morning when Hester had sided with her own generation against their ungrateful elders. Insensibly, from that moment, she began to think of Cecily as a parent.

After tea, it was Derek's turn to walk with Hester along the river bank. Before tea he had dutifully stuck to his father, fetching him various objects from the car—the field-glasses, a bright red cushion—and being given information about how water-mills were operated and why this one could never have been efficient. Long ago, Bennet had known quite a lot about such things.

Some of this information Derek now passed on to Hester, but when she asked how he knew he grinned and confessed that he had learned it only that afternoon. Still, it was probably right, he added; his father was pretty correct about anything to do with engineering.

"He was an engineer himself," he explained.

"I didn't know that. Somehow I thought he had always lived a life of idleness in Mingham."

"Oh no. When they were first married they lived in some dreadful place in the Midlands. But Papa retired quite young, before I was born. They simply hated the Midlands, so they came to live here in the country."

"I suppose he retired because of ill health," said Hester, seizing on this interesting example of a psychosomatic illness caused by hatred of life in the Midlands.

Derek shattered the theory to bits. "Dear me, no, he was as fit as a flea, then. He retired because Mama came into her money."

She hadn't known that, either. Her mother had been Cecily's first cousin, but her mother had died young and the Clifford aunts had not talked much about the Farrimond connexion. She hadn't known there *was* any money, on the Farrimond side.

"You weren't in the running for it anyway," said Derek, who shared his father's interest in genealogies and inheritances. "It came from Mama's other grandfather—not the Farrimond one. And it was tied up in a complicated trust—she wouldn't have got it so soon if someone or other hadn't died unexpectedly. What a glorious surprise for the parents!"

"Yes, indeed."

"Of course, it wasn't an enormous fortune," he said sadly.

"Still, Cousin Bennet was able to retire, and buy The End House," Hester pointed out.

"But I fancy there won't be much left for us. We shall have to toil for our bread all our lives."

"Well, that's what most people do. You'll end up as an important bank manager, very pompous and fussy."

He turned to her. It was on the tip of his tongue to say that he would end up as a famous antique dealer, respected and rich; for at that moment, alone on the river bank with Hester, he felt superbly confident. But as he turned he caught sight of the group in the distance and was fatally—or fortunately—diverted from his purpose. "Why, there's someone else up there!" he said instead.

"It's Mr. Seamark," said Hester, looking round

No need to go back and talk to him, Derek expostulated; but she insisted it would be only polite, when they were picnicking in his park. She led the way back to Cousin Bennet's encampment on the cliff, where he and Maggie and Thomas Seamark seemed to be getting on perfectly well on their own. She was too sociable, Derek thought, suppressing the worse thought that she might prefer Thomas Seamark to himself.

Hester was seldom self-conscious, but even she felt it a little unnerving to have three silent Huttons listening to her efforts to amuse and entertain Thomas Seamark. Cousin Bennet, who was probably thinking he could do it better himself, refused for some reason to be drawn in; he pretended to be dozing in the sun. Maggie was in her most awkward, tongue-tied mood, and occupied herself with collecting the tea things and rattling them together as she tried to pack them into the basket; being Maggie, she could not make them fit in, and kept taking them out and starting again, until Hester longed to remove the basket from her reach.

Derek was simply sulking, which though tiresome of him was understandable. Indeed, Hester found it rather touching.

"Yes, the monks always chose good sites," she said, encouraging Mr. Seamark to admire the site of his own house. And she told him about Fountains Abbey in Yorkshire, and wondered what his Priory had looked like before it was rebuilt.

"Not like Fountains Abbey," he said drily. "It was quite a small place even in its heyday. And most of it was pulled down in Tudor times, for building materials. The Seamarks weren't the first vandals."

Hester thought it wiser to ignore this. "Were there fishponds?" she asked, going back to the safer subject of past times. "I suppose there must have been—for fast days."

She had said the right thing. Mr. Seamark was interested in fishponds, especially in his own, which still existed and could easily be put in order if he had the money and the time. There were three of them, he told her, fed from the river by an ingenious system of sluices and conveniently situated within the big bend of river made just the other side of the Priory.

"Have some cake?" Maggie said, tactlessly interrupting this flow of information.

The cake had been packed and re-packed, and was much the worse for it. Hester thought it very kind-hearted of him to accept the crumbly offering.

"Time we were getting back, isn't it?" said Derek, before Mr. Seamark could finish the cake and go on about the fishponds. "I'll go and help Mama carry her stuff back to the car."

"Mother has been painting a picture of the old ruined water-mill," said Maggie.

"I thought she must be doing that. I saw her as I came by but she didn't see me. I didn't like to interrupt her."

Hester gave Thomas Seamark a good mark for saying that, and she wondered why Maggie laughed.

Cousin Bennet stirred and sat up, a bright-eyed cherub in a good temper. "My wife has a painting craze on at present," he remarked tolerantly. "And it's good of you—very good—to allow her the freedom of the park."

He nodded benignly at Thomas, who looked embarrassed and made protesting noises, as if the freedom of the park had never been in doubt.

But everyone else knew better; and both Bennet and Hester were complacently thinking that but for their tactful interventions Cecily would not be there.

## CHAPTER TWELVE

"IT'S AS FINE as it was wet," said Chrysanthemum Bavington. Sensing criticism in the lack of response, she quickly added: "As fine now, in July, as it was wet in June. Don't you think so, Mr. Hutton?"

"Precisely," said Bennet.

Chrysanthemum was sitting in the back seat of the car. It was difficult to talk to the people in front when you were sitting at the back, but she wasn't easily defeated.

"It's awfully kind of you to give me a lift," she said, for the third or fourth time. "I meant to catch the early bus, 'cos I've got any amount of shopping to do, but I got tangled up with my landlady."

"A knotty complication," Mr. Hutton said, half turning round.

"Oo, yes! I thought I should never get away."

She remembered, just in time, that Mrs. Hyde-Ridley was an old friend of Hester Clifford's people and therefore it wouldn't do to make fun of her, with Hester Clifford driving the car. "Only 'cos of getting into Scorling," she explained. "Otherwise I'd have stayed and helped. I feel awfully sorry for Mrs. Hyde-Ridley, really—I don't wonder she wanted to let off steam."

"What has happened to her?" Bennet Hutton asked avidly.

"'Tisn't her, it's her friend, that Mrs. Vandevint. She fell downstairs and sprained her ankle, and now she's laid up on the sofa and has to be waited on hand and foot. And that half-witted woman who's supposed to come daily hasn't turned up this morning, so I don't know how they're going to manage. Between you and me, Mrs. Hyde-Ridley simply hasn't a clue about how to run a house or cook!"

"I suppose Mrs. Vandevint has been doing the cooking since she came," said Hester.

"Goodness, no! She doesn't do anything. It's all part of their arrangement."

For the rest of the way Chrysanthemum described the arrangement, or as much of it as she had grasped. The ladies visited each other in turns, and whoever was guest expected to be waited on, cooked for, and above all entertained. Each visit was supposed to last the same time—about a month, she thought—but Mrs. Vandevint had pulled a fast one on Mrs. Hyde-Ridley this time; she had let her own house furnished and proposed to remain at *Bonnie Appin* for the rest of the summer. Mrs. Hyde-Ridley had been furious when she found out and she pretended she had someone else coming to stay, so that Mrs. Vandevint would have to go. And Mrs. Vandevint had retaliated by spraining her ankle and claiming that she was unable to travel.

"Masterly," said Bennet Hutton. In gratitude for all this interesting information—and perhaps in hopes of hearing more—he asked Mrs. Bavington to have lunch with him and Hester in Scorling and drive back to Mingham afterwards. She refused the invitation to lunch, but gratefully accepted the lift home.

"I've got to meet Anthony," she explained. "He's coming over from Salchester and we're going to choose the paint, and then we'll have to have an early snack 'cos he has to get back. Thanks ever so awfully."

They dropped Mrs. Bavington outside the post office, having arranged to meet her there as half-past two, and Hester drove Cousin Bennet to the tailor and offered to return and drive him to the Angel where they were lunching. But he said he could walk. The Angel was in the next street, he said, and it would do him good to struggle round there on his own.

She perceived that he wanted to potter about the town by himself, tasting the joys of independence. It was a good sign, she thought, just as it was a good sign that he should suddenly decide he needed a new suit. She drove off to look for a parking place, and since it was market day she had to go quite a long way before she found one, beyond the bus-depot in Station Lane. She took the shopping basket and locked the car and set off to walk back to the shops.

There was a shorter way back to the High Street, down a narrow lane behind the bus-depot; she had come this way with Cecily in the days when they travelled by bus. It was an attractive little lane with a terrace of old houses on either side, and, at the end nearest the High Street, a few shops. Like the houses, they were small and unassuming, and for the most part rather shabby as if business wasn't very brisk. The only one that stood out—and that discreetly—was the antique shop on the other side of the road, and she walked across to look at its window. It had lately been redecorated, she thought; for she did not remember noticing it when she had come this way before.

The re-painting was not quite finished. The fascia-board and the wrought-iron sign were leaf green, but the name on the board was only half done. *Minnie Wildg* . . . it read, from the other side of the road. When she stood below it, looking up, she could see the outline of the missing letters. *Minnie Wildgoose*. What a ridiculous, endearing name. Was there really someone called that, or had the owner invented it to catch the eye of potential customers?

She stared in through the window, looking past the objects in the foreground and trying to see the owner of the shop. The back of the window space was draped with a gauzy net curtain, which was looped up in the middle to give a glimpse of the interior. At first this narrow view showed only a display table and an upholstered early-Victorian chair, but while she watched someone came into sight, carrying a large, recumbent, china cat which he settled carefully on the seat of the chair. He bent down, turning it round so that it nestled comfortably against the upholstery. Hester, with her imagination fixed on Minnie Wildgoose, took at least a minute to register that Minnie Wildgoose looked exactly like Derek.

"It can't be," she said aloud, thinking of Derek doing sums in the bank, of apparitions and psychic warnings and optical illusions and delirium. Then, precisely as he stepped out of the field of vision, her thoughts became realistic and trenchant. She opened the door and marched in.

Derek was at the far end of the shop; she advanced on him with the bright sunlight behind her and gave him no time for recognition.

"Are you Mrs. Wildgoose?" she demanded.

"Do I *look* like—? Well, no madam. Oh golly, Hester, how did you find out!"

The three replies were matched by three facial expressions: indignation, recollected politeness, frank horror. Hester realized at once that this wasn't just a day off from the bank.

"I saw you through the window," she said. "I'm only surprised that you haven't been seen before now. All the Mingham people come this way from the bus-depot."

"But they don't come in here. And I keep out of sight just after the morning bus gets in. I lurk in the back room."

"A fugitive from justice," said Hester. "Or from reality. Do you actually get paid for it?"

"You don't understand. It's my thing—my real thing. What I've always wanted to do. I've found a proper career at last."

"But the bank—"

"Damn the bank," said Derek.

"I suppose they sacked you."

"No, they didn't. I left. I've been wanting to leave for a long time and when I got this marvellous job I left without a qualm."

That wasn't quite true; he had had several qualms, but they were caused by the fear of being found out. Now, that it had happened, however, he was quickly recovering his confidence. It was important to make Hester understand that he was serious about this job; and he felt oddly certain he could convince her.

"I've only just started it," he said, "and I've got a lot to learn. But Mr. Frost is going to teach me. Later on I shall get a job in some bigger place, and ultimately, of course, I shall have a shop of my own."

Hester managed to look sceptical. "Who is Mr. Frost?" she asked. "Is he Minnie Wildgoose?"

"Her nephew. She's been dead for years, but it's a good name. Isn't it?"

"Well—yes. It aroused my interest. That's how I found you out."

"Which just shows," said Derek, not a whit abashed. "I told him we must have the place redecorated, and the name in big lettering. I made him get it started at once, while I was still at the bank."

She wondered how he had managed to impose his wishes on Mr. Frost. Nice as he was, he had never struck her as having a will of his own.

"There are a lot more improvements to come," he said, "but I haven t had time to do them yet. I only put up the net curtains this morning. He had some ghastly old red ones that shut out all the light and clashed with everything. I burnt them."

"Where?" she asked, though she knew it was irrelevant.

"In the yard at the back. I won't show you round now, because the place is so dirty," Derek said primly.

"Where is Mr. Frost? And what is he like?"

"He's gone to a sale today. That's why he needed an assistant —so that he could go to sales. His sister got married and left him in the lurch. . . . Oh, he's quite nice, in a rather dreary way. He knows a lot about the trade. But he has no initiative whatsoever."

"I didn't think you had either."

"You don't know me, Cousin Hester."

The shop was dusty and shabby, but he was standing on his own ground. He was laughing, but he looked quite sure of himself and his *métier*. It was Hester who, to her great surprise, found herself conceding a point.

"No, perhaps I don't," she said.

"You will," said Derek.

Hester pulled herself together and became an elder sister. "The family isn't going to like it," she pointed out.

"But you're not going to tell them. I shall tell them myself, later on. Promise not to tell."

"But that's silly. They'll find out accidentally, and it will be much more of a shock than if you'd told them."

"No, it will be better my way. When I've been here longer this place will be very different, and they'll be impressed when they come and look at it. Besides, I shall be settled. I shall feel settled, so it will be easier to convince them that it's permanent. If I tell them now, they will just say I'm utterly irresponsible, and start counting the weeks till I leave."

"Moreover, you dread the thought of telling them."

"Yes, indeed. I hate unpleasantness, don't you? And this will be extra difficult because of Uncle Malcolm who got me into the bank. The bank was more sacred than my other jobs, if you understand me, because it was tied up with family connexions—and family influence. It will seem like kicking a gift uncle in the teeth." Hester laughed, and he knew he had won.

"But I shall feel very awkward, deceiving them," she said.

"No need to deceive them. You just know nothing about it."

"Your father will want to know what I've been doing this morning, and why I haven't finished the shopping. I'm meeting him—Goodness, it's half-past twelve already!"

"He's not in Scorling?" Derek cried. He turned quite pale.

"Yes, he is. It was a beautiful morning and he suddenly thought he would like a new suit. I drove him in. We're lunching at the Angel. Look, Derek, I must rush off and do some shopping. He's sure to notice if there's nothing in my basket."

"A new suit," Derek said anxiously. "That means he'll be coming in for fittings. Why on earth does he want a new suit *now*?"

"Because he's feeling restored to health. Goodbye."

She hurried to the High Street, flew from the grocer to the chemist, just managed to catch the fishmonger before he shut for lunch, and arrived at the Angel with the shopping basket well filled. Cousin Bennet was sitting in the lounge with two glasses of sherry in front of him, one for her and one for his tired legs.

"I'm sure they deserve it," she said accepting the fiction that the rest of Cousin Bennet wouldn't look at sherry.

"Well, they've carried me here," he said approvingly. "Anywhere else as well?"

"Oh, I examined the shops—just looked in the windows as I came past."

"Good," said Hester. She had feared he might have been to the bank.

"Not good," said Cousin Bennet. "It's a third-rate little town. Jenks is all right—been here for years—but there isn't a decent shop in the place."

Jenks was the tailor. Hester did not want to discuss the shops, in case she found herself talking about the antique shop, so she asked about the new suit. Cousin Bennet described the tweed— though his description conveyed nothing—and they drank their sherry and went into lunch.

"Finished your shopping?" he asked.

"Yes, it's all done."

"I didn't see you in the High Street."

"I expect I was queuing for the fish," she said, thankful that the fishmonger wasn't on Cousin Bennet's route from the tailor to the Angel. He had sharp eyes, and a sharp ear for flaws or inconsistencies in a manufactured story. He had a sixth sense that told him when he was being deceived.

"I hope it was worth queuing for," he said now. "Something out of the common? Some rare delicacy to tempt my appetite?"

"I'm afraid not. There wasn't anything special today."

"Disappointing. You should not have troubled to stand in a queue, my dear Hester, for the kind of fish we can obtain from the perambulatory van."

"I had to stand in a queue to get *any* kind," she retorted with spirit. Nevertheless she felt unnerved, for she had invented the queue to explain her absence from the High Street and his sixth sense seemed to have told him that the queue was a fiction.

Still, it could not tell him that Derek was now an assistant to Edgar Frost, successor to Minnie Wildgoose, and busily re-organizing a business he knew nothing about. No sixth sense could tell one that; it was outside the range of prediction. How extraordinary, she thought, that Derek should show such confidence and resolution . . . no wonder really that Mr. Frost should have been impressed . . . no wonder she had been impressed herself, and persuaded, against her better judgement, to secrecy. He was quite different, she thought, contrasting the determined young man in the antique shop with the charming spoilt-baby-of-the-family at home.

"We should have asked Derek to join us," Cousin Bennet remarked.

Hester wondered whether the sixth sense was partly prompted by telepathy.

"We didn't know we were coming to Scorling, when he left this morning," she pointed out.

"True, true. But you could have gone to the bank. Another time, perhaps . . ." he added vaguely.

"Yes—another time," she replied, willing herself not to think about Derek (since it had telepathic consequences), and copying Cousin Bennet's vagueness.

This pleased him. He did not know why he had suggested asking Derek, whose presence would have turned a pleasant tête-à-tête into a tiresome family party; and he was glad to see that Hester had not wanted him either and was only politely ac-quiescing in the suggestion that he should come another time. Family parties meant arguments and interruptions; one might just as well stay at home.

Chrysanthemum was waiting at the post office, brimming over with gratitude and apologies. The apologies were for the paint— which would take up such a frightful lot of room in the car and she hoped they wouldn't be appalled at her for suggesting it, only it would be such a help, and it was all ready and wouldn't take a moment to stop and pick up, if it wasn't an absolutely frightful bother.

Not at all, said Cousin Bennet, whose curiosity about the uses the paint was to be put to could hardly be restrained. They stopped at the ironmonger's, and he looked at the tins carefully as they were stowed in the back of the car. Bright blue, white, and emerald green; but not a great deal of it; not enough for the exterior of a house.

"This is just so we can make a start," Chrysanthemum explained. "They'll send the rest next week, but Anthony is coming for the weekend and he wants to get going."

Cousin Bennet hardly needed to ask questions; Chrysanthemum talked steadily, all the way back to Mingham. He learned that *Bonnie Appin* was to be painted as well as *Firenze*, at any rate its front, so that it shouldn't look too dreadfully awful beside its rejuvenated other half. Mrs. Hyde-Ridley had absolutely insisted, before she would consent to her tenant's opening a tea-shop, and she had made other conditions as well, in fact she had really put the screw on she'd been much tougher about it than you would have dreamed. But everything was now fixed up. It was all going to be wonderful.

"And of course I feel awfully sorry for her," said Chrysanthemum, remembering her manners. "Her house is so dreadfully un-comfy. I don't blame her at all for sticking out for a bit more rent, you can see she really needs it."

Certainly Mrs. Hyde-Ridley's property looked in the last stage of decay. But after they had left Chrysanthemum at her door, surrounded by tins of paint, Cousin Bennet predicted that it would yet prove a gold mine—for Mrs. Hyde-Ridley.

"She's a shrewd old woman," he said. "And the Bavington is a feckless enthusiast, handicapped by vanity. She thinks she'll make a big profit out of it, but she won't. The profits, indirect but substantial, will be made by Mrs. Hyde-Ridley."

"Well, she'll get a bit more rent, of course," Hester agreed. "And the property repainted. And her tenant's house considerably improved. One cannot serve teas, my dear child, in a near-slum. No doubt that foolish Mrs. Bavington will modernize the kitchen as well, to facilitate her labours. Or is it Anthony who is going to be the cook?"

"Mrs. Bavington, I think. Anthony has the face of a chef, according to Maggie and Derek, but I understand that he's going to be the waiter."

"The easier task," said Cousin Bennet, who had never met Anthony Bavington but felt sure he was a spoilt son.

"I know what he's like from meeting his mother," he explained. "It comes out, you know, it comes out in everything she says. Why, I could tell you their whole history."

It was lucky for Derek that there was a history to be invented, a meeting to discuss, and the hare-brained tea-shop scheme to absorb his father's attention; for earlier in the day Bennet had vaguely suspected that Hester was keeping something from him. It had been the merest shadow of a doubt—an instinctive apprehension of her uneasiness—and he hadn't, at the time, taken it seriously. But he might have remembered it and set his wits to work, if Chrysanthemum's chatter had not given him something new to think about.

# CHAPTER THIRTEEN

CECILY HAD BICYCLED because she didn't like driving the car, and also because Bennet would probably want it for his afternoon outing. She had come through the park, which was much shorter than going along the Monk's Mingham Road, and had spent the day in glorious solitude painting the ruined water-mill, with no picnickers to distract her. It was four o'clock before she felt hungry and thought about eating lunch.

She had worked long enough, she decided; the pangs of hunger would not have made themselves felt if she had still been inspired. She packed up her painting things and loaded them on to the bicycle—some in the big basket, others on the carrier—so that she would not be tempted to continue, and found the packet of sandwiches and sat down under a tree, a little distance above the river. From here she could see the Priory, that dreadful eyesore in an otherwise charming landscape, and naturally her thoughts turned to Thomas Seamark, its owner, and from him to Hester, who would be so ideally suited to him. The idea of their marriage had seemed an inspiration when she first thought of it, and she had been full of plans for throwing them together—like a match-making Victorian mama. But she had done nothing. Even at the picnic when Thomas had so opportunely turned up she had wasted the opportunity through not observing his arrival. And at other times, when she ought to have been thinking constructively about Hester's unhappiness and how to cure it, she had allowed her mind to be diverted by foolish domestic problems which weren't wholly Hester's fault.

Today, in her happy solitude, the domestic problems had lost their importance. She recognized it as one of her "good" days; a day when nothing was too difficult, nothing could vex or depress her, when she felt at the top of her form and able to tackle anything. The power and certainty of this good day had not been exhausted, but the light was wrong now; the temptation to go on painting must be firmly resisted. Filled with energy—which was perhaps what the Victorian mamas had and she normally lacked—she decided to tackle Thomas.

Not in the crude role of a match-maker, oh dear me, no; match-making was both out-of-date and *wrong*. But there was a hair-line, clearly drawn, between match-making and helpfulness—the kind of help one could, and ought to, give one's dear goddaughter and one's bereaved neighbour. The hair-line was perfectly distinct to Cecily as she bicycled swiftly through the park on her helpful mission, and she knew she was well on the right side of it.

Approaching from the Monk's Mingham direction, she came past the stables and down a steep, short hill to the forecourt, instead of by the zigzag drive through the rhododendron tunnel. The return to the stables had been hard on tired horses, old Mr. Seamark used to say; but the descent from the stables, both for horses and bicycles, was quick and exhilarating. She rattled down it at full speed, wondering why the forecourt looked so much darker than it used to, and why the man cutting grass on the bank was shouting.

"Ta, ta!" the man on the bank seemed to be saying.

"Ta, ta!" echoed the man by the front door. But that was Thomas Seamark; he had seen her approaching and was waving a greeting.

Two other men, at the other end of the forecourt, were also shouting something about ta-ta. How strange; how unlike Thomas to shout and joke with his workmen. To a frenzied chorus of ta-ta-ing Cecily flew down the last few yards of the hill and shot out on to the forecourt. Only then did she realize that the shouts were warnings and the greeting a repulse. The forecourt was being resurfaced, and had just received a coating of wet tar.

She bicycled slowly across it, watching the black, sticky mass spread itself round the front wheel, until she reached the steps where Thomas was standing. There she dismounted skillfully, alighting on the lowest step without any help from her host. She looked at her shoes and stockings, spattered but not plastered, and then, propping the bicycle against the step, she looked at the canvas balanced across the basket. There were some spots of tar on the back, but nothing on the still wet surface.

"Thank goodness for that," she said.

"Didn't you *hear* us?" Thomas demanded.

"Of course I heard you, but I thought it was some kind of joke."

"Look at the track you've left."

"Look at my tyres. They're probably ruined. Why didn't you put up a sign or a red flag at the top of the hill?"

"This isn't a public highway," he said coldly.

"And I suppose it doesn't matter to you, if old friends come to visit you and get themselves all covered in tar. Really, Thomas, you don't deserve to be called on!"

He had been fourteen when she first knew him and she spoke to him as if he were still fourteen, and it had a surprisingly good effect. He stopped fussing about the forecourt immediately, and invited her to enter the house.

Cecily usually found the great hall rather overpowering; the stags' heads and foxes' masks seemed to sneer at her and the array of brass ornaments reminded her of Birmingham and the hateful Midlands. But today she did not feel overpowered; she was at the top of her form and invulnerable to sneers and humiliating memories. When Thomas stood still in the midst of his ancestral trophies and started to apologise she took it as a matter of course.

"Of course you couldn't have foreseen it," she said kindly. "It's a long time since I've been to see you, and anyway you wouldn't have expected me to come by the back drive."

"No," said Thomas. "No, I didn't."

If he had been hoping for reciprocal apologies—for being so unobservant, riding so fast, and spoiling the newly-spread surface —his hopes were not fulfilled. Cecily looked about her with interest —a dispassionate, unimpressed interest and asked who cleaned the brass.

"I had to have it lacquered," he said.

He frowned, because the lacquering of the brass represented a victory for his housekeeper and a defeat for himself. He liked to think of the brass being polished every week, just as he liked to think of the house being swept and dusted by a staff of housemaids whose pride and pleasure it was to keep everything in good condition.

"Well, that was a good idea. No one has time to clean brass properly nowadays," Cecily said, observing the frown.

Thomas got her into the library and then began to explain about the housemaids and how much their non-existence mattered. There had been housemaids in his uncle's lifetime; there had been housemaids when he inherited the property; and although he was only fifteen at the time he remembered how nice the place looked, how well kept and cared for. Nowadays there was only his housekeeper and her daughter—both widows, he said gloomily—and the odd-job man who also worked in the garden and a woman who came from Monk's Mingham sometimes to help with the rough. His housekeeper was getting on and she didn't seem able to organize things properly and was always complaining that there was too much to do. He needed someone younger, really; but he couldn't get rid of her, because she was the daughter of his late uncle's gamekeeper and had worked at the Priory all her life.

What you need is a wife, Cecily thought. (She pictured Hester, so capable and energetic; she would be in her element here.) Aloud, she said sympathetically that servants were difficult and it must all be very much worse in a house this size.

He allowed it to be so, but added, rather belatedly, that one mustn't grumble. At least he could just afford to live in it, he explained—which was more than a lot of people could manage. Cecily remembered the Seamark fortune, and Thomas saw that she was remembering it and went on to explain that a large part of the family wealth had been swallowed up in estate duty and taxation.

"And in rebuilding the Priory," she said quickly.

"I thought you would say that."

"Well, it's true. Your grandfather spent a lot of money making the house what it is today."

"I much prefer it to a Gothic ruin."

"Don't be silly, Thomas. No one wants you to live in a Gothic ruin. I only meant that the house is much too big for you."

She couldn't imagine why he should drag in Gothic ruins, or what he was laughing at.

"It's so big—so lonely for you," she went on, deliberately ignoring his laughter. "Especially now, of course."

"Why especially now?"

"I meant—in these last few years."

"You really mean since Beatrice died."

"Of course," said Cecily.

She spoke in a hushed, reverent voice, though Thomas had used the ordinary voice of one who is getting at the facts. It rather surprised her that he should need more than a veiled allusion, until she remembered that Beatrice's death had been too tragic to be discussed and that he was therefore unaccustomed to hearing it alluded to. This explanation, though not wholly convincing, did partly account for his obtuseness about the house being more lonely *now*.

"That's more than four years ago," he said.

Again he sounded more concerned about getting the date right than about his dreadful loss. But Cecily stretched the explanation a little further to include a perfectly understandable masculine dislike of showing emotion.

"Yes, four years ago," she agreed.

"I'm four years older," he said awkwardly.

"We all are, Thomas."

"Yes—but you see—one can't go on . . ."

Light dawned on Cecily; she leant forward and nodded her comprehension. "Of course you can't," she said, "and it isn't right that you should. I knew you were lonely. It was a mistake to cut yourself off—though of course we all understood your reasons. There are some things one *has* to face alone. But no one would ever accuse you of—of disloyalty. We know how you felt, how you still feel, about Beatrice."

"Do you?"

Aware that she was treading on sacred ground, Cecily still trod boldly. It was her good day and she could trust her intuitions.

"Yes, Thomas. And I respect you for it, and wouldn't have you any different. And I'm sure that your friends, anyone who was fond of you, would think as I do. They—she—I mean, no one could take Beatrice's place. But people would understand that. As I said, it isn't a question of disloyalty."

There were times when eloquence wasn't needed—when confused and inadequate remarks could perfectly convey the inspired comprehension one was feeling inwardly. It was so this time; Thomas had understood. He looked at her almost angrily, and she knew it was because, even now, he could hardly bear to talk about his dear, lost Beatrice.

"What do you mean!" he demanded. "Do you really suggest that I should ask some young woman to become my second-best wife? An inferior imitation of what can't be replaced or restored?"

"Don't talk like that," she said gently. "Don't pretend, even to yourself, that you are trying to replace Beatrice. But I know you are lonely—and there are other lonely people in the world."

She had said just enough. Intuition had guided her faultlessly, and now told her not to add another word. She stood up, looking at her watch and carefully avoiding looking at Thomas. It was later than she thought; Bennet would be expecting her; she must be off at once.

Not another word. If she stayed to tea, or accepted his offer to drive her home, she might spoil everything. Talking rapidly (for words of that kind did not count), Cecily got herself out of the house and firmly took leave of Thomas at the foot of the steps. She still had to wheel her bicycle round two sides of the forecourt, which was now being spread with gravel and rolled, but she did not look back. She felt in her bones, where her lesser intuitions sometimes resided, that he had something more to say, but she did not intend to hear it. At least, not today.

It was a long ride home. The bicycle was much the worse for its tarry trip across the forecourt, the brakes would not work properly, the chain kept sticking, and the wheels became incrusted with dust and grit. Its sorry state could not be hidden; and everyone wanted to know why she had gone to call on Thomas, and how they had got on. Cecily had to do a good deal of inventing, which did not rank as lying because it was done in a good cause. In the sunset of the good day she was quite equal to it, and her invented conversation with Thomas was so convincingly dull and neighbourly that Hester and Derek soon ceased to listen to it.

Maggie listened to every word, as she would have listened to a report of Thomas reciting the alphabet, and decided with some relief that her mother had really been quite tactful, since nothing had been said about exhibitions, or restorations, or the Priory's distant Gothic past.

Bennet listened because his curiosity impelled him to listen to everything; the dullest conversations sometimes held the clue to a village mystery or shed new light on a hitherto obscure character. He listened patiently to "I said's" and "he said's," to reported remarks of the most extreme, and realistic, banality, to the description of the tar-spread forecourt and to the description of the terraced garden seen from the library window, and to what Cecily had said about it, and what Thomas had replied, as they stood at the window discussing such plausible subjects as gardens, the weather, and the bad state of the road between Mr. Headley's house and Monk's Mingham.

He listened patiently, and pigeon-holed every statement for further consideration. He considered them in the interval between supper and his bedtime, sitting by himself in his study and sometimes rubbing his hands together and saying, "Choo, choo!" But he wasn't annoyed—only intrigued and excited by his growing conviction that his wife had made up the whole conversation from beginning to end. Except, perhaps, the bit about the tar.

"Did Derek clean your bicycle?" he asked, when Cecily came in to say goodnight.

"He said it was too late to start. He'll do it on Saturday."

"But you'll need it tomorrow. This picture isn't finished?"

"I can't go tomorrow anyway. Mrs. Hyde-Ridley is coming to tea."

Bennet had not forgotten that, though he pretended he had.

"Both of them?" he asked, yawning.

"Yes. Hester is fetching them in the car because Mrs. Vandevint can't walk properly yet."

"Pity. You could have taken the car."

"It doesn't matter at all," Cecily said. "I don't think I want to do any more to the picture at present. I spoil things by tinkering at them."

No assignation for tomorrow, he thought. Not that assignation was the proper term; but he had wondered whether she was plotting something with Thomas, some plan that couldn't be revealed. But Cecily wasn't a plotter; nor, for that matter, was Thomas. They were the kind of people who might really have had the kind of conversation she had invented.

A quarrel, he thought. (Stupid not to think of it sooner.) She quarrelled with him, and doesn't want to admit it.

He yawned again, staving off the goodnight kiss without seeming to.

"You ought to have asked Thomas to tea tomorrow," he said sleepily. "He'd enjoy meeting them."

"I never thought of it. Would you like to ring up and ask him in the morning?"

Bennet shut his eyes to hide his disappointment. (Not that Cecily would notice; she never noticed fleeting expressions or betraying gestures; yet his disappointment was so acute that it seemed positively unwifely of her not to observe it.) When he opened them again the room was in darkness. She had switched off the light.

"Cecily, Cecily!"

"What is it, darling? I thought you'd dropped off to sleep."

The room wasn't quite in darkness, she had the torch she always carried in her dressing-gown pocket, since the time when he used to lie in a dark room and complain that switching on the light to see if he were asleep was man's final inhumanity to man. But the torch gave so feeble a glow that he could hardly see her.

"Come back. Turn on the light."

"But why? It's your bedtime and you're frightfully sleepy. It's such a pity not to go to sleep when you *are* sleepy, when there are so many nights when you want to feel sleepy and can't."

Nevertheless she turned on the light, gave him a drink of water, and automatically felt his forehead for the temperature which would explain the sudden frenzy of the recall.

"Perhaps he wouldn't like it, after all," he said.

"Who? Oh, Thomas. Well, there's no harm in asking him. In fact, I think it's quite a good idea," Cecily said calmly.

It was a calmness she couldn't possibly have assumed, if she had quarrelled with Thomas. But Bennet had already discarded this hypothesis and was working on another one.

"Better to have him at the weekend, when Derek and Maggie are at home," he suggested.

"Yes . . . yes, it would be better. They could play tennis."

She hoped Hester would be good at tennis.

"Maggie would enjoy that," Bennet said casually.

Because Cecily's thoughts were fixed on Hester she did not immediately respond. Then, remembering that Maggie was her daughter, she blushed guiltily and responded with exaggerated enthusiasm.

"Oh yes, I'm sure she would. It's a *very* good plan. I've been rather worried about Maggie lately—I mean, about her future. This farming . . . and never seeing anyone. I feel it isn't really what she wants."

In fact it was some weeks since these particular worries had last troubled her; for the return to painting and Hester's more obvious predicament had driven them out of her head. But now, prompted by Bennet's casual remark, she did her best to atone for her maternal negligence.

"Maggie can be so difficult, but tennis is a good idea because it will give her something to do. Not just having to talk, I mean. I wish I could help her, but it isn't easy—she isn't a bit like what I was at her age. I got on very well with my mother, but Maggie is so—so reserved. She needs help, but she'd hate to know I was trying to help."

"Better not let her find out then," Bennet advised.

He yawned once more, a genuine yawn this time, and tilted his head for the parting kiss. "Goodnight," he said, and instead of looking at the wardrobe he looked at his wife, not without admiration. He reserved some admiration for himself, because he had found out why she had been to see Thomas and could guess what they had talked about.

Plotting and scheming. Of course it must have been a round-about conversation, a spying out of the land with a view to a future campaign. Women—mothers—could legitimately engage in these conversations on behalf of their marriageable daughters.

For a moment, on the edge of sleep, Bennet wished he could be a woman and a mother, because he would do this sort of thing better than Cecily. Still, judging by her air of contentment, she hadn't done too badly. She hadn't—he felt perfectly certain—met with a rebuff.

# CHAPTER FOURTEEN

ANTHONY BAVINGTON was a very quick painter indeed. His mother said so, and the exterior of *Firenze* proved it. In no time at all— well, just a weekend—the blistered woodwork turned white, bright blue, and emerald green. Only the attic window and the gutters and eaves remained in their former state, because he had not been able to borrow a ladder long enough. But the rectory possessed such a ladder and Mrs. Merlin had promised to lend it when Anthony started his holiday.

"Professional decorators always begin at the top," Hester pointed out.

"Anthony says it doesn't matter a bit. This is a jelly paint so it won't run down on the bits he's already done. Doesn't it look absolutely smashing?"

Chrysanthemum beamed with pride and Hester said politely that the house looked quite different and very gay. Then the front door of *Bonnie Appin*, outside which she had been standing, opened cautiously, and Mrs. Hyde-Ridley peered round it and exclaimed:

"Oh, it's you, Hester! How nice to see you—do come in quickly as I thought it was my tenant as I know she's hanging about trying to get me alone. Mrs. Vandevint has gone to the doctor as he didn't call yesterday and I'm not surprised after all the fuss she made the time before. She's awfully nervous about herself as it comes of being a V.A.D. and seeing all those awful amputations. Come in, come in!"

During the course of this welcome, Chrysanthemum had withdrawn behind her own front door. She had popped out when Hester rang the bell of *Bonnie Appin*, just to tell whoever it was that both the old ladies had gone to the doctor and to gather a few compliments about the beauty of the new paint. "She thought you were both out," Hester said to her hostess, defending Chrysanthemum against the charge of hanging about, which was repeated as soon as they got indoors; but Mrs. Hyde-Ridley replied sharply that if her tenant said that she was lying.

"She knows Mrs. Vandevint went alone as she was watching from her front window as I *saw* her! She seemed quite a lady when she was new but she isn't really—she stands at the window and looks out as bold as brass."

Mrs. Hyde-Ridley gave a satisfied glance at her own front window, where the net curtains were carefully pinned together down the middle to give cover to ladylike espionage.

"Still, she's quite a good tenant, isn't she?" said Hester, who had learned not to argue with her Clifford aunts about whether being a lady mattered.

"I suppose so but I wish I could get the Leverett-Mannings back. They were here in the war, you know, as they came to escape the noise as their own house was right in the path of all the enemy bombers and they never got a single night's sleep! He'd been an ambassador and knew everyone and all the diplomatic gossip, and she was a Crosby from Harlington where all my people are buried so we had lots to talk about."

Derek used to say that all the tenants became retrospectively grander, as time on its ever-rolling stream bore them away from Mingham; and Hester noted with interest that the Leverett-Mannings had now acquired ambassadorial rank, as well as having one foot, so to speak, in a family mausoleum.

"You must miss them," she said politely. "But it's nice that you've got Mrs. Vandevint here. I don't know how my aunts would exist, if they hadn't got each other to talk to, now that they're—Well, they don't go out a great deal, these days."

"That's because they're delicate," Mrs. Hyde-Ridley asserted, firmly repudiating the suggestion that she or her contemporaries were feeling their age. "I remember they were awfully delicate as girls, as they always had to rest before balls, even the balls at Alassio which were really only hops. And their aunt who chaperoned them—that would be your great-aunt Mellicent Clifford, Aunt Mel they called her but I know it was Mellicent really—was always on at them about wrapping up well as the weather is so treacherous in Spring and she was afraid they would get pneumonia as they had been so ill with it when they were children, and she made them wear their thick combinations always. And sometimes later on, when it got really hot, they used to slip into my room and borrow my thin ones and change there so she wouldn't find out, as they said they simply couldn't bear the tickly feeling any longer. Oh, what fun we used to have in the dear old days at Alassio!"

Hester's Clifford aunts were her father's elder sisters; even when she was a child they had seemed old and staid. And as tough as old boots. Whatever the nature of their youthful illnesses, which hadn't to her knowledge been pneumonia, they had certainly outgrown them by then. Just as they had outgrown being frivolous and going to hops and defying the commands of their chaperone. And Great-Aunt Mellicent was to Hester only an ancestor whose portrait hung on the stairs; it was a shock to learn that Mrs. Hyde-Ridley had known her in the flesh. The whole thing was a shock —it was like being whirled away on a time-machine into a gay, ridiculous past that one hadn't dreamed existed.

"I know they used to go abroad a lot, when they were young," she said, "but somehow I imagined it was all culture and sight-seeing."

"Oh, you're thinking of Rome! Of course they spent the whole winter there and did the antiquities and the Vatican and everything, as they had to winter there as their lungs were so delicate and their Aunt Mel saw to it that they didn't waste their time. Yes, they used to complain of all the sight-seeing they had to do and say how glad they were to get up to Alassio—that was in the Spring, you see, when the weather got warmer and they could come north. Of course I was never with them in Rome as it was too far for me but I used to hear all about it! They could afford to spend the whole winter abroad in those days as it was before your family had the lawsuit and lost it, as you know it went on for years and broke your grandfather's heart and I expect your father's too!"

"But he lived for years after that," Hester protested. "The lawsuit happened long before I was born."

"But he was never the same man, was he? Oh, it's such a pity, Hester, that your aunts never took you abroad as their aunt did them!"

Hester thought so, too, because she was still seeing the aunts through Mrs. Hyde-Ridley's eyes. Then, remembering what they were like today, she laughed and shook her head.

"No, it wouldn't have worked. And they'd given up that sort of thing long before my time. Anyway, they're too—too poor to afford it."

She stopped herself from saying "too old." Poverty was allowable, poverty happened to everyone. Mrs. Hyde-Ridley was already agreeing that the cost of travel was simply awful nowadays—even in England, even just getting to Folkestone which was as far as she ever went. For a moment Hester pictured her making a romantic excursion to the limits of where Abroad started and gazing nostalgically at the departing cross-channel steamers; but then she remembered that Mrs. Vandevint lived at Folkestone and that they visited each other in turns. She asked whether Mrs. Hyde-Ridley would be going back with Mrs. Vandevint when the present visit ended. Mrs. Hyde-Ridley grew shrill and indignant as she explained that Mrs. Vandevint was staying for the whole of the summer.

"She's let her house! Ten guineas a week and she won't make a penny out of it, as everyone knows furnished tenants are worse than a fire! Fancy never telling me and pretending it was just a month as usual! And then planning to fall downstairs instead of going to her sister as she said I'd said she was to! Though of course I was only joking. Falling from the top instead of only from halfway as she'd planned was a judgement on her, and I can only be thankful poor Pussy wasn't killed, as she knew perfectly well poor Pussy always sits on that top step and it would have been all her fault if he had been!"

"Yes, indeed," said Hester.

It was ten minutes before she could ask whether Mrs. Hyde-Ridley needed anything from Scorling, and another ten minutes before she could get away. But a late start to the morning's shopping was part of her plan (as ingenious, in its way, as Mrs. Vandevint's) for filling in the time. The precious car was sitting outside *Bonnie Appin* in full view of half the village, some of whom would certainly tell Cousin Bennet about it if he thought of checking up.

Cecily had not wanted to come to Scorling herself, and Cousin Bennet could not come because he feared he was starting a cold. But both of them had thought that Hester could easily do all the shopping and be back for lunch, and at first she had been hard put to it for a reason not to be. Then she had thought of offering to shop for Mrs. Hyde-Ridley; and here she was, with half the morning gone before she had even left Mingham. Even Cousin Bennet would not find any flaws in her story this time.

When Hester reached the antique shop it was nearly one o'clock. She walked in, and Derek came out of the back room to greet her. As soon as he had done so he hung a card on the door handle and turned the key. "Closed for lunch," he explained. "But some people can't read so I lock the door as well."

"But you've locked us in."

"We're lunching here. Just a picnic, but it's quite cosy. Come and see."

"Will Mr. Frost mind?"

"Of course not. He's gone to a sale. . . . Why, Cousin Hester, surely *you* don't mind?"

"No," she said. "No, I'm not expecting you to give me a rich lunch at the Angel. Only—"

"Oh, I couldn't possibly afford that. I'm saving up, you know. Only—what?"

"Nothing at all," she said. She was pleased to hear that Derek was saving up, it seemed to make him more serious and reliable. She walked into the back room and Derek followed her. "There you are," he said complacently. "Much nicer than those dreary little caffs near the station."

On her earlier visit she had not seen the back room so she could only guess at the miracles Derek had accomplished. It was clean and tidy, the overflow from the shop stacked round its walls like a three-dimensional jigsaw, the big desk under the window a model of business-like order, the card table in the middle covered with a white cloth, on which the picnic lunch had been set out with as much elegance as circumstances permitted. The window looked on to a small yard, and she could see that this too was swept and tidy. There was a bowl of flowers on the window-sill and a fine Persian rug on the floor.

"You live in style," she commented. She was sitting on a Sheraton chair and eating off a Rockingham plate.

"Today is a special occasion, naturally. But even when I'm alone I like to have things clean and decent. Old Frost used to eat fish and chips off a newspaper, until I stopped him."

"How squalid," she said gravely.

"And very bad for his digestion."

Today was a special occasion. Hester, too, was aware of it, though she told herself there was nothing "special" about lunching with Derek, whom she thought of as a younger brother needing sisterly support and good advice.

"I'm glad you are saving up," she said. "Do you get commission on the things you sell?"

"Yes. I'm saving up to buy a share in the business."

"But that's—I mean, won't it take half a lifetime?"

"I hope not," said Derek. "I hope Mama will advance me a bit, when she realizes I'm serious. Of course I shall have to have some savings of my own as well, just to show her that I am. And then Frost will want to keep me, so he'll probably let me have a share for very little. After all, he hasn't got a wife and family to provide for. All he needs is a fair income for himself—and he'll get that, with me as his partner. I don't see why I shouldn't have a share in this business—well, quite reasonably soon."

It's sheer fantasy, Hester thought. She smiled kindly at her young brother Derek and said she would look forward to seeing his name over the shop in place of Minnie Wildgoose's. Though it wouldn't be so eye-catching, she added.

"Oh, I shan't change the name for a long time. It's too fetching—besides, he wouldn't like it. I know you're only humouring me, Hester; but just wait and see. You don't mind waiting, do you?"

"Oh, I'm quite prepared to wait."

"Good," said Derek.

For a moment Hester felt oddly confused, as though she had somehow missed a bit of the conversation and come out with the wrong response. She had not meant . . . but surely there was no question of her being intended to mean . . .

"Did you have any trouble getting away?" Derek was asking. "You were rather late—I was afraid the parents had changed their minds and decided to come too."

"No, I was late on purpose."

She told him about visiting Mrs. Hyde-Ridley, so that there should be a good reason for a late start, and explained that she had got involved in reminiscences of the distant past. Soon she was telling him about the aunts at Alassio, those frivolous young girls whose existence she had never imagined, and about Great-Aunt Mellicent, who had changed from an indifferent oil painting into a remembered chaperone, and about her own feeling of being caught up in a time-machine and transported to a happier world.

Derek was a good listener. He enjoyed the reminiscences as much as she had done; he laughed without sneering and did not need to have things explained. It was as though his friendly interest in people could bridge all the gaps. She found herself thinking of Raymond, who had never been able to understand why she "bothered" about her old aunts in Yorkshire. But Raymond, she thought now, wasn't interested in people.

"Of course it seems a happier world, in comparison," Derek remarked. "But it's partly because the distant past always looks so delightfully sunlit, and partly because your own past has been so cluttered up with misfortune. I expect your poor aunts once thought their hearts were broken, just as you think now."

"I don't—"

"Thought, then. I strongly approve of the past tense, but it seemed unsympathetic to use it."

"It's a horrible expression, anyway."

"A broken heart? But, my dear Hester, it's a *cliché*. *Clichés* really do describe emotional experiences, you know. The mere fact that hundreds of people use them proves it. People who are truly suffering don't bother about looking for elegant new ways of expressing their feelings."

Hester did not know why she found this nonsense soothing. Perhaps only because it allowed her time to stifle the sad, meaningless cries her mind gave when it thought of Raymond.

"All right. I had a broken heart," she said.

"Because you were in love with him and he jilted you. 'In love' is another *cliché*, of course, but I'm not sure about 'jilted.'"

"It might be nicer to say he let me down."

"We are talking about *clichés*, Hester dear, not about euphemisms."

Once again she found herself laughing instead of crying. Not that there was any likelihood, now, of her bursting into tears as she had so humiliatingly done when she was ill; but it had been a moment for sorrow and now it was a moment for gaiety.

"All right. He jilted me," she said cheerfully. "Now tell me what happened to you."

"I didn't get jilted," Derek said primly. "But then I wasn't properly engaged. Mama has probably told you I was, but she's mistaken. *Did* she tell you, Hester?"

"Two girls—one in Aldershot and one in Germany."

"Oh dear, that makes me sound so volatile. And of course I was. But you must remember I was much younger then."

"Young and impressionable," she said.

"Irresponsible, you mean. I do hate being called irresponsible. I suppose I used to be, but I'm not any longer—only they don't see it."

As an elder sister, Hester might have pointed out that no reformation was yet visible. Derek had impulsively abandoned a career in banking for a precarious job in an antique shop; he was weakly postponing the day when he would have to tell his parents of his action; he indulged in childish daydreams instead of facing facts.

It was all true. But there *was* a change; she had felt it before and she felt it now. In the antique shop Derek showed qualities that never appeared at home, a self-confidence and determination that inspired belief and somehow lifted him right out of his allotted role of younger brother. She could tease him but she could not snub him. Indeed, she did not want to.

"It's a label round your neck," she said. "Just as I've got 'broken-hearted' round mine. I think that's worse than being labelled irresponsible, because people think they have to be sorry for me. I hate being pitied as much as you hate being misjudged."

"No, you don't," Derek said firmly. "You may think you hate it, but you've come to expect it, and even regard it as your due. Of course that's very natural, but you'll have to fight against it all the same."

"I don't expect it. I hate it! Don't talk nonsense."

"You see? You're angry at once, because I don't show respectful sympathy for your grief. That's what it is, Hester: because you're still feeling sorry for yourself you still expect sympathy from other people. Not in words, of course, but a sort of warm, cosy atmosphere to protect you from harsh reality."

"Well!" she said. "Well, really."

It was Derek, not she, who disliked harsh realities. It was Derek who went in for warm, cosy atmospheres, fantasies of making his fortune and proving his family wrong. While she sought for words to correct this absurd reversal of identities there was a moment's silence, in which she heard the chiming of the clock on the mantelpiece and another one in the shop. Derek looked at the clock and then stood up.

"A quarter past two—time to open the shop," he announced. "Sorry, Hester, but I can't afford to shut out potential customers. You must come a bit earlier next time, because for some reason there are never any customers after half-past twelve so we shan't be disturbed."

What makes you think there will be a next time? Hester thought but did not say. Still, it must have been written on her face; Derek turned back from the door and scrutinised her anxiously.

"You're not taking umbrage, are you?" he asked.

"Of course not."

"Please don't forget that I'm on your side. I feel even more strongly about it than your Yorkshire aunts. But you must see that just pretending to forget it, and hanging on to it with the other half of you, gets you nowhere at all. And too much sympathy is dreadfully enervating."

It was his primmest voice: sedate, elderly-baby, easy to ridicule. Nevertheless Hester's umbrage (which she had untruthfully denied taking) faded as quickly as the shadow cast by a racing cloud. The sun shone out again; for no reason at all.

Looking for a reason afterwards, she found it in his allusion to the Yorkshire aunts. It had recalled his earlier interest in them, and his liking for people and his perceptiveness. All the qualities that contrasted so pleasantly with self-satisfied indifference. One really could not be angry with anyone as warm-hearted as Derek . . . or at any rate, not angry for long.

# CHAPTER FIFTEEN

JULY IS THE month for church fêtes. June seems too early in the summer, and the disadvantage of having them in August is that many people go away for holidays or have children at home from school, and cannot therefore undertake to assist at the stalls, or with the teas, or in the less important but still necessary tasks of selling raffle tickets or taking shillings at the gate. Moreover the Saturdays in August are reserved for outings; the choir-boys, the choirmen, the members of the Mothers' Union and of the Sunday school all expect to be taken in motor coaches for a long day at the sea, or a mystery tour, or a visit to the most distant cathedral city that can be reached in the time. Their tastes differ, they cannot all go on the same outing so each group needs a different Saturday. There are no Saturdays in August to spare for church fêtes.

"Or the equivalent," added Mr. Merlin, who was aware that it wasn't exactly a church fête that was under discussion. In some ways he wished it had been.

"The trouble with us is that we've got into a rut," Mrs. Merlin retorted.

By "us" she meant, of course, her husband; it could be taken as a comment on his long, pedantic explanation of why church fêtes, or their equivalent, must always be held in July.

"We are limited by circumstances," Mr. Merlin protested. "There are, for instance, only four Saturdays in August—"

"Five this year."

"I beg your pardon. Five. And they are already—"

"And only four outings," Mrs. Merlin cut in swiftly.

"The choir-boys, the Mothers' Union—"

"Yes, yes, Gregory, I *know*. Four outings—five Saturdays. And as for the novelty of having it in August, that's just what I'm counting on." Mrs. Merlin flung out her arms in the maenad's gesture she always used to promote frenzied enthusiasm. "Something new in August—out of the rut!" she cried incoherently.

"But people like being in ruts, especially the people in this village. Custom, tradition . . ."

It was no good; the very names of custom and tradition were anathema to Mrs. Merlin, when they conflicted with her wishes. And church fêtes were anathema, too, because there had been far too many of them in the past. This year everything was going to be different.

She had begun by planning a simple display of country dancing, to be held on Pooley's Piece. Then it had been transferred to the park, by kind permission of Mr. Thomas Seamark; and as the new location would undoubtedly attract a larger audience Mrs. Merlin had arranged for the sale of ice creams and had persuaded a team of country-dancing experts to demonstrate the higher branches of the art; and after some thought she had decided to have two stalls as well, one for home-made cakes and jam and the other for arts and crafts, which people could patronise in the intervals between the dancing. There was also the question of serving teas, which had not yet been settled.

To the Rector and the organising committee it had begun to sound like a church fête with all the profitable side-lines omitted (jumble and white elephants, raffles and bowling for the pig), but Mrs. Merlin insisted on calling it a Country Dancing Fiesta and confidently believed that people from all the surrounding parishes would flock to see this novelty, as well as the inhabitants of Mingham itself.

And now she was proposing to postpone the affair until August. The Rector felt sure they were heading for a disaster, but he felt equally sure that no words of his would convince his wife of her mistake. She was not in the mood to be crossed; she was in the mood when argument merely made her more contrary. If he went on arguing, they might find themselves holding the Country Dancing Fiesta in October.

"I'll tell the committee this afternoon," Mrs. Merlin said happily.

Mr. Merlin assented with a sigh, knowing that he would get no help in that quarter. Mrs. Merlin had unfortunately alienated all the capable women who had formerly helped to run church fêtes, and her present colleagues were, like herself, more enthusiastic than efficient. They were mostly country dancers; or they played recorders or wove homespun yarns into narrow lengths of loose material which eventually became very baggy skirts. Excellent women, Mr. Merlin reminded himself, but collectively, alas, a broken reed.

The committee received the news with relief. They knew what Mr. Merlin did not—that the local dancers needed much more practice. Mrs. Merlin had changed the programme so often that her teams were in a dreadful state of confusion: with so many dances half learnt, some of the performers never seemed to know which one they were dancing. It was all Mrs. Merlin's fault, but the committee did not tell her so; instead, they spent the afternoon discussing such minor details as new ribbons for the maypole and whether the children's team should wear green socks.

Miss Cardwell, the village school-teacher and the only member of the committee with any talent for organisation, heard about the change of date only after it had been eagerly adopted. She could not be present at many of the committee meetings, because of her work in the school, and she suspected Mrs. Merlin of holding the meetings at these inconvenient hours on purpose to thwart her. It was with a fine sense of being about to have her revenge that she approached the rectory that evening, after tea and after the arrival of the bus bringing her friend Miss Knapp back from work. Miss Knapp worked in the Scorling branch of the county library and frequently did not get home till past eight o'clock, but today she had been on the early turn, which meant that she got away at five. Miss Knapp accompanied Miss Cardwell to the rectory gate, but excused herself from going further.

"You know I can't stand any unpleasantness," she said.

Miss Cardwell, who could stand a lot of it, went through the gate and vanished down the path that led to the back door. It was Mrs. Merlin, not the Rector, whom she wished to interview, and she knew where to find her. Miss Knapp thought about going into the church and then thought not; she strolled up to the lych-gate and back again, and wondered whether it would be seemly to sit on the low wall that enclosed the rectory garden. While she was still undecided the gate in the wall on the other side of the street opened, and Bennet Hutton looked out.

That wall was quite a high one and the gate was also high, so she did not see him until he came out and greeted her. But he had seen her, from his bedroom window, and had come hastening down to find out what was happening. There was no reason at all why Miss Knapp should not take a stroll up the village street to the church, but she wouldn't have done it unaccompanied. Miss Cardwell wasn't in sight, therefore she must have entered the rectory. Why hadn't Miss Knapp gone in too?

Miss Knapp played the recorder, also the violin (which she called a fiddle) and the glockenspiel. She was very versatile. With fiddle or recorder she had often accompanied the rehearsals of country dancing on Bennet Hutton's lawn, so she knew him quite well and thought him quite Dickensian. The smiling, benevolent kind, of course, not a Quilp or a Mr. Dombey. She was pleased to be shown the garden, though she insisted on coming back to the gate every so often to see if Miss Cardwell had reappeared. And although she would not have dreamed of discussing the committee's decisions with any outsider she did not think of Mr. Hutton as an outsider. He had lent his lawn for the rehearsals and was therefore identified with the project.

"It's to be in August now, if Mrs. Merlin has her way," Bennet Hutton told his family that night. "But Miss Caldwell wasn't consulted and she says it can't be in August because she and Miss Knapp are going to Bournemouth for a fortnight. Miss Cardwell is not only a prancer but she trains the junior prancers, the school-children, and no one else could ensure that they all turn up. And Miss Knapp, of course, is part of the orchestra."

"How awkward for Mrs. Merlin," Cecily said, with a touch of satisfaction.

"Does Thomas know the date has been altered?" Maggie asked.

"I don t know. Still, he can't plead that the park will be needed for something else."

"But he'll have to be there himself . . . it mightn't be convenient. Poor Thomas, I do think Mrs. Merlin should have asked him first."

Bennet noted that his daughter had a one-track mind. Very nice and touching.

"Does poor Thomas know there's to be a maypole?" he asked. "And two stalls and an ice-cream van and possibly a tent for teas? And a hundred and fifty folding chairs coming in Rudd's breakdown truck, for the people who will pay half-a-crown extra to sit down?"

Maggie was appalled. She was sure Thomas knew none of these things.

"It will be a sort of imitation church fête," she said, voicing the unspoken thoughts of the Rector and the committee. "But he thinks it's just a few people coming to watch some country dancing. He won't want hordes and hordes."

"He won't get hordes and hordes," said Bennet. "Where would they come from? Why should they bother to come? And another thing; they're charging far too much for everything. Miss Knapp said so, and I entirely agree with her."

He thought how much better he would have organised it, if he were ever permitted to organise anything. He was a good organiser—far better, for instance, than Cecily—and there was no phase of village life, from running the house to running the church fête, that he couldn't have handled. But he was never consulted; he had been relegated to an armchair and the boring life of an invalid. He had become redundant.

He did not admit to himself that there were advantages in being an invalid, for latterly the advantages had been less apparent than the vexations. Everyone agreed that he was recovering, yet he was still treated as a sick man; his invalidism clung to him like a bad reputation and he felt he would never live it down. For this he blamed his family, who persisted in humouring his whims and ignoring his intelligence. But in rare moments of insight he also blamed himself.

Tonight he wasn't blaming himself. His urge to play a more active part had been thwarted by his family; in particular by Derek, who brusquely rejected his offer to mend the faulty electric light in Maggie's bedroom.

"Oh, don't trouble yourself, Papa," Derek said. "I expect it's only the fuse and I can manage that without good advice."

Naturally Bennet would not have done the crawling about on the floor by the power point, or the climbing of the housemaid s steps to reach the fuse-box high up on the cellar wall; but he had intended to do more than merely advise. The rejection put him back among the bystanders, among the incompetent and the unwanted. He brooded on it for a time, sitting alone in his study (with four other people in the house and none of them sparing a thought for his solitude), and then he went quietly into the hall and put on his hat and overcoat. It was only half-past nine and a fine, warm evening, but the habits of an invalid were strong in him. And it was months, perhaps years, since he had last ventured out after supper.

He was not going far—only across the street to the rectory—but his *sortie* had the qualities of an adventure. He left his own house as if he were escaping from a prison camp, and took great care to shut the gate noiselessly. With the rectory gate he was less successful, for it could not be opened or shut without a loud, betraying squeak from its rusty hinges, but that did not matter because he was now, so to speak, across the border. He stood still, just inside the gate, recovering from the excitement and considering his next move.

The Rector was spraying the roses; a task which he enjoyed, but for which he could seldom find time. It was strange, he thought, that country clergymen in fiction had all the time in the world to cultivate their gardens and pursue their hobbies. They grew prize-winning carnations or became famous as local geologists or antiquarians, or were free to devote hours to solving local murders which had baffled the best brains of Scotland Yard. In his experience there was never time for more than the minimum of garden upkeep—mowing the lawn, pulling up the biggest weeds, and planting out the lettuces for the slugs to eat—and hobbies were out of the question. He must be, he thought humbly, a very poor organiser.

His wife had gone to bed early, with a headache which she attributed to the unpleasantness with Miss Cardwell. Without admitting that it was a relief to escape the post mortem on Miss Cardwell's visit which would have occupied the evening if his wife had not retired, Mr. Merlin was frankly enjoying his solitude in the garden. The squeak of the opening gate fell on his ears as the least welcome of sounds. Yet, having heard it, he could not ignore it. He put the syringe in the bucket and walked round to the front of the house to meet the caller.

There was no one there. For a moment he hoped his ears had deceived him; then he looked towards the gate and saw a tubby, well-muffled figure shuffling slowly up the drive.

"My dear Hutton!" he exclaimed solicitously, advancing to meet an invalid whom only dire emergency, it seemed, could have brought out at this hour.

"Evening, Merlin," Bennet Hutton chirruped back. "Fine summer evening. Must make the most of it. Thought I'd come across for a chat."

Never had Bennet Hutton shown a neighbourly spirit; why did he have to be neighbourly now, on one of the rare evenings when one was enjoying blissful solitude? Mr. Merlin could not help asking himself this question; but he immediately silenced the inner voice and tried to forget it.

"A beautiful evening," he agreed. "And your being out so late is, I trust, a sign of returning health? Not that it is really late, of course, but by *your* standards . . . The standards, I should say, that an invalid is compelled to—"

"Precisely," Bennet said quickly. A good fellow, Merlin, but it was fatal to let him start qualifying his qualifying clauses. "A beautiful evening. A convalescent invalid. You have it in a nutshell."

And you have me, he thought kindly, to advise and assist you in your difficulties. A lucid intelligence, coupled with a talent for diplomacy.

"Shall we stroll round the garden?" he suggested. "You were, I imagine, musing among your roses when I arrived . . ."

"I was spraying them," Mr. Merlin corrected him.

"Ah, you gardeners! A rector's roses are as cherished as a spinster's parrot."

This time Mr. Merlin did not bother to correct him, for he felt it was useless to stand out against the country clergymen of fiction. They walked back to the lawn where the roses grew in their star- and crescent-shaped beds (a setting devised by some past incumbent who really had had time for gardening), and began to pace up and down the weedy, overlong grass. The Rector permitted himself a regretful glance at the syringe as he passed it, but Bennet did not even notice it was there. His attention was fixed on something quite different; he saw himself, as if from some celestial vantage-point, walking up and down a rectory lawn by the side of a perplexed clergyman and solving his problems for him.

"I gather you're having trouble with the village about the date of the—er—display," he said.

Mr. Merlin could not quite repress a shudder. Not this, not this again, his shudder said. But to Bennet it was a straightforward symptom of bewilderment, and he dealt with it graciously.

"Very difficult, trying to please everyone," he sympathised. "But you want to take a practical view—remember you *can't* fit in with everybody, and settle in your own mind what would be best. Then, when you've got it all clear in your own mind, you can explain it clearly to the—er—dissatisfied. You'll have your arguments, your reasons, all marshalled. And of course you will also use diplomacy."

"How do you know?" Mr. Merlin asked.

"My dear Rector, I feel sure you are capable of using diplomacy in a good cause. . . . Oh, you mean how do I know of the trouble?"

He paused to consider this; he wasn't sure whether it would be wise to admit having heard about it from Miss Knapp. The pause gave Mr. Merlin time to summon up his powers of resistance.

"It is indeed difficult to please everyone," he said. "Nor is it always wise even to attempt to do so. Moreover there are times when too much discussion, too much debate, even when conducted in the most helpful spirit—as, for instance, yours now—can be a positive hindrance. Or, if that sounds too harsh, let me say that they tend to cloud, rather than to clarify, the issues. In short, and if you will forgive me for saying so—but remember, my dear Hutton, that I am speaking to a neighbour, and, I trust, a friend—"

"A neighbour and a friend. In a nutshell. My own thought when I crossed the street. I came to help."

Bennet's staccato interruptions had no more effect than tintacks scattered in the path of a steam-roller. Mr. Merlin swept steadily on.

". . . In short, there are already quite enough people arguing about matters connected with the Country Dancing Fiesta. The committee, and—well, the committee. It is, after all, their business. Let us leave them to settle it."

"As you wish. Of course. Only hope they settle it sensibly."

"Look at my poor roses," Mr. Merlin said humbly. "A great plague of greenfly, I'm afraid. I am trying soapy water, but perhaps you know of something better."

This attempt to soothe hurt feelings did not succeed. Bennet Hutton had come there to deal with more important matters than a plague of greenfly; and if his advice wasn't wanted, he would go home again.

Let them manage matters in their own stupid way, he thought; the thing would be a flop and that would be a lesson to them. The foolish Rector and his equally foolish wife deserved to be taught a lesson.

He crossed the street with his eyes on the ground, brooding on the snub he had just been given and on ingratitude in general. He exaggerated his slow shuffle, to demonstrate what an effort it had been for a poor invalid to visit the rectory and try to help. Not until he reached his own gate did he look up; and then it took him a full minute to appreciate what was wrong with the familiar outline of The End House.

But when he had taken it in he smiled cherubically, his more recent snub quite forgotten.

The house was in total darkness.

# CHAPTER SIXTEEN

IT WAS NOT really Derek's failure to mend the electric light that made one anxious about him, Cecily said. But that failure was a kind of symptom of other things, and naturally one couldn't help worrying if one was his mother.

"What other things?" Hester demanded.

"Oh, you know, dear. I sometimes think he's no good at anything because he has a—a sort of will-to-failure."

Hester found herself defending Derek with vigour.

"He has nothing of the kind," she said. "He's ambitious and energetic. He really means to get on. And I think he deserves to."

"I hope the bank thinks so too," Cecily remarked doubtfully. "I might write and ask Malcolm if he's giving satisfaction. That's my elder brother, who got Derek into the bank, though of course he doesn't work here himself, he's in the head office and—"

"Oh, I shouldn't bother him, Cecily. In fact, I think it would be a tactless mistake."

Hester drew a graphic picture of busy men in head offices resenting having to answer inquiries about junior recruits in distant local branches. To her relief Cecily found this convincing and agreed not to write. She admitted that her brother Malcolm did not like being bothered, and never corresponded with her unless it was something important.

"We've grown apart," she said rather sadly.

"Then it would be *much* better not to bother him."

How deceitful of me, Hester thought. But her instinct to save Derek from exposure had operated much faster than her conscience.

She supposed it was because she really believed, now, that he had found his vocation and should be given a chance to prove it. Exposure at this stage, with people scolding and deriding him, might sap his new self-confidence.

"Derek has a very nice nature," she said, switching from careers to personalities. "He's always so kind and helpful."

"Helpful! What about the electric light?"

"Well . . . he was trying to help."

Trying to mend the light in Maggie's bedroom, he blew the main fuses and put out every light in the house. "That's not helpful."

Hester admitted it was not. She might have argued that it was the good intention that counted, but an inner voice warned her that she had said enough. You are overdoing it, said this cautious commentator; adding very quickly and firmly that friendship was always liable to be misunderstood, and that was why she must play it down.

"It was lucky Cousin Bennet was able to cope," she said.

"Yes, wasn't it? That reminds me, Hester. Thomas wants to show you his fishponds."

One thing leads to another; but there seemed absolutely no link between Cousin Bennet's skill with electricity and Thomas Seamark's fishponds. For Hester did not know that Cecily had been telephoning to Thomas while she and Derek were down in the cellar mending—or wrecking—the electric light.

"Oh, does he?" she said, non-committally.

"He asked us to tea on Saturday. I knew you'd love to see the fishponds so I said Yes."

Hester remembered that the establishment of an *entente cordiale* between the Priory and The End House had been one of her self-allotted missions. She had not given it much attention lately, and it was time she did.

"Good," she replied. "Yes, I remember him talking about the fishponds at the picnic. It was quite interesting."

"Thomas *is* interesting," Cecily said firmly.

Thomas had given the invitation without stating whether he meant all of them or just herself and Hester. But since her talk with him—that pathetic all-but-open declaration of his hopes—Cecily could feel happily certain it was Hester he wanted to see, and that the fewer people who accompanied her the better. So she set out tea on the trolley for those who would be staying at home, and made it clear to Bennet and Derek that they had not been asked to the Priory.

She thought she had also made it clear to Maggie. But when she came downstairs her daughter was standing in the hall, wearing a clean cotton frock instead of grubby gardening clothes, with her hair brushed into something like neatness and her sun-tanned face heavily powdered. She even had stockings on, and a pair of white shoes she hadn't worn since Cecily bought the n for her last summer. At any other time Cecily would have been pleased to see Maggie taking trouble with her appearance, but now she stood still in dismay.

"Are you ready?" Maggie asked. "Hester's got the car outside, and I've shut the yard gates."

"But you're not coming," Cecily cried. "I mean—I thought I told you, darling—Thomas didn't say all of us."

"He didn't say just you and Hester, did he?"

Cecily hesitated. "I think that's what he meant," she said.

"I don't," said Maggie. "Not unless he actually said so. Thomas always used to ask the lot of us—when he did ask us, I mean. He never left people out. It's against his principles."

She opened the front door and walked out to join Hester, who was apparently expecting her. Cecily followed feeling both surprised and annoyed, surprised by Maggie's vehemence, and annoyed by her contrariness. It was so like Maggie, she thought, to insist on coming when she wasn't wanted, while obstinately refusing the invitations her mother wished her to accept.

Just because it was "so like" Maggie, the significance of her action passed unnoticed. Cecily was busy reorganising her plans, considering how Thomas and Hester could be sent to look at the fishponds alone—a simple matter, if she had been the only other person present—and, with another part of her mind, regretting that she had put on a hat. It had seemed a good idea when she did it, but now she feared that a hat would make the tea-party seem too formal.

The sight of the Priory, across the spotless new surface of the forecourt, paused both Hester and Cecily to break into heartless laughter. "It's just not true!" Hester exclaimed. But the sight of Thomas, coming round the corner of his house to welcome his guests, put an end to their mirth. They got out of the car and greeted him with hypocritical delight, pretending to think every-thing was absolutely wonderful.

That was Maggie's view of it, admittedly a prejudiced one because she could not be loyal to Thomas and wholly fair to other people at the same time. Moreover, now that she was here, she was assailed by a horrible doubt about whether he was really expecting her. The doubt, and the wish to dissociate herself from false effusiveness, combined to render her greeting as brief as possible. "Hullo," she said curtly.

"Hullo, Maggie," said Thomas. "I'm glad to see you."

Maggie was assailed by more doubts. Did this mean he had *not* been expecting her and was politely trying to hide it? Alone with Thomas, she would have asked him, but somehow her mother's presence always made her feel shy and tongue-tied. And all wrong, she thought bitterly, scowling down at the white shoes. "No one else?" said Thomas. "I expected all of you."

Maggie looked across at her mother. In an instant her doubts were banished; the fleeting guilt on Cecily's face, and Thomas's words, convinced her that all was well. "We didn't know that," she exclaimed triumphantly. "Mother thought—"

"I thought three would be quite enough of us. In any case, Bennet had a bit of a headache . . ."

Intent on stopping Maggie, Cecily was forced to give Bennet the headache she had designed for herself, after tea when it was time for the fishponds. But that did not matter because now she would have to see the fishponds; she would have to pair with Maggie and detach her from Thomas and Hester. Maggie had no *savoir-faire* and would never dream of detaching herself, unless she was made to.

Tea on the upper terrace was delightful, Cecily thought; it took her back to the years soon after the war, before Thomas's marriage, before Bennet's illness, when she had so often sat here drinking tea, and talking to Thomas and Bennet with one eye on the children playing on the lower terrace to see that they did not fall into the river. Maggie and Derek always gobbled their tea in a hurry; they liked the lower terrace so much that they grudged every minute away from it. They had a special game, with stick boats that were launched from the upstream end of the terrace and raced to the downstream end, and sometimes Thomas played it with them; while she sat here in the sun watching, and thinking how nice it was that the war was over and they could settle down to a peaceful, lazy existence. . . .

Time seemed to be standing still when one looked back at it, and it was forever summer. Today, because it was summer again and she was back on the terrace, Cecily found it easier to remember those earlier summers than the ones that followed, when the children were growing up and Bennet was turning into an invalid; when Thomas's marriage and the death of his wife were taking him away from them, and the tea-parties had become rare and formal and had then ceased altogether.

The fishponds lay some distance downstream, beyond the walled kitchen garden and a steeply sloping "wild" garden, which was now much wilder than its designer had intended.

"A shame to let it go," Thomas said ruefully.

"I don't know. There's something about a ruined garden . . . an enchantment that well-kept ones somehow miss."

Cecily paused to look back at the hillside, the wooded slopes enclosing this charming confusion of meandering paths and overgrown bushes. A stream ran down through the wild garden, crossed by a rustic bridge at the foot of a small cascade. It was quite delectable.

"Oh no, you mustn't touch it!" she cried.

"I can't afford to."

They walked on, down the bank of the stream and across the stepping-stones at the foot of the hill. Suddenly Cecily realised that she had been walking beside Thomas ever since they left the terrace; it was she, not Maggie, who was being tactless. She paused again, on the last stepping-stone, and said abruptly: "Don't wait for me."

"Why not?" Thomas asked in surprise. He was on the bank just ahead of her, holding out his hand to pull her across the gap. "Why not? Don't you want to be helped?"

"I just want to stay here. It's too beautiful."

The stepping-stone was a large, flat one; Cecily could stand on it without wobbling, as she turned round to stare back at the wild garden. "I'll follow you," she called. Lost in the contemplation of beauty (the only excuse that had presented itself), she heard Thomas walk away, and as soon as he had gone a few steps she looked quickly over her shoulder to see where Hester and Maggie had got to. They were a good way ahead, walking together as she had feared, so in a minute or so she would have to go on and detach Maggie.

And Thomas was striding after them, with something in the set of his shoulders and the back of his head that suggested a kindly contempt for artistic ladies rooted to the spot by a glimpse of the picturesque. He has no taste, she thought; but she thought it quite fondly, seeing in the man walking away from her the shy boy of her first acquaintance and the lost friend of those summers after the war. Before he married Beatrice.

The three fishponds lay full in the sun, and down here by the river there wasn't a breath of wind to temper the heat. Perfect, Hester thought; if one could just sit sunning oneself without listening to a lecture. She cautiously withdrew a short distance and then lay down on the dry, warm turf. If he wanted to show them the other sluices, she would say she was waiting for Cecily.

"My uncle didn't understand the importance of the sluices," Thomas was explaining. "He simply puddled up the leaks in the banks, and then planted his water-lilies."

"If only he'd mended the sluices," said Maggie, "you wouldn't have had all this trouble."

She looked sadly across the fishpond which like its two fellows was more marsh than pond, with a little water in the middle and a wide margin of mud.

"Yes. He didn't understand. He thought the stream from the dell would be enough to keep them filled. In fact, the stream hardly helps at all, as he'd have found out, if he'd bothered to calculate the rate of flow. The monks built these ponds to be fed by the river, and a very good job they made of it."

"How beautiful they would look, if you could get the sluices repaired, and all those mucky weeds cleared out."

Water-lilies, Hester thought. Not mucky weeds.

"Horrid mess, isn't it?" said Thomas. His voice was warm with approval; he did not seem to mind Maggie's criticism at all. But of course she was agreeing with him about mistakes made in the past.

"All that boggy decay round the edges," Maggie said distastefully.

"Yes. If I could get the sluices put right the ponds would be full right up to the banks."

"Oh, Thomas, can't you do it? It would be such an improvement—"

They think exactly alike, Hester told herself, with a trace of superior amusement. Neatness and order. Not a mucky weed anywhere. She raised her head and propped herself on one elbow to look at them.

They were standing only a few feet away, though it was clear they had forgotten all about her. They were discussing what would have to be done, the best way to do it and what it would cost. They were talking loudly and animatedly, sometimes interrupting each other, but without any suggestion of disagreement; indeed, their good humour—and Maggie's talkativeness—was what struck Hester first. She thought she had never before seen Thomas in a really good temper, and what struck her next was the difference it made to his looks.

This is the *entente cordiale* all right, she thought; I don't need to do anything more about it. She straightened out and lay full length on the grass, basking in the sun and feeling pleased and a little complacent. For the re-establishment of good relations between the Priory and The End House had been all her doing; if she had not coaxed Cousin Bennet to take the first step, organised picnics and cooked an emergency dinner and constantly reminded them of Thomas Seamark's existence, the Huttons would simply have continued to think of him as a man who had chosen to become a recluse. They might have regretted it, but none of them would have taken any action.

Maggie and Thomas had walked a little way along the bank; the sound of their voices had diminished but she could still hear what they were saying. They were lamenting the difficulties caused by Thomas's uncle, who had dumped quantities of clay against the sluice-gates to make them watertight, instead of putting them into working order.

"It was a bad mistake," Thomas said severely. "Those sluice-gates were still working in the middle of the eighteenth century. There's a record in one of the old estate books about re-stocking the ponds with fish."

"What sort of fish?"

"It doesn't say."

"Carp, I should think. Will you get some carp, Thomas, when you've mended the sluices?"

"I haven't thought. The thing is, it may turn out to be too big a job. Too expensive to be justifiable."

"Yes, I know," said Maggie. "But perhaps you could do it in stages."

They went on talking. Hester listened, half asleep and too lazy to join in, although she could have joined in without raising her voice. Besides, it was a very dull conversation and they didn't want her.

The oddity of the last thought jerked her awake. That was wrong, said her waking intelligence; it was a very dull conversation *but* they didn't want her. That did not seem to make sense either; and yet, in a way, it did. A dull conversation about fishponds. Why should it sound like the conversation of lovers?

How stupid of me, she thought, watching them as they moved away along the bank . . . how stupid not to see a thing so obvious. She watched them with interest and amusement, though the amusement was partly at herself, clever Hester who thought the *entente cordiale* was all her doing. Bossy I may be, she thought, but I'm not responsible for *that*.

Behind her, walking fast to make up for lost time, Cecily approached rapidly. It was just as she had feared: Maggie wasn't giving Thomas a chance to talk to Hester.

"I'm so sorry," she cried breathlessly. "I only meant to stay there a minute—I just sat down in the sun . . ."

"I expect you went to sleep. I'm nearly asleep myself. Come and sit down here."

"No, no, we must see the fishponds. We'll catch them up and then Thomas can tell you about them."

"I've heard quite as much as I want to."

Cecily looked so disappointed that Hester thought she must have a particular affection for the fishponds, based, perhaps, on their mediaeval origin.

"Oh, Cecily, they *are* interesting," she said quickly. "I only meant that Thomas has already explained all about them how the sluices work, and everything. And now he's gone round to the other side with Maggie to look at—well, another sluice-gate, I think—and I thought it would be nice if we just stayed here in the sun, till they come back."

"We could walk round the other way and meet them."

"Don't let's. It's too hot."

Reluctantly, Cecily sat down.

"It has been such an agreeable afternoon," Hester said. "I've enjoyed it immensely."

She was still trying to atone for her indifference to the beloved fishponds; but for Cecily the words had a different meaning.

"I'm so glad, dear," she said encouragingly. "I've enjoyed it too. Tea on the terrace, and Thomas being as he used to be. He really is—I mean, he *has* got over it."

Hester realised that what was so obvious to herself was still unperceived by Cecily, and an instinct of caution stopped her from even hinting at it. But she saw no harm in putting in a good word for Thomas.

"Yes," she said, "he's not a recluse any longer. I've felt that too, today—as if I were seeing the real Thomas for the first time."

"And you do like him?"

"Oh yes, very much. He's far nicer than I thought at first."

Things were going well, Cecily thought. In spite of Maggie's intrusion and her own failure to detach her, the afternoon could be counted a success.

# CHAPTER SEVENTEEN

THE COUNTRY Dancing Fiesta was to have been held in late July and was now postponed to August. Luckily this news had been spread by word of mouth (together with the news of the unpleasantness between Mrs. Merlin and Miss Cardwell, which had nearly led to there being no Fiesta at all), so that no one was deceived by the posters still advertising the original date. And in due course the date on the posters was corrected by Mrs. Merlin, who toured the village with a sheaf of gummed strips printed in black on red, which she stuck diagonally across every poster she could find.

At the school she met with a rebuff; the poster by the gate had already been corrected by Miss Cardwell, who would have done the others as well only she didn't care to presume. Mrs. Merlin accepted the rebuff meekly, because she knew that without Miss Cardwell's co-operation the Fiesta could not take place, but inwardly she felt far from meek. She thought about Wrightley, that wonderful parish where everyone had been so keen and energetic, and the thought added fuel to her inward flames. When she got to Rudd's Garage and found that the poster had been taken down and thrown away, the flames burst out in open rage.

"There's no excuse at all, Mr. Rudd! You knew it was only postponed. What's the good of having all these corrections printed if the posters are thrown away?"

"No good at all, when they doesn't come in time," Rudd said calmly. "It's past the date on them posters, Mrs. Merlin, and that's why I took mine down. No sense in keeping an out o' date poster up, is there now?"

"It's not my fault that the printers were so slow!"

"Ah, but you could have told us they was on the way, couldn't you? Come to that, I could have done them myself."

Too late, Mrs. Merlin remembered that Rudd owned a machine that printed handbills, tickets for whist drives, and other small items. It was her failure to remember these things that was always getting her into trouble, and now, for the second time that morning, she had to placate a parishioner whose co-operation was essential to the success of the Fiesta.

"I'm sorry, Mr. Rudd, that I didn't think of asking you. I didn't realize! You see, you're always so busy—mowing-machines and cars and everything, what we should do without you I simply can't think! But I'll certainly remember next time."

"Let's hope it don't get put off again, Mrs. Merlin."

"Oh, I didn't mean that!"

Smiling, praising, apologising, Mrs. Merlin beat a retreat. She hoped she had smoothed things over, but she did not dare to mention the breakdown truck which was supposed to be transporting the chairs from the parish hall to the park. Another visit, nearer the day, would be needed to settle that.

Mrs. Merlin habitually walked with her head poked forward and her eyes on the ground, too intent on her errand or her grievances to observe her surroundings. It was a habit that did her no good in Mingham, where people expected the Rector's wife to notice them and wish them good-day; and this morning it must have accounted for her walking right past *Firenze* without seeing the metamorphosis it had undergone. But on her homeward way she heard a noise and looked up. She was surprised, indignant, and dazzled.

Indignant, because it was the long rectory ladder that was propped against the gable. But then she remembered that she had promised to lend it; and almost at the same moment Mrs. Bavington came running out of the house, bubbling over with pretty apologies.

"Your ladder, Mrs. Merlin! I do hope you'll forgive us for taking it! Anthony went up to the rectory this morning, and you weren't there but he explained to the Rector. You did promise to lend it but I 'spect you've forgotten all about it—it's so long ago."

"No, I remember perfectly," Mrs. Merlin protested.

"Oh, good! The Rector didn't seem to know about it and I was afraid you might have forgotten. Please, please forgive us for helping ourselves!"

To be receiving apologies instead of giving them was a pleasant change, and moreover Mrs. Merlin was gratified to see one of her posters displayed in *Firenze*'s front window. Chrysanthemum saw her looking at it, and explained that she had got it from a member of the committee who lived at the bottom of Endless Lane where no one ever went.

"She was going to put it on her gate, but what was the good of that?" she said laughingly. "So I said, 'Give it to me and I'll stick it in my window where everyone's bound to notice it.' You don't mind, do you?"

"Miss Barter," said Mrs. Merlin, identifying the committee member.

"That's right. She buys cakes from me."

"I didn't know you sold cakes."

"I've only just started. Come in and taste them. On the house, of course! You know we're opening next week!"

Chrysanthemum jumped up and down in childish excitement, and a voice high above their heads said:

"Steady on, Chrissie! You're jogging the ladder."

"Sorry, darling. Oh, I forgot—you don't know Anthony, do you? My son, Anthony—Mrs. Merlin, who lent us that ladder." Mrs. Merlin looked up. She saw a plump young man, foreshortened against the roof-line, whose face was dimly familiar to her. She knew he often spent weekends at Mingham, but as he never came to church she was not officially acquainted with him.

Anthony acknowledged the introduction politely, and went on painting. His mother said proudly that he never wasted a moment, and renewed her invitation to coffee and cakes. Mrs. Merlin delved in her bag for a gummed strip to bring the poster up-to-date, and explained to Mrs. Bavington that it must be stuck on diagonally. She was sorry, she said, that she could not come in that morning, but she would look forward to visiting the tea-shop when it opened. Chrysanthemum said that the first time any of her friends visited the shop their teas would be on the house.

Mrs. Merlin went on her way, feeling soothed and cheered by this encounter with really friendly, really keen people. At the back of her mind was the thought that they might be roped in to help with the teas (if teas could be arranged), and that in any case the young man might be asked to help with the erection of the maypole. He could hardly refuse, since she had lent them the rectory ladder.

Hitherto Anthony had spent his Mingham weekends sitting in a deck chair in the back garden, or in an easy chair indoors, reading crime stories or biographies of successful men and listening to dance music on his portable wireless. So he knew hardly anyone, and had acquired the reputation of being spoilt and idle. His emergence as an energetic though slapdash painter surprised the whole village.

"Of course his mother works just as hard as he does," Mrs. Hyde-Ridley remarked. She was annoyed because the exterior painting of her own house, which had been part of the bargain, had got no further than the lower half of the front, and because Anthony had left splashes of paint on the window-panes and hairs from the brush on the front door. But Chrysanthemum had promised faithfully that the front should be finished before the tea-shop opened and that the back would be done in the first slack period.

"There's so much to do, and we've simply got to open on August Bank Holiday," she explained. "August is the best month —we simply can't afford to miss the rush!"

Mrs. Vandevint sniffed at the idea of there being any rush in Mingham, but Mrs. Hyde-Ridley saw the point. Bank Holiday meant customers, and customers meant profits, and profits were needed to pay the rent.

Much had already been done before Anthony appeared on the scene; a new stove had been installed, and chairs and tables and crockery, and Chrysanthemum had had her drawing-room furniture carried up to her bedroom and her bedroom furniture carried up to the attic. (Mrs. Hyde-Ridley hoped the roof was more watertight than *Bonnie Appin's, but did not like to enquire.) But after Anthony's arrival the pace of the work quickened, and to the ladies next door it seemed that Anthony and his mother spent all night as well as all day hammering and scraping and scrubbing and arguing. Mrs. Hyde-Ridley bore it with surprising patience, and even Mrs. Vandevint showed a gleam of interest as opening day approached. Without admitting it, they were both looking forward to a new entertainment.

"Of course we shall go to tea there on the first day," Mrs. Hyde-Ridley told Hester. "She wants people to come, as the fuller it is the better as that will show the trippers it's popular. You'd better come with us."

"I expect Derek and Maggie and I will come together," Hester said hastily. She wondered why she could never go into the post office without meeting Mrs. Hyde-Ridley.

"Oh well, if you're all coming . . . ! Anyway, it's 'on the house.' She said so."

"Surely not! How is she going to make it pay?"

"Oh, only the first time we have tea there. All her friends, she said—as of course she wouldn't be giving free tea to the trippers!"

Until that moment Hester had not thought of attending the opening; and she had dragged in Maggie and Derek simply to stave off a session with Mrs. Hyde-Ridley and her friend. But when she told Derek about it he said it would be fun. Not as good as a lunch party in *his* shop, but still fun. They would see the transformed inside of *Firenze*, and the trippers if there were any, and Anthony doing his stuff. And if it was for free, better still.

"All right," said Hester. "I'll tell Maggie."

"Oh, why bother? I mean, it wouldn't amuse her. She doesn't share our intelligent curiosity about how other people live."

"But it's August Bank Holiday, and I know she's spending the day at home. We can't just go off and leave her here with the parents."

"That's the worst of home," Derek said. "Every jaunt turns into a family outing."

She knew what he meant. Since the day when she had lunched with Derek all her visits to Scorling had been in company with either Cousin Bennet or Cecily, and instead of being free to visit the antique shop she had spent her time heading them off the street it was in.

"All your own fault," Derek said, watching her. "If you hadn't persuaded Papa to let you drive the car, it wouldn't have been available. Then he wouldn't have thought of getting new suits and having fittings for them, and Mama wouldn't have thought of popping in for a quick look round the shops. You should have stuck to the bus."

"Anyway, it's very lucky they don't have their banking accounts at the bank where you worked. Or you'd have been found out long ago."

They laughed at each other, with the shared secret linking them together and separating them from the others, who would not understand and must be prevented from finding out. Nevertheless, Maggie could not be left to spend the afternoon by herself—or with her parents, which came to the same thing. Even Derek saw that.

"Oh, well," said Maggie. "I suppose I might as well come with you."

It was Monday afternoon and they were standing at the gate. Maggie had seemed oddly reluctant to commit herself to the jaunt, and even now she was in two minds about it. The reason for this became evident to Hester just as they were starting, when a car came slowly out of the narrow lane beside the rectory and turned down the street towards them. Maggie watched it approaching and said in a casual voice, "That's Thomas's car."

Was it intuition that had urged her to stay at home, or did she know he might be coming? Hester hadn't time to decide; the car drew up at the gate and Maggie walked out to greet its owner. Derek gripped Hester by the arm and whispered: "We must make him come too. Be firm. Or else we shall all find ourselves sitting round the table here, entertaining him."

"But—"

"And be quick about it. Otherwise we shall have Papa on the scene, and no escape for anyone."

Mrs. Hyde-Ridley and Mrs. Vandevint were adepts at getting the best places, and they had got them today; they were sitting at the table in the bay-window with a good view up and down the street. The bay-window was a small one and just accommodated a table for two, with other tables grouped closely round it and no room to put anything down or alter the position of one's chair. That was a mistake; but they bore with it nobly, keeping their voices low and even ceasing their criticisms when Anthony was near at hand. Besides, there were things to praise as well as things to criticize: the decor, and the excellence of the cakes. They were able to eat as many as they liked, knowing that the tea was "on the house."

The phrase had delighted them, as soon as they found out what it meant. It had been incorporated in Mrs. Hyde-Ridley's local news bulletins, and since her information was known to be accurate it had brought in a number of people who could claim to be acquainted with Chrysanthemum Bavington and therefore thought themselves eligible for free teas. Miss Barter was over by the fireplace, Miss Cardwell and Miss Knapp were sharing a table with two hefty young women in khaki shorts (who might or might not be their friends), Mrs. Edwards from the post office was sitting with the Rudds from the garage, and other familiar figures kept appearing in the doorway, looking for an empty seat or being directed to the overflow tables in the dining-room. With so many Mingham residents present there was not much room for the paying public; still, as Mrs. Hyde-Ridley said, the place was packed out and that was a very good advertisement.

"Full up!" she screamed through the window, to three total strangers who were hovering in the street. The strangers turned away towards the bus-stop and Mrs. Hyde-Ridley nodded her garden-party hat in triumph. "They'll tell everyone how popular it is," she said.

"And they'll come earlier another time," Mrs. Vandevint prophesied.

The ladies continued to eat, disregarding Anthony's annoyance and the fact that there had been, after all, a vacant table in the middle of the room. But when a car came slowly down the street and drew up outside they stopped eating and gave it all their attention. A car was different, and moreover it was a car they felt they ought to recognise. The only thing that stopped Mrs. Hyde-Ridley from identifying it was the extreme unlikelihood that Mr. Seamark would wish to patronise the *Firenze* tea-shop on an August Bank Holiday.

The car stayed there for a full minute and then moved on. Just as the watchers in the window were commenting on the oddness of this behaviour—no one getting out, or even *looking*—it stopped again, fifty yards down the street, and Mrs. Hyde-Ridley had to lean sideways and peer round Mrs. Vandevint's feather boa to make out what was happening. "Two getting out now," she reported excitedly. "They're walking back as the car isn't staying there as I suppose they were only getting a lift. Though they didn't need one as they've only come from The End House as it's Hester Clifford and Derek Hutton!"

"No," said Thomas. "No, I can't face it."

An ordeal, certainly, for one who was lately a recluse, Hester thought. As the car moved away she had a brief glimpse of Mrs. Hyde-Ridley and Mrs. Vandevint in the bay-window, resplendent in best clothes and transfixed by curiosity, which suggested that the *Firenze* tea-shop was not the best place for a private jaunt with Derek. But it was not of Derek and herself that she was thinking, of course, but of Maggie and Thomas; and the plan that now presented itself was all for their benefit.

"Stop," she said peremptorily.

Thomas stopped, opposite the post office, and while Maggie was protesting on his behalf that the tea-shop would be horrid and crowded and no fun at all, Hester opened the door and got out, followed by Derek.

"You needn't come," she said kindly to Maggie and Thomas. "But Derek and I must go, because we said we'd be there and I think Mrs. B. is counting on getting a full house."

Faint-hearted protests could be ignored. Hester walked briskly away from them, and heard the car drive off.

"Masterly," said Derek.

It was one of his father's favourite words for describing a successful manoeuvre, and she could not but feel she deserved it.

"I thought it best," she said modestly.

"And I entirely agree with you."

They walked past the window, returning the smiles and waves of the alert spectators, and entered the tea-shop. It was still crowded, and fortunately the only vacant table was at the opposite side of the room from Mrs. Hyde-Ridley's. After waving again, and making a non-committal response to a remark she did not catch, and congratulating Anthony Bavington on the success of the opening day, Hester sat down with her back to Mrs. Hyde-Ridley. Reminiscences of her aunts were all very well, but she did not want to be given them across a crowded room.

"Of course I was all for getting rid of Thomas," Derek said. "Still, there would have been a certain interest in seeing his reactions to all this. Talk of bad taste! It would be like Greek meeting Greek."

Hester blinked at the candy-striped walls and star-spangled ceiling. "Yes," she said thoughtfully. "Yes, but—I mean, it was for Maggie—"

"And Maggie too. You got rid of them beautifully."

There was a misunderstanding somewhere; the chief reason for the manoeuvre did not seem evident to Derek.

"But don't you see . . ." Hester began, and then stopped, because it was impossible to discuss Maggie's and Thomas's situation in a tea-shop in Mingham. Someone would be sure to overhear; the grapevine would grow rampant on it.

"Cheer up," Derek said. "We're going to eat a large free tea and then go for a long free walk. Think of all the money I am saving. Bank Holiday is the cheapest day of the year."

It wasn't so difficult to discuss the antique business, because they had talked about it so often and had already invented a private code in which they could allude to it while ostensibly alluding to something else. They played this game with discretion (and never when Cousin Bennet was present), and now they flattered themselves that they could outwit any clueless grapevine.

But Bank Holiday wasn't, after all, the cheapest day of the year. Murmurs of disappointment and annoyance could be heard on all sides, as the Mingham residents finished their teas and found themselves looking at the bills. Chrysanthemum had retired to the kitchen, and Anthony seemed unaware of his mother's generous offer; he handed out bills to everyone and was deaf to the murmured protests. No one liked to do more than murmur, and although everyone admired Mrs. Hyde-Ridley and Mrs. Vandevint, who simply left the bill lying on the table and walked out without paying, no one dared to follow their example. Anthony's expression, as he watched them go, made it clear that there would be very strict limits to the Bavington hospitality.

# CHAPTER EIGHTEEN

"I'm sorry," said Thomas. "I hope you didn't mind."

He drove on in silence for a minute, and then tried again.

"You weren't committed to it, were you? You don't mind giving it a miss?"

Maggie woke up abruptly, to assure the real Thomas of what the dream one already knew.

"Oh no, I didn't want to go at all," she said. "I'd much rather be here."

"Good. I only thought—"

"*They* wanted to go—Hester and Derek—and of course when you turned up . . . Well, Hester is like that, she just drags people along without asking them."

"It would have taken a lot of dragging to get me into that tea-shop."

Neither of them remembered that it was Hester who had spared them; in retrospect she played no part at all. Thomas had acted decisively, Maggie had simply accepted her dream-like good fortune. They drove on, talking happily about their escape, until the country road became a street again—the main street of Scorling, which on a Bank Holiday afternoon was conspicuously shut up and deserted, except for the big new cafe beside the cinema and the Angel hotel. Couldn't have tea there, Thomas said firmly; he drove through Scorling at speed, looking with equal disfavour at the smaller cafes in Station Lane and the crowded Lido Restaurant by the river beyond the town. Maggie foresaw, with loving equanimity, that they would not be having tea anywhere.

Thomas hated crowds, noise, and fuss; he had expected to be entertained in The End House's drawing-room and she was still surprised that he hadn't gone straight back there. But they were out on the Warnford road now, beginning a tealess but beautiful climb to the bare downs above Warnford Castle. It was a long time since she had been that way, and when they had passed the awkward corner and emerged on the long straight incline she made him stop, so that she could look at the view—the wide valley, and the bird's-eye view of the castle directly below them with its turrets and formal garden.

"How sweet it looks," she said. "So neat and trim."

"Not bad," Thomas said. "He's certainly tidied it up a lot."

"He must be having a party. Look at all those people on the terrace. They've just come out of the house and now they're going round the gardens."

"Conducted party, not his friends. Not even conducted, I believe. He just lets them loose."

Maggie had not known that Warnford Castle was open to the public, and she stared with interest at the small figures now thronging the formal garden.

"What a lot of them," she exclaimed. "It must be awfully profitable."

"This is the first year he's done it, and I believe it's paid him handsomely. Charges them half-a-crown to see everything. Of course he had to spend a lot on the place first, putting the grounds in order and re-arranging the rooms. Half the house has been shut up, ever since the war."

Looking down on them from this distance, she could not think of the sightseers as a human crowd with all its tiresome characteristics of noisiness and unruliness and irritation-for-Thomas. They were as quiet and orderly as a procession of ants. Moreover, they had each paid half-a-crown.

"Thomas, that's what you ought to do," she cried. "It would pay for the new sluice-gates and everything!"

"Good heavens! Do you seriously suggest—"

"Not when you're at home, of course," she said hastily. "But you go away a lot. The Priory could be open then."

"I don't go away much nowadays. Haven't you noticed?"

"How should I notice? I never see you."

A short time ago, the sight of his car on the Scorling road had counted as "seeing Thomas." Now, it didn't. But she couldn't explain this, any more than she could explain, even to herself, her new freedom to argue and protest. It was as though the high barrier of the past had melted like an iceberg.

"You never see me because you're always at Scorling Gate farm," he said.

"Well, why shouldn't I be? I work there."

"Or at the far end of the garden. Or handing out tracts round the village."

"The parish magazine, not tracts."

"Pretty much the same thing," Thomas said crossly.

He had been absurd and unfair and now he was cross. The time when he telephoned and she had been in the garden, the time when he came in for a drink and she was doing the magazines, had been isolated occasions, and Scorling Gate farm was her *job*. And the argument had somehow got turned topsy-turvy, for it had begun by her protesting that she never saw Thomas and now he was protesting that he never saw her. But why argue at all, she thought— the whole thing was ridiculous, and worse than that if it made dear Thomas cross and spoilt the afternoon.

"You're seeing me now," she said tranquilly. "And I was only joking about opening the Priory for sightseers. At least, I had forgotten how impractical it would be."

"You mean you had forgotten to allow for my prejudices?"

"Oh, no," said Maggie, deeply shocked, "I don't mean that at all. You aren't being prejudiced, Thomas, you're just being perfectly reasonable. It's different for Lord Warnford, of course, because he lives in the dower house and so he isn't disturbed by the sightseers, as you would be if they were tramping all over the Priory. I hadn't thought of that, but I see now that it would be horrid for you. You'd have no privacy at all."

She did not know why Thomas laughed.

"Nothing for him to do but count the half-crowns," he said. "Don't apologise for it, Maggie—it's not a bad idea at all, even though I haven't got a dower house to retire to. How would it be if we opened the park and the gardens, and kept the house to ourselves?" She knew better than to take this seriously; his saying "we" made a game of it, an amusement for a summer afternoon.

"We couldn't charge half-a-crown just for the garden," she said, throwing the ball back. Thomas said they could include the stables and the ruins of the water-mill. They argued light-heartedly about whether people should be allowed on the upper terrace, and Maggie suggested they should be charged sixpence extra, to compensate him for being peered at through the library windows. This brought them back to the question of the entrance fee (double-price for children under ten, they agreed), and Thomas then remembered hearing that the Warnford scheme included a separate charge for the gardens alone, to catch all the horticultural enthusiasts who would not want to be bothered with the house.

"Artful of him," said Maggie. "People like Mrs. Headley would think it sheer waste of time to walk through those rooms when they might be walking round the garden. I wonder what it costs without the castle?"

In the end they got into the car and drove back to find out.

The Warnford scheme, as Thomas called it, had been designed to catch everyone, even the passing motorists who might never have heard of Warnford Castle or thought of going there. There were large posters in all the local villages, pointing fingers had been added to old signposts and new signposts had been erected where they were needed, to keep people from wandering off down byroads and to remind them of the attraction ahead. No one could possibly have failed to find his way to Warnford Castle. Moreover, the scheme ensured a smooth flow of traffic even on Bank Holidays. Arrows directed motor coaches to one entrance, private cars to another, pedestrians to a short cut from the bus-stop to the nearest lodge. There were car-parks inside the gates, said the notices; and all parking on the roadside or on the common was strictly prohibited. Maggie and Thomas discovered the reason for this when they had driven through the main entrance and reached the appropriate carpark, where an old retainer touched his cap in a practised servile gesture and demanded sixpence. A nominal charge for the use of the ground, he said glibly, which his lordship was forced to make.

"We never thought of parking fees," Maggie whispered to Thomas, who replied rather unkindly that his lordship had thought of everything.

"Now we're here, we'll see how it works," he added. "You'd like to go round the gardens, wouldn't you?"

"Yes. If you don't mind."

"Mind? Mind what?"

The crowds, she could have said; but she didn't, because she didn't want to put Thomas off. And the crowds were leaving now, it was getting late and the castle itself was closed, though the gardens would be open for another hour. People were coming back towards the car-park; and the orangery (teas half-a-crown) looked quite deserted. They walked past the orangery to the gate that gave admittance to the gardens, where Thomas bought the tickets and waved aside a small guide-book (half-a-crown, with map and coloured frontispiece).

"How much?" she asked.

"One and six each. Did you want the guide-book?"

"Certainly not. We can find our way without spending half-a-crown."

"We never thought of that, either. Could you write a guide-book to the Priory, Maggie?"

"*Two* guide-books—one for the house and one for the gardens, at half-a-crown each. Yes, I could do it. Or perhaps Hester would do it better."

"Perhaps she would. The wonderfully efficient Hester."

"Don't laugh, Thomas. Hester *is* efficient but I wasn't making fun of her. I mean, she's very nice as well as being very efficient."

"In fact, you like her better than you did."

"I never said I didn't like her," Maggie protested.

"But you didn't, did you? You harped on her virtues and said how nice it was having her, but it wasn't at all convincing. And then you were annoyed because I said she was pretty. Don't you remember? That evening you were trying to warn me not to believe Mrs. Merlin."

"I didn't. I wasn't! Not annoyed, I mean . . . Oh well, it's true that I didn't like her so much at first, but everything's different now. I suppose I've got to know her much better."

It embarrassed Maggie to know that Thomas had observed her annoyance. Although she noticed everything he said and did, she had never thought of his noticing her in the same way and remembering what she had said, quite a long time afterwards. It was embarrassing but also rather gratifying.

"Warning you about Mrs. Merlin wasn't much help," she said.

"At least I know about the maypole and the stalls and the ice-cream and the threat of a marquee. If you hadn't warned me," he said indignantly, "I should still have been expecting a small village gathering, a—what did she call it?—a simple little display for a few enthusiasts. Really, that woman is thoroughly unreliable."

He was speaking of the second warning, given on the day they went to see the fishponds. Maggie laughed, but protested that Mrs. Merlin was not unreliable, only rather silly and, yes, inefficient —the very opposite of Hester.

"Well-meaning but tactless," she added.

"A great handicap to her husband," said Thomas, who took a landowner's interest in the parish and counted himself a supporter of the church although he did not attend it more than six times a year. "The Rector," he said firmly, "is a very good man."

"Oh, look," said Maggie. "There they are, just ahead of us!"

"Talk of the devil!"

Thomas quickly stopped himself, aware of the impropriety of talking of the devil when referring to a clergyman and his wife. "Lucky you saw them first," he went on. "If we go down to the right, along that path, we'll avoid them. Don't look at them, then they won't recognise you."

The Merlins were coming towards them but were still some distance away, and both of them had their heads turned to the long herbaceous border. "I suppose it's a holiday for him, too," said Maggie, following Thomas along the escape route. "I suppose they came over here to get away from the parish, so perhaps they won't want to meet us, any more than we want to meet them."

"They'd want a lift home. They haven't got a car so they must have come by bus."

"Oh—do you think we ought to . . . ?"

"Later," he said. "We'll look out for them later, if you think we must."

Maggie said nothing. She did not want the company of the Merlins, but she did not like to think of them going back by bus when they might have gone by car. It would be hot and crowded. They would have to change buses in Scorling. How tiresome of them to be here . . . no, how selfish of her to think it. Why couldn't Thomas have agreed that the Merlins would prefer to be left to themselves?

The path had brought them to an enclosure surrounded by yew hedges. "This is the knot-garden," Thomas said. "At least, it used to be. They've altered it since I last saw it. It used to be all beds, with narrow grass paths between them—sort of layout that needed a lot of work to keep it tidy."

The knot-garden now had a grass plot in the centre, with a lily pool and two marble benches, and the intricate planting was confined to four beds in the corners. It was quiet and deserted, and the high yew hedges cut it off from sight. A good place to hide from the Merlins, Thomas said with satisfaction. They would never find their way down here.

"How did you find the way? Did you say you'd been before?"

"A long time ago. I came over with Beatrice. She'd thought of making a knot-garden at the Priory and we asked Lord Warnford to let us see this one. That was this man's father, must have been the year before he died. The place was shut up at that time and the grounds were in a very poor state. We could only guess what the knot-garden had been like in its heyday."

"Oh," said Maggie. "How—how sad it must have looked."

The description still seemed to her appropriate; for the past had crept up like a dark cloud and she could only think of Thomas sitting on this bench with Beatrice, whom he had loved so dearly.

"Very sad," she repeated lamely, wishing there was some way of comforting Thomas without intruding on his grief. For he, too, was bound to be thinking about the past, in this garden he had visited with Beatrice.

"No sadder than it does today," he said. "It's the yew hedges . . . I suppose."

"Yes," she said obediently. It could be anything he liked to pretend.

"Or are you thinking that it's sad for me because of Beatrice?"

"I do understand, Thomas. I really do. Let's—let's go somewhere else. Or would you rather stay here a bit longer? I dare say—"

"You really don't understand. You never have. This legend—well, it was partly true, I suppose, and all my fault. I let it grow up. No, I didn't realize how it was growing. And then, when I did, it seemed too late to do anything. And wrong, in a way like defacing a pious memorial. A tablet commemorating all the virtues of my late wife."

"What legend? I don't know what you're talking about."

"The legend of my broken heart," he said.

Maggie could see Thomas quite plainly. He was standing just in front of her, near enough to be touched. But his voice seemed to come from far away and to reach her in snatches, so that she could hardly hear him.

"Beatrice was very beautiful," he was saying. "I fell in love with her, and we got married, and just at first we were happy, and then we weren't so happy. It wasn't . . . it was because we were so different. She disliked the Priory, you know, and living down here in the country, and I disliked her friends and the kind of life she enjoyed. She wouldn't settle here; we had the flat in London. Do you see, Maggie? It wasn't a total failure, but it wasn't what you all think."

"But she died," Maggie said. "And you minded terribly."

"Yes, I did," said the voice from far away, speaking to itself. "Why did I mind so much? It was partly remorse, I suppose—and shock. She'd gone abroad with friends, I didn't even know she'd gone. And she'd gone because we'd had a quarrel . . . I was haunted by the feeling that I'd killed her."

"No, no," she said.

"I shut myself up and brooded on it, and that made everything much worse. Because the legend grew up. It cut me off, somehow, from the people round me; it forced me to go on remembering the past and being the man I was supposed to be. At first,

I didn't realize it was happening, because I was feeling wretched and guilty and only wanted to be left alone. And then it seemed impossible to deny the legend."

"I know," said Maggie. "I've felt like that about other—legends. Family traditions or beliefs or whatever you like to call them. It's impossible to deny them—and you have to go on living up to them because everyone expects you to."

"Something like that," he said, "but more my own doing, really. The legend flourished because, at first, I let it. I morbidly enjoyed being a recluse."

"Don't say that. It was our fault—everyone's—wanting romantic legends and distorting the truth to get them. Oh, Thomas, I'm so sorry! All this time we've been hanging on to the legend—"

"Don't accuse yourself, Maggie. You showed it up for what it was."

The knot-garden had appeared sad because of a mistaken belief in its sacred associations. The legend had been dragged into every meeting; it had cast its shadow over every thought. So how could Thomas say, with such assurance, that she had shown it up?

She might have asked him, but the moment had gone by. The moment of silence, while she looked back at her own belief in the legend, was broken by the sound of voices. Distant voices, becoming louder; people approaching the knot-garden and congratulating each other on having located it. Their shadows came ahead of them, stretching down the grass path which was the only way into the enclosure. At the other end of the shadows were the Rector and his wife.

"It's our free day," said Mrs. Merlin, after making all the usual remarks about the strangeness of meeting one's near neighbours in another part of the county. "So we came over this morning and we've seen everything there is to be seen. We nearly missed this little garden, but fortunately Gregory remembered reading about it in the local paper when the place was first opened. Really, they ought to put boards up, to show you the way."

"They expect you to buy the guide-book," said Maggie.

"Oh, I wouldn't do that. Half-a-crown is far too much. I'm charging a shilling for the programmes and people can give more if they like."

The programmes were of course for the Country Dancing Fiesta, and once Mrs. Merlin got going on this subject it was impossible to stop her.

"My dear, the bus," Mr. Merlin interrupted anxiously.

Somewhere in the distance a bell was ringing for closing-time; and even further away—to judge by Mr. Merlin's expression—a bus was about to depart for Scorling. But Mrs. Merlin knew there was no need to hurry, because Mr. Seamark would certainly have come by car and would be bound to offer them a lift home.

"That will be very nice," she said, accepting the invitation with an adequate show of surprise. "Now we can have a little talk about the arrangements for Saturday. I'll sit in front with you, and we can settle all those tiresome details. It's unbelievable how things keep cropping up."

Poor Thomas, Maggie thought. Then she corrected herself; for, in spite of having to endure a little talk all the way from Warnford to Mingham, he need no longer be pitied.

"Yes," she said, echoing Mr. Merlin's happy phrase. "A truly wonderful day."

# CHAPTER NINETEEN

IT WAS AN eventful week, with the Country Dancing Fiesta looming up at the end of it as the event to outshine all others. Bank Holiday was an event for everyone, and on Tuesday a number of Mingham residents shared in the excitement of seeing *Bonnie Appin*'s attic window fall out in one piece, frame and glass together, and end up as countless pieces of wreckage on the pavement. This disastrous event was attributed, by Mrs. Hyde-Ridley, to Anthony Bavington's carelessness with the ladder (leaning it against the window-frame, as everyone *knew* that would weaken it), and by the Bavingtons to Mrs. Hyde-Ridley's neglect to maintain her property.

On Wednesday two members of the Fiesta committee resigned, after an eventful meeting during which Miss Cardwell was reported to have thrown the ink bottle at someone, though other observers declared it had only got knocked over. On Thursday, in response to an appeal from the Rector, Maggie left Scorling Gate farm at lunch-time and bicycled into Scorling to find out what had happened to the programmes.

"They may be at the bus-depot," he said. "Or alternatively, still at the printers'. We have tried telephoning, but it was unsatisfactory. Several persons are on holiday, and the woman who answered appeared to know nothing about it. And time, alas, is running short."

Everyone else was too busy to go; a series of minor difficulties had, as Mrs. Merlin put it, cropped up, and the loss of two helpers had weakened the morale of the rest. Mrs. Merlin was needed in Mingham to keep things together, and the Rector was needed as her personal assistant and whipping boy. Fortunately Mrs. Enderby, of Scorling Gate farm, felt a great sympathy for the Rector and encouraged Maggie to take the afternoon off, and the rest of the week too if it would help the poor man to survive the day. The day of the Fiesta, she meant; for her sister who lived in Endless Lane next door to Miss Barter had told her all about the plans for the Fiesta and it was perfectly clear to Mrs. Enderby that they were silly plans, and that the Fiesta would be a dead loss.

"Poor man, it's a shame," she said. "I know he wanted a proper fête himself, but he was overruled. Who's going to come and watch the school kids, that they can see every day for nothing? The only thing wrong with the Rector is, he can't say No to his wife."

"Perhaps if we get a glorious fine day . . . ?"

"It'll have to be as fine as the Day of Judgment," said Mrs. Enderby, who for some reason always pictured this last day without a cloud in the sky, as if the preliminary tempests and lightnings could be counted on to clear the air. "And that we're not likely to get, with the glass falling already. You get off as soon as we've finished dinner, and I'll tell Mr. Enderby not to expect you till Monday. Oh no, you're starting your holiday Monday, aren't you?" Only if Mr. Enderby was not planning to start cutting the thirty-acre field, Maggie explained. She could take her holiday when it suited him.

"You have it now as you arranged," Mrs. Enderby advised. Mr. Enderby was not there to be consulted, having gone to visit his son over on the other side of Scorling; but although, unlike the Rector, he was quite capable of saying No to his wife at times, Maggie decided to take the advice and chance it.

"Very well, I'll be away for a week from Monday," she said.

"And tomorrow as well. That's all right—you've done the wage sheets and he can manage the rest. It'll make a change for him," said Mrs. Enderby. Change and decay, said the hymn, but she didn't agree with that; change kept you young and therefore helped to stave off decay.

Bicycling into Scorling, Maggie hoped Mr. Enderby would not think she was letting him down. Hitherto she had always been glad to stay late and work hard at busy times, and to have her holiday in a slack season and at short notice. It was Hester who had suggested her taking a holiday now, pointing out how nice it would be for both of them, and how much more beneficial than a cold, wet week in November. Hester had been rather managing about it; but in spite of this Maggie felt grateful to her. And also to Mrs. Enderby, who had been so understanding about the Rector's difficulties and the missing programmes.

I hope I shall be able to find them, she thought, pushing her bicycle up the steep hill from the bridge. It was a task which would have suited Hester; but Hester had gone up to London for the day and therefore was not available. A terrible waste of a day, in Maggie's opinion, not only because most of it would be spent in trains but because London itself was a waste of time. She didn't know how Hester could bear to live and work in London, which, on the rare occasions she had been there, had seemed to bear a fairly close resemblance to hell. The thought of

living in a town— worst of all, in London—was always a power-
ful antidote to any discontents about living in Mingham.

Thomas hated it too, she thought. He couldn't ever have
been happy with Beatrice if she despised the Priory and insisted on living in London. Not blissfully happy, as the legend had
ordained.

Beatrice had been very beautiful, and when she died he had
been terribly unhappy for a time. Even allowing for the shock
and his feelings of guilt, Maggie perceived that the death of Beatrice had hurt Thomas badly, so that, in a way, the legend was
true. And yet it wasn't. It was a distorted, falsified version of
the truth, turning both Thomas and Beatrice into travesties of
real people.

In the legend Beatrice had been a story-book heroine, as
good as she was beautiful. In real life she had been selfish and
stubborn, and almost openly contemptuous of the dull people
she met at Mingham. (Maggie remembered how the tea-parties
and other Priory entertainments had gradually stopped, how
rarely Beatrice had undertaken the duties of a landed proprietor's wife, opening fêtes or giving out prizes or even visiting
her neighbours.) In real life Thomas had differed from Beatrice
as much as he loved her, he had been made to do things he did
not want to do, such as living in London, and no doubt he had
argued about it and been cross and resentful. "It wasn't a total
failure, but not what you all think."

So now she could think about it quite differently; it was a
sad, true story and she could think about it without exaggerated sympathy or unacknowledged envy. She did not grudge
Beatrice the love that had been hers; indeed an unloving, un-
caring Thomas would have been a dreadful disillusionment. But
he was neither a tragic hero nor a man without a heart; he was
simply Thomas, seen at last in clear daylight. The shadow of the
legend had gone for good.

At the top of the hill she got on her bicycle and made for the
bus-depot, where the parcel of programmes might be waiting
for someone to put it on a Mingham bus. She bicycled along the

High Street and turned off at the cross road before the Angel, which would take her to Station Lane where the bus-depot was.

Round the corner, a few yards down the narrow lane, there was a new antique shop; or perhaps not new but merely under new management, for she remembered a dingy little shop here in the past and the name over the door seemed familiar. *Minnie Wildgoose.* There were three lustre jugs in the front of the window, and she stopped and went back to look at them; in ten days' time it would be her mother's birthday and she had not yet bought her a present. A lustre jug seemed coals to Newcastle, because The End House already housed a large collection of them, but her mother always appeared to welcome new additions so perhaps one of those in the window would do as a birthday gift. If they weren't too hopelessly expensive.

She opened the door and walked into the shop.

It was quite small, and there were two other customers in front of her, with a small child, taking up most of the room. They had their backs to her and were discussing the purchase of a wedding present, arguing with each other about whether "this table" would do. Maggie could not see the table, for her view was blocked by the two solid backs, and she turned to look through the net curtain at the lustre jugs in the window. Half listening, immersed in her own thoughts, she heard another woman's voice coming from the back of the shop.

"This is a drum table," it said. "A nice old piece, and in very good condition. Of course we guarantee it to be genuine."

A persuasive, competent voice. Perfectly familiar. But of course it couldn't possibly be Hester, because she was in London. And even if she wasn't . . . !

Maggie turned round abruptly and pushed her way between the child and a wing chair. Edging round the two customers, she confronted the saleswoman, who gave her a startled glance and turned bright pink.

"Hester!" she said, softly and incredulously.

"I shan't be long. Wait for me in there."

Hester managed to speak quite calmly, and as she pointed to the door behind her there was only the fading blush to show she had been taken by surprise. But when the customers had left the shop and she had come back to join Maggie in the little room it was clear that this calmness was only assumed. Just for once, thought Maggie, Hester was really shaken.

"I sold it," she began quickly. "I sold the little table! I thought they weren't going to buy it but they did. They decided—"

"I heard them," Maggie-interrupted. "And you. You were very efficient."

Hester abandoned the pretence of being calm. She hesitated, and then said awkwardly, "This is my new job, you see. Very part-time."

"You didn't tell us. And you said you were going to London."

"I didn't tell you, because—Oh, it's no good, you'll have to know and be sworn to secrecy. I knew Cecily was going painting and Cousin Bennet wouldn't come without being driven but I never thought of you! Derek said—"

"Derek," Maggie exclaimed. In a flash of light she saw what was coming. "You mean it's *his* new job. Just another new job for Derek!"

"Oh, Maggie, do listen. You don't understand at all."

The room behind the shop was a testimonial to Derek's industry; at least it would have been, if Maggie had seen it before. (Hester had quite forgotten that she too had had to take the evidence on trust.) Running an antique shop was his *métier*, his vocation, the career he had been unconsciously looking for in all his past experiences. Anyone could tell he would get nowhere in a bank, but here he would make his fortune.

"And what about Uncle Malcolm?" Maggie asked coldly.

"That's just it. That's why you mustn't tell the parents. There'd be a terrible fuss about his leaving the bank, because his Uncle Malcolm got him in there. And he must have time to—to feel that he's really settled and making a success of it, before he tells them. Of course he *is* making a success of it, but a family row at this stage would be very demoralising. Don't you see? He's learnt to think of himself as a failure, and it's most important that he should get back his self-confidence. . . ."

The words poured out: explanations, justifications, defensive apologies. For the first time Maggie felt herself to be older and wiser than Hester; or at any rate calmer and less embarrassed. As if they had somehow changed places.

"I suppose Derek told you about leaving the bank because he needed sympathy," she said—as Hester might have said herself.

"He didn't tell me! I found out by accident, just like you."

"And now you're helping him to run the business."

"No, no. This is the first time. It was important, you see. Mr. Frost wanted him to go to this sale with him. Derek has got to learn the trade, you see. Sometimes they've been to sales together on early-closing days, but this isn't early-closing day."

"Jolly lucky for Derek, having you to mind the shop while he learns the trade."

"It's time poor Derek had a bit of luck," Hester said warmly. The street door was heard to open. Hester sprang to her feet and hurried into the shop. Maggie was left in the little room, surrounded by all the evidence of Derek's industry, to consider these surprising revelations and decide what to do about them.

Hester, she thought, had acted very foolishly. It was true that she might have felt obliged to keep Derek's new career a secret, since she had discovered it by accident; but it was silly of her to believe it would last, and how much sillier to encourage and actively assist him, and to embark on complicated deceptions like this pretence of going to London for the day. Not the sort of thing one would have expected of Hester.

Nevertheless, her foolish behaviour was rather endearing; just as her bossy efficiency had been putting-off. "They're bound to be found out," Maggie reflected, seeing Hester and Derek as a pair of childish conspirators; and she felt quite sorry for them, especially for Hester who had had no experience of Father's sarcasm and who need not have been involved in the fearful trouble that was coming to Derek. Poor Derek—but still, he was asking for it. Fancy Hester, so practical and hard-headed, actually approving of his throwing up the bank!

"No good," said Hester. "One of those silly women who couldn't make up her mind. If there had only been one lustre jug she'd have bought it, but with three to choose from she couldn't decide."

She looked quite disconsolate, as if the sale of a lustre jug had really mattered to her.

"That's what I came in for," Maggie said. "I saw them in the window and thought I'd get one for Mother's birthday present. How much are they?"

She hoped this would cheer Hester up, but it didn't. "Of course you can't buy one," she said, quite crossly. "Cecily would want to know where it came from, and Derek would know you'd been here."

"But aren't we going to tell him?"

"Much better not. If he knows you know, it will make him more nervous about what he says at home. More self-conscious, I mean. I think it would be far kinder not to tell him."

"What nonsense," said Maggie. "Really, Hester, it's wheels within wheels! It's ridiculous! What does it matter whether Derek feels nervous and self-conscious? Why do you make such a fuss about him?"

"I don't. I just think he's never had a fair chance."

Maggie could have gone on arguing about that, but she suddenly remembered the programmes. "All right," she said brusquely. "I'll pretend to know nothing and Derek won't know I know and you'll pretend I don't know and we'll all go on deceiving each other like mad and then Derek won't have anything to be nervous about until Father finds out. And now I must *go* and look for the programmes."

"What programmes? Oh dear, how complicated family life is."

"It isn't," Maggie said with exasperation. "You make it so."

The programmes were in the parcels office at the railway station. The clerk had reckoned that they ought to have been sent to the parcels office at the bus-depot, seeing that Mingham wasn't served by rail, but had naturally waited for someone else to put things right. However he obligingly lent Maggie a hand-cart to wheel the bundle down the street to the bus-depot, and the clerk there promised to put them on the evening bus. The conductor would drop them off at Rudd's Garage. Rudd would transport them to the rectory.

But Rudd might wait till tomorrow, so Maggie thought it kinder to tell the Rector of the success of her mission as soon as she got back to Mingham. The door of the rectory stood open and she found him standing in the square hall, looking anxiously at the barometer.

"Good," said the Rector. "Very good. I am much obliged. This evening or else tomorrow? Ah yes, Rudd will bring them. Of course. No, Maggie, I quite realize you couldn't bring them yourself, on your bicycle. Far too big a parcel. Quite so."

His anxious duckings ceased. He pointed to the hand of the barometer, which had gone back some way from the movable pointer. "I set it this morning," he said sadly.

"Perhaps it will go up again before Saturday."

"Have you looked at the sky?"

"M'm, yes," said Maggie. She had been looking at the sky all the way back from Scorling. "Perhaps it will hold off," she said hopefully.

She felt so sorry for Mr. Merlin, whose last hopes of a successful Fiesta were plainly dwindling, that she willingly agreed to assist with preparations the next day. "Friday—yes, I know, but I've got the day off," she explained. "And of course I shall be at home on Saturday as well."

"Friday and Saturday, then," said the Rector. He looked faintly cheered, and confided that they were short of helpers, and that any extra hands would find plenty to do.

Maggie did not discover what the extra hands were to do on Friday. Two days—or a day and a half—seemed longer than was needed for putting up a maypole and setting out the chairs and two stalls; and anyway, the chairs and stalls could not be set out till the day. But she promised to be at the rectory early the next morning, ready for anything.

# CHAPTER TWENTY

ON FRIDAY MORNING the glass was still falling and the sky looked more unsettled than it had done the evening before. But it wasn't raining, and Maggie still hoped the rain would hold off till the Fiesta was over. She told Hester about the shortage of hands, and Hester volunteered to help if she was needed. They walked across to the rectory soon after breakfast to find out what was to be done; though both of them agreed that it seemed too soon to start preparing for an out-of-doors event on Saturday afternoon.

The front door of the rectory stood open, as it had done last night. The square hall was empty, but the sound of voices indicated that there were people in the drawing-room on the right, and in the dining-room on the left; some of them children, some of them adults, and all of them in a state of nervous excitement or near-hysteria. Hester rang the bell but no one answered it, so after a minute she and Maggie advanced to the drawing-room. There they found a number of small girls trying on their new costumes, with Miss Cardwell and Miss Knapp making last-minute alterations. Miss Cardwell, with her mouth full of pins, mumbled that Mrs. Merlin was in the dining-room and they'd better ask her if she needed any help.

"Surely the dresses could have been fitted before now," Hester said, when she had shut the drawing-room door behind her.

Maggie pointed to the door opposite, which was half open. It was unlikely they could be overheard, but Hester's nod agreed that it was better not to risk it. They crossed the hall again, and knocked at the open door. A knock seemed a polite way of interrupting the heated female dispute going on inside the dining-room.

"Of course there's time," Mrs. Merlin said shrilly.

"Not enough time, not enough time!" the other voice kept repeating.

"Plenty of time!"

"Not enough time!"

Hester knocked again, very loudly, and pushed the door open.

The programmes had been unpacked, and were stacked in piles on the dining-room table, and on the floor. There appeared to be thousands of them. Mrs. Merlin and Miss Barter were standing on either side of the table with fountain pens in their hands, which they were using like daggers to menace each other. It was lucky, Hester said afterwards, that the table was a broad one.

"What is it? Oh, Maggie—and Miss Clifford! Come in, come in. Now there will be *plenty* of time—see, Miss Barter, two extra people to help us!"

Miss Barter sat down suddenly, as if it was all too much for her. "We can never do it," she wailed. "Three misprints—and all these programmes. We can never do it!"

Hester did not see why they should. Maggie agreed with Miss Barter that there would not be enough time to correct the misprints in every copy of the programme, which was the task Mrs. Merlin was insisting should be done. While the three of them were trying to calm Mrs. Merlin down and convince her that the misprints did not matter, Miss Cardwell burst into the room and announced that Miss Knapp wasn't feeling at all well and might not be able to come tomorrow. Since Miss Knapp was the leader of the five players who were to provide the music for the dances this was a more serious disaster than the faults in the programmes; and Mrs. Merlin acknowledged it by instantly rushing away to minister to Miss Knapp, who was lying on the sofa in the drawing-room feeling not exactly faint and not exactly sick but as if she was in for one of her attacks.

Miss Knapp was given brandy in warm milk flavoured with cough-mixture; for the rectory brandy was kept in a medicine bottle that had formerly contained cough-mixture, and the flavour still clung to it. "A terrible combination," said Hester, who had been sent to ask the Rector for the brandy (which was kept locked up in his study) and had officiously taken the cork out and smelt it. But it seemed to do Miss Knapp good; at any rate she was able to stand up and declare her intention of crawling home and going straight to bed. Miss Cardwell had to go too, to look after her; the school children were dismissed with half the alterations unfinished; the programmes lay forgotten in the dining-room. For Miss Barter was right; there wasn't enough time to do half the things that still needed to be done, and now with Miss Cardwell and Miss Knapp out of action there were still fewer hands to do them.

"It's ridiculous," Hester said at lunch. "They've been weeks and weeks planning it, and nothing is ready."

Cousin Bennet looked pleased. "I might have helped—if I'd been allowed to," he said.

"You can help now," said Maggie. "You can go across this afternoon and help the Rector to write numbers on dozens and dozens of labels. To tie on the chairs."

It was not the kind of help Bennet had proposed to give. He pointed out, sensibly enough, that there was no need to number the seats; and there wouldn't be enough people to fill them anyway. But Mrs. Merlin had got books of numbered seat-tickets and thought it essential that the chairs themselves should be numbered to match.

"She could have written the labels weeks ago," said Hester.

In the afternoon Hester and Maggie were detailed to accompany Mrs. Merlin to the park, to unload the folding chairs from Rudd's truck and stack them on the ground. Hester had suggested that this would be done on Saturday morning, but it seemed that Friday afternoon was the only time Rudd could transport the chairs from the parish hall. However, he was lending a big tarpaulin to put over them and protect them if it rained during the night.

Mrs. Merlin's idea had been that she would sit in the driving-cab with Rudd, while Hester and Maggie perched on a pile of chairs in the back of the truck. Hester had a better idea, and persuaded Cousin Bennet to let her take the precious car—not, of course, to transport the chairs, but to convey Mrs. Merlin, Maggie and herself. He agreed quite readily, because the loan of his car was a way of helping, and freed him from further obligations.

The site of the Fiesta was some distance from the entrance gates, but apart from this drawback it was well chosen. There was an area of level and fairly smooth turf for the dancers, partly surrounded by higher ground which would make a grandstand for the spectators. At the other side of the arena the ground sloped gently to the river, which could be seen winding through the water-meadows—a very pretty view, Mrs. Merlin said with satisfaction—and by good fortune there was a cart-track leading off the main drive at this point, so that people coming in cars would be able to drive nearly to the top of the grandstand-bank.

"The ones without cars will have a longish walk," Hester said thoughtfully.

"That doesn't matter because they will be so interested to see the park. It's a real draw, you know—it hasn't been open to the public for years."

Hester drove slowly along the bumpy track (not a surface the precious car was accustomed to) until she could go no further. While they were waiting for the first truck-load of chairs Mrs. Merlin showed them where the stalls would stand—one under this oak tree, and one under that—and where the ice-cream van would be stationed. The stalls were simply trestle-tables and Rudd would bring them with the chairs. The ice-cream van would come under its own steam. It was a pity she had not been able to serve teas, but with so many people away, or not co-operating, it could not be arranged.

The afternoon wore on. There were tedious waits while Rudd went back for more chairs, and arguments about how many more he should bring, and a query from the loading-party at the parish hall about which trestle-tables were meant. The two long ones, said Mrs. Merlin; but as soon as Rudd had departed with this message she remembered that she needed a third table—a short one—on which to display the books about folk-dancing, and photographs of international festivals, which the county team were bringing with them from Salchester as propaganda for the Cause.

"If Mr. Hutton can spare the car we could bring the table here tomorrow morning," she said. "It isn't heavy. The table part would go on the roof."

Hester knew the precious car would never be allowed to carry a table on its roof. "No," she said firmly, "I'm afraid I can't promise it. But I'll drive you back to the parish hall now—we'll be there before they've got the others loaded—and then you can find the one you want and Rudd can bring them all together."

Mrs. Merlin gladly agreed to it. She had remembered something else, a telephone message for Gregory which had come that morning while he was out and which she had forgotten to give him when he returned. It was from the man who was coming to preach on Sunday, to say he couldn't, and she ought to let Gregory know at once so that he could start writing his sermon. There would not be time to write it tomorrow.

Maggie watched the car disappear. "Shan't be long," Hester had said; but she had spoken ironically and Maggie knew she was thinking that Mrs. Merlin was bound to remember other things and that they might be gone for hours. Poor Mrs. Merlin; the cloudy sky and the falling glass had so unnerved her that she couldn't really concentrate. But then, organisation had never been her strong point.

Maggie finished stacking the folding chairs in a big pile, but she could not spread the tarpaulin over them unaided. There was nothing more to do, she might just as well have gone back in the car. But she was glad they had left her behind, because now there would be time to walk down to the river before they came back.

The Priory was out of sight, hidden by the wooded ridge to the west. But the fishponds must be quite near, just beyond the point where the trees came down almost to the river bank. There was a track along the bank and a stile in the fence at the edge of the wood, and beyond the stile the track turned uphill through the wood and led to the wild garden which the wood enclosed.

She remembered the way so well, though it was a long time since she had walked along that track. She remembered the steep place where you had to scramble and the barrier of rhododendrons where the path seemed to end. But there was a way through, if you knew it and didn't mind stooping, or a way round if you went higher up the hill. Maggie stooped, diminishing herself to the height she and Derek had been when they found the way through, and crept along the secret path which had once been a route for smugglers or Red Indians. It brought her to the edge of the wild garden, about half-way up the hillside; she pushed aside the rhododendron branches and stepped out into the daylight.

The silence in the garden was broken by the noise of the stream, splashing over the rocks of its little cascade. It sounded quite loud, because everything else was so quiet. For a long minute Thomas and Maggie stared at each other across the stream as if neither of them had ever expected to see the other again.

"What are you doing?" Maggie said at last, forgetting to explain what she was doing herself.

Thomas said he was going to put wire across the ends of the rustic bridge, so that no one would try to cross it and perhaps cause it to collapse and break his or her foolish neck. It was obviously quite rotten, but people never thought of looking.

"Oh—the people at the Fiesta tomorrow? But surely they won't come here."

"They might walk up from the river," he said. "The way you came."

"Not my way," said Maggie. "I came through the wood."

"Is that how you got here? I thought I was dreaming. I couldn't believe you had come up the path through the garden without my noticing you."

"I thought I was dreaming, too."

There seemed nothing more to be said. Unhesitatingly Thomas walked across the bridge which he had just declared to be obviously rotten, and took Maggie in his arms and kissed her fondly. Unhesitatingly Maggie returned his kisses. After an interval of time which neither of them could have measured, Thomas asked her to marry him and Maggie gave an incoherent reply which meant Yes.

On the other side of the wood Hester and Mrs. Merlin and Rudd struggled with the tarpaulin, lamenting the absence of a fourth person for the fourth corner. When they had got it fixed to Mrs. Merlin's satisfaction (though not entirely to Hester's), they carried the trestle tables to the shelter of the nearest big tree. Then Rudd drove off in the truck, and Mrs. Merlin showed Hester again where the tables were to stand and where the chairs were to be set out. After this there was no reason for remaining and Hester said they had better go back.

"But where has Maggie got to?" Mrs. Merlin demanded, as she had been demanding ever since her first glimpse of the deserted scene.

"I don't know. Perhaps she thought she'd walk home by that path beside the river."

"She wouldn't do that—not go off without a word. Maggie wouldn't leave me in the lurch."

"I'm sure she wouldn't. But there really wasn't anything more to do, was there? She knew Rudd would be here to help with the tarpaulin."

"Oh dear, I do believe that's a spot of rain!" Mrs. Merlin cried dolefully.

"I ought to go back, and explain," Maggie was saying to Thomas. "Only what shall I say?"

"I'll drive you back. Later on. I suppose I ought to see your father."

"I suppose we ought to tell Mother and Father first before we tell anyone else."

It was an admission that other people existed and would eventually have to be told. They existed somewhere far away, on the other side of the wood or the other side of the world, but sooner or later they would close in, a circle of tiresome relatives and friends, exclaiming and asking questions.

"Yes, we must tell them first," Thomas agreed. "It wouldn't please them to hear about us through the grapevine." He looked at her rather anxiously. "I'm afraid it may not please them at all—"

"Why not? Oh, darling Thomas, what does it matter! But why shouldn't it please them?"

"I'm not sure. I just have a notion."

The notion applied chiefly to Bennet. Thomas would once have expected more opposition from Cecily, but since their talk last month he had come to feel reasonably hopeful that she had nothing against him. True, her maddening belief that no one could replace Beatrice had shown a strange disregard for Maggie's happiness; but at least she had not raised any objections. In fact, she had seemed to be encouraging him.

"Your father can be rather difficult," he said.

"Yes, indeed—poor Papa. But he won't be difficult about you. He likes you. Only he'll talk and talk and we shall have to humour him. You don't mind, do you?"

He laughed. "I'll humour everybody," he said. "Your parents and Derek and Hester and everybody—provided you're going to marry me at the end of it."

"I'm going to marry you anyway," said Maggie.

They had gone back to the Priory. The time for humouring people, for answering questions and listening to exclamations, could be postponed a little longer. It was Maggie who first thought of postponing it till the next day.

"Till the Fiesta is over," she said. "The Fiesta will be quite bad enough, without being badgered. And even if we only tell the parents it's quite likely they will tell other people. I'm sure Father would tell Mrs. Pilgrim anything."

The thought of being badgered in his own park, of being at the mercy of any Mingham resident who chose to buy an entrance ticket, dismayed Thomas as much as anything could dismay him; he was pretty well proof against it at this happy moment, but he agreed that they would do better to tell no one until the Fiesta was over.

"You're perfectly right," said Maggie, as if it had been Thomas's idea. "But where have I been all this time?"

"Helping Mrs. Merlin to muddle through the preparations."

"No, darling—you forget that Hester was there. She was there and I wasn't, and she'll want to know where I got to. Shall I say I went for a walk?"

"So you did."

"Yes—but why? Why did I suddenly go for a long walk?"

"You felt an irresistible impulse to visit Monk's Mingham."

"To make sure they'd been told about the Fiesta."

"To warn them that it's going to rain and remind them to bring their umbrellas."

"Something like that," said Maggie. "Well, slightly more plausible, of course. It's raining now, so I shall say I went for a walk and met you and came back to the Priory to shelter. An edited version of the truth."

# CHAPTER TWENTY-ONE

"IT'S JUST A little drizzle," Mrs. Merlin insisted. "It may make the ground a bit damp but that can't be helped."

It had rained on Friday evening, but not for very long. There had been no rain during the night, and for a short time after breakfast the clouds had seemed to be lifting. By midday they had come down again, but no one could say it was raining heavily.

"And they forecast 'bright intervals,'" she went on.

Mr. Merlin knew better than to argue. In any case, a Fiesta was not like a church fête, it could not be transferred to the parish hall, because there would not be enough space for the dancers to give their performance. It was bound to be held in the open; or not at all.

"I don't suppose they'll have it at all," Mrs. Vandevint argued, peering at the rainswept street.

"Of course they'll have it," Mrs. Hyde-Ridley declared. "This is just a clearing shower—my glass hasn't moved an inch—I expect it will be blazing sunshine by three o'clock as we won't be starting till then as it's no good being there too early before things have really got going! I told Rudd to call for us at a quarter to three as that will be just right as he is always late. I suggested Chrysanthemum should come with us and pay for half the car, but she says she can't as she expects to be busy this afternoon as lots of people are sure to want tea and there isn't any in the park."

"They won't come all the way back here to get tea," said Mrs. Vandevint.

But she felt mollified; Violet was hiring a car and that certainly counted as entertainment. She had been prepared to say that her ankle would not permit her to walk as far as the park, but if she was being taken in a car that was different.

"But I shan't wear my best hat," she said.

"You could wear your blue straw as it's summer as your felt one is really an autumn hat. I shall wear my black and white one as Mr. Seamark will be there and he'll be bound to ask us to shelter in the house if there should be another shower. I dare say he'll show us all over it!"

Mrs. Hyde-Ridley did not know that the site of the Fiesta was some distance from the Priory; unwittingly she gave the impression that there would be shelter close at hand.

"In that case I *shall* wear my best hat," Mrs. Vandevint decided. "My blue straw won't quite do if we're going to meet Mr. Seamark and be shown round the Priory."

"Those chairs will be soaked already," Hester told Derek. "We spent the whole morning setting them out and it was utter waste of time. No one is going to pay an extra half-crown to sit on a wet chair, when they can get wet through for free just standing up."

"Perhaps we needn't go," said Derek, looking hopefully out of the kitchen window.

"Oh, we've got to go. Even your papa is going. It's lucky for you that you have to work at the bank on Saturday mornings, otherwise you would have gone this morning as well, like Maggie and me."

"The bank" meant the antique shop, and the glance that accompanied it was a conspirator's secret signal.

"I might have asked the bank for a morning off," said Derek, "if I'd known that you and Maggie were toiling and moiling by yourselves."

"Not by ourselves. We did the chairs and Mrs. Merlin and the Rector and what's left of the committee fussed about with the maypole and rigged up a little tent to store the stuff that's going to be sold. They couldn't set it out on the stalls because of the rain. And Thomas Seamark came to see how we were getting on, and he commanded a farm roller to come and roll the arena. Even so, it will be heavy going for the dancers."

Hester looked round and made sure the kitchen door was shut and Mrs. Pilgrim safely on the other side of it. Though goodness knew why she was still in the house, because it was after one o'clock and she should have left half an hour ago.

"I'm sure I'm right about Thomas and Maggie," she said. "You're all as blind as bats not to see it for yourselves."

"And your eye for romance, dear Hester, could be better described as a magnifying glass. There isn't any romance, in the accepted sense of the word, between Thomas and Maggie. Your warm heart has most commendably deceived you. All the more honour to it, with such prosaic material to work on."

"Oh, rubbish. You've never been in love."

"Haven't I?" asked Derek.

The kitchen door opened and Mrs. Pilgrim marched in with the cleaning rags and tin of brass polish, which she dumped on the table by Hester's elbow. Hester was mixing a dressing for the salad; Mrs. Pilgrim was just going to give a once-over to the two copper preserving pans before she departed. It was her familiar method of staking her claim to the table—and indeed to the kitchen—and the only thing that surprised Hester was its happening so late in the day.

"I reckon they don't know nothing about it," said Mrs. Pilgrim, addressing the four walls of her own kitchen and her own neat table with its plastic cloth, and incidentally Mr. Pilgrim who was sitting opposite.

"That so?" he responded.

"I waited on to have a word with Mrs. Hutton and kind of sound her, which I couldn't do any sooner because she was up in that attic painting all the morning, and that just shows, doesn't it? For if she knew about Miss Maggie and Mr. Seamark she'd hardly have settled down to painting just as usual, even if it *was* still a secret just among the family. I mean to say, they'd have been talking it over among themselves, not just going on as usual, as if nothing had happened."

"That's right," said Mr. Pilgrim.

"She doesn't know a thing about it, I'm certain of that. 'Course I'm only guessing myself, with hearing from Mrs. Merlin's Enid this morning about how Miss Maggie left her in the lurch yesterday afternoon and then Miss Maggie saying how she'd gone for a walk and then hearing about her being at the Priory and Mr. Seamark driving her home. But it stands to reason, doesn't it?"

"That's right."

"'Course I wouldn't say a word to anybody, and you make sure you don't either."

Silence came easily to Mr. Pilgrim, whose passive role in conversation was by now habitual, and to this directive he merely nodded.

"Derek and that Miss Hester, they don't know neither," Mrs. Pilgrim continued. "Though I'm surprised in a way, because she's sharp enough to see through a brick wall backwards. Still, they were quite as usual and no feeling at all that they were keeping something back from me. *They* don't know."

Mr. Pilgrim cleared his throat, as a preliminary to asking a question. But before he could frame it Mrs. Pilgrim had answered him.

"I couldn't catch the master alone," she said regretfully.

Bennet had had a busy morning. He had been across to the rectory to commiserate with the Rector on the unpromising day, and he had then walked down the street as far as *Firenze* to find out what, if anything, was happening there. He did not like being left out; and he had a feeling that there was more going on than he knew about, and that it wasn't all to do with the Country Dancing Fiesta.

It had been a busy morning, but a barren one. Everyone else was busy too, no one remembered to ask after his health, Chrysanthemum was making cakes and Anthony told him the tea-shop was not open in the mornings; even the Rector was rather short with him, making the excuse that he had an important letter to write before going off to the park. Cecily was painting, Hester and Maggie were in the park, and Bennet was quite glad to see Dr. Jamieson's car coming up the street, not ten minutes after his own return from *Firenze*. Unlike the Mingham neighbours, Dr. Jamieson was less busy than usual and was easily persuaded to stay and have some sherry and a long chat.

Then Derek returned from Scorling, and a little later they had lunch, everyone obsessed by the weather and wondering whether it would keep fine. The rain had stopped but the wind was increasing, it was a nasty, blowy, chilly afternoon and the last sort of day for an invalid to attend a function in the open air, especially when he had been out and about all the morning. But Bennet was determined to be present at the Fiesta, not only because he wanted to see the prancers in action but because his sixth sense had told him that something was being concealed from him and he wanted to know what it was. At the Fiesta, he thought, he would find out.

They were late starting. Cecily couldn't make up her mind what to wear, Bennet decided to wear his thin black shoes and found they had not been cleaned. Maggie and Derek and Hester were ready and waiting, while the parents fussed about upstairs as if there was all the time in the world. Three months ago Hester would have been upstairs as well, encouraging Cecily and cajoling Cousin Bennet; but today she belonged to the group that muttered impatiently, "Oh, the parents! Why can't they hurry up?" Happily unaware of their status, Cecily and Bennet at last appeared in all the glory of best clothes which they thought suitable to the occasion, and the party set off.

*

"Perhaps we're not as late as we thought," Hester said doubt-fully. "Perhaps there are still a lot of people to come."

"Choo, choo! The prancers outnumber the audience."

Cousin Bennet was exaggerating, but from the top of the bank where they were standing the scene below looked pitiful-ly empty. On one side of the arena was the block of chairs, with three people in the front row, and on the other side was a thin line of depressed-looking spectators huddled in mackintoshes and clutching umbrellas. Beyond them a few more people were wandering round the two stalls and the ice-cream van, and in the foreground the members of the visiting country-dance team were reluctantly taking off their coats and preparing to go into action.

"Anyway, Miss Knapp has made it," said Hester, counting five musicians all looking rather blue. "There she is in the pixie hood —I hope someone remembered to bring the brandy."

"And there is Thomas," said Maggie.

He had paid half-a-crown for a seat because Mrs. Merlin had demanded it, and now he was compelled to sit through the next dance on the programme because he was too conspicuously placed to stand up and walk away. The only other seated spec-tators were the two people beside him, to whom he had been introduced by Mrs. Merlin but whose name he had not grasped and did not want to know. They were husband and wife; the wife had something to do with country dancing and her husband was a prominent citizen of Salchester and had been brought over to open the Fiesta.

Thomas himself had been invited to do this but he had re-fused, pretending that he might be away; it was quite enough, he thought, to allow them to use the park and to give a hand-some donation to the church funds. If it had not been for Maggie he would have postponed his arrival till later; and now she was standing at the other side of the ground and he was stuck here until the next interval. He clapped the dance perfunctorily, not-ing with impatience that it was the first of a group of three, and made polite, absent-minded replies to the enthusiastic woman beside him, and watched with a sinking heart the approach of the Rector, who was bringing two more people who had been cozened into paying their half-crowns.

"I believe it's going to rain again," said the woman beside Thomas.

"The Priory isn't even in *sight*," Mrs. Vandevint said indignantly to Mrs. Hyde-Ridley.

"It's quite all right as I've bought seat-tickets as Mr. Seamark is sitting there," Mrs. Hyde-Ridley hissed behind the Rector's back.

The dancers trooped out of the arena, and the Rector stopped to speak to a parishioner. Mr. Seamark stood up. In another minute he would have escaped them, but Mrs. Hyde-Ridley rushed past the Rector and neatly waylaid him before he could turn away. How nice to see him, she shrieked, as it was a long time since they'd met as he never gave parties as his uncle used to do; and this was her friend Mrs. Vandevint who had known Mingham for years and yet had never seen the Priory as she'd always wanted to as it was such a wonderful old house! And she was sure he wouldn't mind if they went on up the drive as it would be a pity for Mrs. Vandevint not to see it as it was so near.

"It is quite a long walk," Thomas said, looking at the two old ladies and wondering where they bought their hats. "And I'm afraid it's starting to rain."

"Then we'll get Rudd to drive us," Mrs. Hyde-Ridley said triumphantly. "He can drive us there and come back—he'll want to come back as his daughter is dancing round the maypole. It will only be a shower as my glass hasn't moved an inch—but if it *should* turn heavy perhaps we could go indoors and shelter, as I'll tell Rudd not to come and fetch us till the maypole's over,"

On the other side of the arena Bennet stood under an oak tree, holding over his head an umbrella borrowed from Miss Knapp. In theory he was holding it over Miss Knapp and himself but in practice she was getting the drips from the ends of the spokes. However, she had her pixie hood and her raincoat, and since she always enjoyed talking to Mr. Hutton she bore the drips without complaining.

"If the rain lasts we shall not be able to continue," she said.

"Very brave of you even to start."

Miss Knapp smiled heroically. "It was my duty," she said. "Yesterday I hardly felt equal to it—but I couldn't let them down."

"Precisely. Your devotion does you credit. A pity there are so few people to applaud your performance."

They were off. Miss Knapp knew of several reasons for the Fiesta's lack of success, and Bennet could think of plenty more. These were—of course—the weather, and the distance from the village, and the date in August instead of in June. But in addition to these obvious reasons there were others which they discussed in soft voices: feuds and dissensions and stupidity and forgetfulness. It was an enjoyable conversation, and Bennet was sorry when Miss Cardwell pounced on them like an outraged school-teacher—which of course she was—and scolded Miss Knapp for her folly in standing under a damp tree and bore her away to one of the two small tents in which the dancers and musicians were sheltering from the rain. Miss Cardwell's solicitude also reminded him of his own neglected state, forgotten by his family and left to fend for himself. Cecily should have been urging him to go home.

But he had no intention of going home. The Priory was nearer, and Thomas would be glad of an excuse for leaving this dismal scene and driving him there; and then they could return if the weather improved. He began to look round for Thomas, whom he had observed earlier in the afternoon but who had now temporarily vanished. His own family had vanished too, but they must all be hidden in one of the groups which were clustered under the oak trees. They were not under his own oak tree. Still holding Miss Knapp's umbrella, which he had forgotten to give back and which she had been too flustered to demand, he walked across to the nearest group in search of Thomas—or of Maggie or Derek who could be sent to find him.

None of them was there. But on the edge of the sheltering group stood Mrs. Hyde-Ridley and Mrs. Vandevint, peering out at the rain and measuring the distance between themselves and Rudd's car, which was parked at the top of the grandstand-bank with Rudd sitting inside it.

"We must make a dash for it," Mrs. Hyde-Ridley was saying. "Your hat won't be hurt, Dulcie, as it's only a shower and won't take us ten seconds!"

Mrs. Vandevint, who wasn't built for dashing, retorted angrily that her hat would be quite ruined.

Bennet's chivalry in offering the use of his umbrella—or rather, the gay little tartan umbrella that belonged to Miss Knapp—was rewarded by his discovery that the ladies were going to the Priory. Rudd's car was a large one and there would be plenty of room for him. Thomas would be sure to turn up at the Priory soon (if he wasn't, as Bennet strongly suspected, already there), and Rudd was coming back to the Fiesta and could give a message to Cecily, to instruct her to send Hester with his own car to fetch him home.

He still felt that something was being concealed from him, but it was no good pursuing inquiries here, with everyone huddled into compact groups where every word would be public. Moreover, Mrs. Hyde-Ridley was as good a source of information as he could hope for, if it was anything to do with the village.

Driving back up the cart-track, he was too much absorbed in the flood of information already being divulged to spare more than a glance at his own car, which was parked at the side of the main drive where the track began. His mind merely registered that it was still there, at the place where he had made them all get out and walk because of the danger to the car's ancient springs.

"I bet you brought it further than this yesterday," Derek had said, when he and Hester got back to the car.

"Yes, I took it down the track to the top of the bank. But your father wasn't in it."

"He'll be sorry he didn't let you bring it any nearer today. He's probably looking for you now, to send you to fetch it so that he won't get his feet wet."

With a callous disregard for Bennet's wet feet, Hester and Derek got into the car and lit cigarettes and settled down to watch the rain and talk about their own concerns. The Fiesta was out of sight and out of mind; and when Rudd's old car drove past they hardly noticed it, or observed that it turned towards the Priory instead of towards the village. Nor did they notice its return. But soon afterwards they were compelled to notice Cecily, who pulled the door open and asked indignantly if they had been there all the time.

"Yes, Mama. We prudently took cover from the rain. Come and join us."

Cecily got into the back of the car and took off her hat and shook it. "It will never be the same again," she said disconsolately.

"Then you can buy a new one," said Hester.

"Where is Maggie?" Cecily asked. "I thought she was with you."

"And where is Papa? We thought he was with you."

"He's at the Priory," said Cecily. "He sent a message. I suppose we'd better go and fetch him, and then we can all go home and change. Everyone is leaving—I've been looking for you everywhere—why on earth didn't you tell me you were going to the car!"

"I'm sorry," Hester said soothingly. "We thought you'd be sure to come back here."

It crossed her mind that she had never thought of Cecily at all —or of Maggie, or of Cousin Bennet, apart from an unsympathetic thought about his wet feet. To make amends she hastily offered to go and look for Maggie while Cecily and Derek went to fetch Cousin Bennet. But Derek said it would be better to go to the Priory first in case Maggie was there.

"No point in your getting wet," he said kindly, "when she may be there with Thomas."

Hester knew this was a mocking allusion to her romantic theories. But Cecily took it seriously and rebuked Derek for thinking that Maggie could be with Thomas when Thomas had official duties to attend to and no time to bother about—well, about people like Maggie.

"Still, we'll go to the Priory first," she added, "because Maggie might have gone with your father and Mrs. Hyde-Ridley. Rudd didn't say whether she was with them—I didn't think of asking him."

# CHAPTER TWENTY-TWO

MRS. TURLE, who was Thomas's housekeeper, had not gone to the Fiesta because that sort of thing did not appeal to her, especially on a day which anyone could see was bound to turn out wet. She had let her daughter go, and since she expected to be alone she had invited two friends from the village to come and have tea with her. Mr. Thomas had not said he would be bringing his own friends to the Priory, or sending people there to shelter from the rain; and if it hadn't been Mr. Hutton with the ladies she would hardly have known what to do. But seeing that it was Mr. Hutton she reluctantly admitted them and escorted them to the drawing-room, which Mr. Thomas never used these days but which was clearly the proper place for chance callers. She shut the door on them and went back to her interrupted tea-party, not caring whether they found it damp or not.

Shortly afterwards, when she ushered in the second lot of callers, she noticed with grim satisfaction that the first lot looked quite subdued. It was the room, of course; for even in August it had a sort of gloom about it, due to its size and facing east and never being used. And naturally it looked a bit dusty and bare, with most of the ornaments put away and the upholstered chairs shrouded in holland sheets, but that couldn't be helped—it was their own fault for coming uninvited, or Mr. Thomas's fault for not warning her there might be company.

"Why on earth did she bring us in here?" Cecily exclaimed, as soon as Mrs. Turle had left them.

"Because she's a stickler for etiquette," said Bennet. "And to show us that we weren't wanted."

"Absolute nonsense," said Mrs. Hyde-Ridley. "Mr. Seamark invited us himself!"

She believed this to be true, and so did Mrs. Vandevint.

"There's no point in staying, as Thomas isn't here," said Cecily. "We'd better take you home, Bennet, before you catch a chill."

This was what she should have said at the Fiesta; but it was now too late for wifely solicitude, because Bennet was determined not to go home without finding out what Thomas was up to. Why wasn't he here? What was keeping him out there in the rain? If he wasn't out there in the rain, where was he lurking? Luckily there was a good reason for not leaving at once; or at any rate a good excuse. They could not abandon Mrs. Hyde-Ridley and Mrs. Vandevint, who would have to remain until Rudd came to fetch them.

"We will all wait here," said Bennet, settling himself into one of the holland-covered chairs and making a warning face at Cecily, who was capable of suggesting that all six of them could squash into his precious car. "No doubt Thomas will turn up soon, and make amends for this somewhat chilly reception. As Mrs. Hyde-Ridley has pointed out, he—er—knows we are here."

"He doesn't know *we're* here," said Derek. "We only came to fetch you."

"Then your presence will be a pleasant surprise for him," Bennet said tartly.

Mrs. Hyde-Ridley and Mrs. Vandevint, sitting together on a shrouded sofa, were deep in reminiscences of other drawing-rooms, of which this one somehow reminded them. Its carefully shrouded state rather impressed them, because it suggested a well-trained staff in the background who knew how a house should be run. This was how drawing-rooms had looked in the old days, when the family was setting off for Scotland or for Italy, and the fact that Mr. Seamark wasn't setting off for anywhere did not matter; it just showed that he was a man of property with more rooms at his disposal than he needed.

"Quite twenty bedrooms," said Mrs. Hyde-Ridley, "and that's not counting the attics!"

"Twenty-four," said Bennet, choosing a number that sounded artistically right though it bore no relation to the truth. "And that's not counting the haunted one, which has never been used since a psychic investigator went mad in it."

He settled down to pass the time and enjoy himself in his own way, doubling the size of the Priory and inventing two good ghost stories and some dubious Seamark history in a suitably distant past. His elderly auditors listened enthralled, while his family looked at its watches and wondered what had happened to Rudd, and to Thomas, and—as an afterthought—to Maggie.

All three of them, with the Merlins and a few staunch supporters, had been engaged in rescue work—the removal of what could be moved and the protection of what couldn't. The dejected performers went first, with the musicians and the stall-holders; the county team had its own transport, but Rudd and Thomas drove the others home in relays, and then loaded their cars with the squashy home-made delicacies from the produce stall, and the sodden arts and crafts, and dumped the lot in the parish hall for someone else to deal with. In the meantime the other rescuers stacked the chairs and spread the tarpaulin over them, and Mrs. Merlin insisted that the maypole should be lifted out of its socket and laid on the ground so that she could rescue the ribbons.

"They'll run in the rain," she said; but Maggie could see they had run already and were hardly worth rescuing. Mrs. Merlin, however, was so distraught that it seemed unkind to point it out— better let her occupy herself with winding up the wet ribbons and then perhaps she wouldn't notice that one of the tents had split.

"It said bright intervals," Mrs. Merlin kept repeating; and again Maggie had not the heart to point out that a bright interval was fast approaching, now when it was too late and everyone had fled. For the rain had almost stopped, and there was even a gleam of watery sunlight on the woods beyond the river. By the time Thomas returned from his last journey with the arts and crafts it was not raining at all.

"I thought we should never get away," Thomas said, when he and Maggie were safely in the car.

"But we couldn't abandon them, could we? Though it was bad luck on you, darling. If you hadn't been with me, Mrs. Merlin would never have dared to ask you to help."

Thomas denied this quite indignantly, especially the suggestion that it was bad luck being with his beloved.

"Well, it was good luck—for them—that you had the car," Maggie admitted. "But I meant that it wasn't your sort of thing, and not what you bargained for when you agreed to her having the Fiesta in the park. . . . Oh dear, do you think we should have taken the Merlins' home?"

"No!" said Thomas, adding more calmly that Rudd was coming back to fetch them. Moreover, he said, he had spent the greater part of the afternoon talking to Mrs. Merlin and her colleagues instead of to Maggie, and he never wanted to talk to them again. Bar the Rector, he said prudently, with whom conversation would be essential when it came to arranging a wedding.

Maggie laughed and agreed. She could not but agree that talking to other people was a fearful waste of time; nevertheless she saw that Thomas had enjoyed his rescue work more than he would admit. Or, if he hadn't exactly enjoyed it, he had at any rate done it quite willingly, accepting all the obligations of being a Mingham resident.

"You didn't really mind, did you?" she asked.

"My dearest Maggie, I am quite prepared for the next Country Dancing Fiasco to be held on the terrace, so that everyone can take shelter in the house when it rains."

"Then it won't be a Fiasco but a riotous success. Why are we going to the Priory now, darling?"

"For a respite. Just a short respite before I take you home and tell your parents. We'll have a drink and plan how to break the news. Or are you wet through?" he added anxiously. "Would you rather go straight home and change?"

"I'm not at all wet. Miss Knapp lent me her mackintosh when she went off in Rudd's car. I could see Miss Cardwell didn't approve, but Miss Knapp was in one of her self-sacrificing moods and Miss C. couldn't stop her."

Maggie was still wearing the mackintosh, which was much too big for her and singularly unbecoming. Cecily would have despaired of her, but Thomas thought she had never looked more enchanting. He stopped the car to kiss her, and then drove on down the rhododendron tunnel for the promised respite before they had to start talking to other people. He swung the car into the forecourt and narrowly avoided hitting another one, which had been inconsiderately parked just beyond the bend.

"Damn!" he said.

"That's ours," said Maggie. "What a mercy you didn't hit it, because Father would never have forgiven you."

Just for a moment Thomas did not care whether Bennet would have forgiven him or not. "If he doesn't want it to get hit he shouldn't have left it there," he said crossly.

"I know. It's utterly maddening of them. What are they doing here? I thought they'd gone home long ago. But parents *are* maddening, Thomas. You don't know how lucky you are being an orphan and not having to bother with them—though I suppose you'll have to bother with mine, now."

There was a slight delay, while Thomas assured Maggie that the privilege of marrying her would more than make up for any bother whatsoever. Then they got out of the car and walked up the white steps, hand in hand because it was a symbolical moment. They were entering their home, and very soon they would face Maggie's parents and ask for their blessing. Or, as they expressed it themselves, they would tell them at once and get it over.

Thomas opened the door. Still hand in hand, they crossed the threshold; and then very quickly drew apart, in silent but complete agreement about the need to appear as disengaged as possible. For in the great hall were not only Cecily and Bennet, who were to be told at once, but also Derek and Hester and Mrs Hyde-Ridley and Mrs. Vandevint, whose presence made the telling unthinkable; at any rate for such haters of the limelight as Thomas and Maggie.

Bennet was halfway up the lower flight of the staircase, with Mrs. Hyde-Ridley and Mrs. Vandevint a few steps below him.

Cecily was sitting down, reading a book, and Derek and Hester were inspecting the trophies of the chase that hung on the walls.

The entry of the Priory's owner took them all by surprise; there was an instant of confusion—on both sides—before Bennet collected himself and justified his position.

"Too cold in your drawing-room, Thomas," he said reproachfully. "The ladies were freezing."

"I am sorry to hear it. Wouldn't they be warmer in the library?"

"We are on our way there," Bennet retorted. "I was just showing Mrs. Hyde-Ridley and her friend—as we went past—that interesting portrait of—of—"

"The Seamark whose ghost drove people mad, as I was so interested as there's another ghost like that in a house in Scotland as they've had to nail up the door of his room. Is your ghost's room's door nailed up, Mr. Seamark?"

Thomas said firmly, "There are no ghosts in this house. Never have been."

He was thinking of Maggie, who might reasonably object to sharing a house with a ghost that drove people mad. It did not occur to him that Bennet had invented the ghost to while away a tedious hour; otherwise he would have backed him up and explained to Maggie afterwards.

Bennet descended the stairs in an offended silence, while Cecily asked Maggie, not for the first time, what she had been doing; and Mrs. Hyde-Ridley and Mrs. Vandevint shrieked and muttered, respectively, their complaints of Mr. Hutton's inaccuracy: and Hester, standing a little apart, asked Derek whether he thought Thomas had heard what they were saying about the trophies of the chase when he came in.

"I don't think so," said Derek. "He's only taking umbrage about being saddled with a ghost."

". . . And where did you get that perfectly dreadful old mackintosh?" Cecily demanded. "Take it off at once—you look quite—"

"No ghost at all! Just fancy, as Mr. Hutton seemed to know so much as naturally I believed every *word*!"

"Maggie has been working hard, in the rain," Thomas said coldly to Cecily. "If someone hadn't lent her a coat she'd have been soaked through."

"But she doesn't need to go on wearing it!"

"I don't believe Mr. Hutton knows anything."

"Oh, Mother, what does it *matter* if it's too long!"

It was a long time since the great hall had rung with voices, all speaking at once. Hester noticed what a difference it made, as if the house were coming back to life; but Rudd, standing at the open door, thought sourly that it was worse than the zoo. He raised his own voice to its full parade-ground volume, reducing the opposition to a stunned silence.

"*If* you're ready, ladies! Otherwise I'll have to go. Can't leave the Reverend Merlin standing out there in the rain."

Rudd's parade-ground voice, so seldom heard in civilian life, frightened Mrs. Hyde-Ridley and Mrs. Vandevint into instant obedience. With hasty farewells they hurried after him and were bundled into the car; not until they were half-way home did it occur to them that they had hired it, and that the giving of a lift was a matter requiring their consent. But by that time they had picked up the Merlins and it was too late to protest.

There hadn't really been a quarrel, Cecily thought—it was just that they were all feeling cold and tired and irritable. It had been awkward, Thomas walking in like that and finding them making free with his house; and she hoped he had not noticed that she was reading the old Visitors' Book, which she had taken out of a drawer in the gate-legged table where she knew it always used to be kept. Of course it dated from long before his ownership of the Priory, it recorded the names of people who had stayed there when he was a boy, and she a newcomer to Mingham; but still, he might be annoyed that she had opened the drawer and ferreted about for the book.

It had been right at the back, buried behind a lot of things that belonged to Thomas himself. What a pity, she thought; for the long disused book seemed to summarize all that was wrong with the Priory, its chill emptiness and ugliness and isolation, as if life had passed it by.

But Hester would change all that, she thought. Relaxing a lit-tle (for they were now in the library, the only room in the house where relaxation was possible), she allowed herself to drift into a daydream of the happy future, only slightly disturbed by a dim sense of continuing strain and awkwardness in the present. But that, of course, was Bennet's fault for insisting on staying when the rest of them wanted to go home; and it was for Bennet to deal with it.

He dealt with it drastically, merely waiting till he had been ensconced in the most comfortable chair with a little rug over his knees and a cushion behind his head—attentions which were no more than his due.

"You let me down badly," he began, with an accusing look at Thomas. "You made me feel a fool. I suppose I shouldn't complain —it's your own house and your own ancestors. Still, I wasn't criticizing 'em, you know. I was simply giving our guests—*your* guests—a little harmless entertainment."

"He invented the ghosts," said Hester.

"He entertained Mrs. Hyde-Ridley and Mrs. Vandevint by telling them ghost stories," said Derek, who believed that the Seamarks needed very lucid explanations.

"Just a joke," Bennet said sadly. "Harmless. You should al-low an old man the harmless pleasure that remains to him." He huddled into the chair, fragile and feeble. "I didn't think you'd grudge me that, Thomas."

Thomas drew a deep breath. If he wasn't to quarrel with his old friend (which in the circumstances was unthinkable), then he must silence him. For Bennet in this mood was more irritat-ing than anyone he knew.

"Never mind the ghosts," he said. "Maggie has promised to marry me."

This wasn't how he had planned to break the news; it sound-ed both too abrupt and too casual. But it silenced Bennet as effectively as a baize cloth thrown over a canary's cage. There wasn't even a twitter.

"Wonderful," said Derek. He was looking at Hester, but nei-ther Maggie nor Thomas noticed. Hester stepped forward and kissed Maggie and burst into a flood of congratulations, and almost at once Derek was joining in. He saw as well as she did that the parents needed time to recover.

"This is a great surprise," said Bennet.

False words, but necessary. They were a modulation from one key to another, from peevish accusations to indulgent approval.

Inwardly, he plumed himself for having known that something was up.

"Oh—what is it?" cried Cecily.

Immersed in her daydream, she had not heard Thomas speak. Immersed in her daydream, the outburst that followed seemed for an instant like the daydream come true—congratulations, kisses, excitement—and then like the daydream gone mad.

"What is it?" she repeated faintly, though by this time she was aware what it was. Hester turned round and gave her an encouraging glance. "Aren't you delighted?" she said briskly, and then quickly turned away, standing between Cecily and Thomas so that he should not see how far she was from being delighted or even acquiescent. How long can we keep it up? Hester thought, waiting to take over from Derek if he ran out of words. But the other parent was smiling cherubically and uttering preliminary chirrups, which were an artistic indication that the great surprise had been a pleasant one.

Bennet enjoyed himself enormously, giving a father's blessing to an engagement which he had long foreseen and approved. He did not say that he had foreseen it, but he said everything else that needed to be said, and a good deal, in the opinion of his auditors, that didn't. He went on too long; he enlarged on his own feelings and embarrassed Thomas and Maggie by alluding to theirs, which they strongly held to be none of his business; he strayed into reminiscences of Thomas's uncle and of Maggie's childhood, which were both irrelevant and boring, and he could not refrain from bringing in the ghosts, with a very handsome apology for having sullied the reputation of a ghost-free mansion. Nevertheless, his lengthy speech was a success; it dissipated the explosive atmosphere and gave Cecily time to get her feelings under control.

And that, Hester thought, was probably his reason for making it.

# CHAPTER TWENTY-THREE

ON SUNDAY, the day after the Fiesta, Cecily had the odd sensation that she had become invisible.

This was an exaggeration, because no one bumped into her or commented on her apparent absence. But it felt like invisibility because no one seemed to guess what she was thinking or to notice that she wasn't joining in. Bennet and the children, and even poor Hester, were all in remarkably good spirits, and from the start of the day she was sharply aware of the difference between their mood and her own. It was their blank imperception of any difference that made her feel invisible.

Cecily did not observe that none of them was ever alone with her; she was too wrapped up in her dismay to notice the significant avoidance of tête-à-têtes. In the morning Hester went to church, accompanied—rather to her godmother's surprise—by Derek, and Bennet and Maggie worked companionably in the garden until Thomas arrived to take Maggie out to lunch. Cecily was invited to join the church-goers, and she refused; she was pressed to join the gardeners and she refused again, on the plea of having to cook the family lunch. This excuse also served to cut short her meeting with Thomas, whom Bennet insisted on asking in for a glass of sherry; drinking them out of house and home, thought Cecily, and quite unnecessary after last night.

Last night had been unnecessary too; bringing Thomas back for dinner and opening champagne and letting poor Hester slave away in the kitchen after her exhausting day at the Fiesta; it had been unnecessary and frightful and Cecily did not know how she had got through it. But today she had the excuse of the Sunday joint, she was able to slip away after only a few minutes' talk, and she did not go back. The sherry-drinking was prolonged by the return of Hester and Derek; then it was time for lunch, and after lunch Hester and Derek did the washing-up and Bennet said very firmly that he was going to sleep and retired to his bedroom, quietly locking himself in. But Cecily knew it would be useless to try and discuss the engagement with Bennet—as she certainly intended to do—on a Sunday afternoon when he wanted to sleep.

Hester and Derek finished the washing-up and crept out to the garden, hoping that Cecily, too, would go to sleep. Perversely, it was a much better afternoon than yesterday, though still rather windy and cold. They went to the far end of the garden and found a sheltered place at the foot of the bank which divided the garden from the fields—not only sheltered, but out of sight.

"No parent will track us down here," said Derek, leading Hester through the gap in the hedge which grew on top of the bank. "This was one of Maggie's and my best hiding places, when we were young."

"You always make it sound such an infinitely distant past."

"That's how it seems. Infinitely distant, because we took so long to grow up. Haven't you noticed what a long time we Huttons take over everything?"

"Yes," she said. "When I first came here I thought you were the most slothful characters I had ever met. Totally lacking in energy and initiative."

"You know better now," Derek said smugly.

"I still think—"

"Of course you do, because you make up your mind so quickly and then you don't like to un-make it. But you really do know better, don't you?—if you'd give the facts a chance!"

He was joking; but it mattered. "Oh, I know better about you," she answered quickly. "But for the others, I'm not quite sure."

"When you first came here I wondered whether you could be 'not quite sure' about *anything*."

There was a pause. Then Derek said, "Sorry," and Hester said, "All right. But don't tease me about it." And then, with one accord, they began to talk about the parents.

"Mama is taking a long time to calm down," Derek said, as if they had been discussing them all the while.

"She's got something against Thomas," said Hester. "I thought last night she was just dumbfounded because it was a totally new situation which she'd never dreamed of. But you can see she's just as much against it today."

"Yes, that's what *I* thought—that she needed time to get used to the idea of Maggie marrying Thomas who's supposed to be a recluse."

"And living in that horrible house she so much despises."

"Still, she's had time to get used to the idea by now," said Derek.

"That's what I said. It must be something else, something *more* than shock."

"But what could she have against a blameless character like Thomas?"

"His age?" Hester suggested.

"Well, he's a good bit older than Maggie, of course. He must be thirty-five. But I don't think that really matters, do you?"

"Not if they suit each other."

"Anyway, I don't think it's his age. Mama thinks young men— that's me—are frightfully irresponsible, so logically she can't object to his age."

"Logic doesn't come into it," said Hester. "But I don't think it's his age, either. And then, she has always seemed to like him— I've often heard her praising him and saying how good and kind and intelligent he was. A very paragon."

"Oh well," said Derek. "It's just one of her quirks. She doesn't want Maggie to marry a paragon. But luckily Papa is all in favour of it."

"I'm in favour of it myself."

"That's your romantic unconscious coming out. But it *is* lucky Papa is in favour of it, because if he wasn't he would be very difficult to deal with. One can't get really tough with an invalid."

"But he has quite recovered," said Hester.

"He could easily have a relapse," said Derek. "That's one reason why I have postponed telling him about my new career. He could easily have a relapse and I don't want him to. Not until—"

He broke off. But Hester did not ask why Cousin Bennet's relapse must be postponed; she was too busy considering the original cause of his illness.

"I suppose it never was a real illness," she said. "It was a protest against—well, what? Being made to retire to Mingham, and having nothing to do?"

"Indeed and indeed it was a real illness. Specialists, nurses, losing the use of his legs, why, Hester, it was *serious*."

Derek sounded so serious himself that Hester at once discerned in him a latent interest in invalidism. But this (though it was a warning to be heeded) did not stop her from thinking at the same time how much nicer he was than the rest of his family. She had often thought so before, but never with such overwhelming certainty; it was as though all her other thoughts had been pushed aside as unimportant.

"It must have been very trying for you," she said, inadequately. "I'm glad he got over it."

"There is always the danger of a relapse, as I said. Still, he *has* got over it," Derek agreed.

He turned towards her and added in a matter-of-fact voice, "You've got over it too, Hester. You've stopped feeling sorry for yourself at last."

"How horrid you were, that day in the shop."

Derek was not to be side-tracked. "I wasn't horrid," he said calmly. "I was merely truthful. You were angry with me then, but you're not angry now. That proves that you're not still demanding sympathy."

Whatever it proved, she certainly wasn't angry with him. "I've stopped feeling sorry for myself," she agreed. "And I've stopped pining for Raymond."

"Are you quite sure?"

"Yes, I am. I stopped pining before I stopped sorrowing."

"Good," said Derek. "If you're really sure."

Well might he doubt it; this wasn't the first time, or the second, that Hester had insisted that she wasn't pining for Raymond. But now she had no need to insist; for the name evoked no sad, tumultuous cries in her own heart, to be silenced by emphatic pronouncements. It would have been easy to explain this to Derek—there wasn't, any longer, a reluctance to talk about it—but she judged explanations unnecessary. He was quite clever enough to work out for himself that lack of insistence meant certainty.

"We see, we've all got over things," she said. "Thomas has got over being a recluse."

"That only leaves Mama to get over Thomas."

Once again, without awkwardness or hesitation, they exchanged one subject for another. But they had scarcely begun on Thomas —his recoil from isolationism, and the probability of his staying to supper when he and Maggie returned from wherever they had gone—before Bennet tracked them down.

He knew they were somewhere in the garden because he had seen them creeping out by the door from the yard; he had watched them from his bedroom window and had guessed that they were dodging Cecily. (The possibility that they were dodging himself did not occur to him.) He had come out to find them before tea, so that he would not be exposed to arguments over the tea-cups. There was a time and a place for everything—a time and a place of his own choosing.

It was a big garden, but there weren't many places to hide; this particular place was not nearly so parent-proof as Derek imagined. Bennet found them quite easily, guided by the sound of their voices and their laughter. He did not attempt to go through the gap in the hedge, which had been made by persons younger and slimmer than he, but he stood in the orchard behind them and chirruped loudly until they responded.

"Tea-time, Hester! It's time for tea!"

Presently they joined him, Hester saying he shouldn't have bothered to hunt for them, and Derek saying it wasn't tea-time yet.

"Your mother is getting it," said Bennet.

He strolled back to the house slowly, holding Derek's arm and sometimes laying his other hand on Hester's, and talking to both of them about nothing in particular.

"No, no, Cecily can manage," he said, when Hester offered to go and help.

It was perfectly clear to him that Cecily disapproved of the engagement, but he had not yet found out why. Last night, after the celebratory evening, he had gone to bed quickly and pretended to be asleep when she came to say goodnight; like Hester and Derek, he had thought she was suffering from shock (she had always reacted badly to surprises, even when they were pleasant ones), and that she would see things differently in the morning. But he had been wrong; there was something he didn't understand.

He would find out what it was tonight; and he wasn't going to have Hester finding out first. (A dear girl, Hester, but not the right person to handle Cecily.) So he kept her beside him, and after tea he invented various tasks to keep her and Derek occupied, with himself supervising them, and after supper he made them play three-handed bezique until his bedtime. By then Cecily had already retired on the plea of being quite worn out. Bennet knew perfectly well that she would not forgo the goodnight ritual, but this was what he wanted. It was the time and place of his own choosing.

Waiting for her to come, he nibbled a biscuit and reflected on what he already knew. She had been all in favour of the marriage; she had actually gone to call on Thomas of her own accord; and although he did not know what had been said on that occasion he knew they had not quarrelled. She had invented a conversation about weather and gardens, therefore the real conversation must have been about something else. No doubt it had been allusive and indirect, a mere probing of feelings or— on Cecily's side—a manifestation of maternal goodwill (and how much better he would have done it himself, Bennet thought enviously), but at least it had been a satisfactory beginning. No quarrels, no doubts; she had been pleased with herself, that night, and she had had the air of one who has carried out a delicate mission with conspicuous success.

So what had Thomas done, since then, to make himself ineligible? Cecily was no good at hiding her feelings, it had been clear as daylight that she thoroughly approved of him after her visit to the Priory, and it was equally clear now that she thoroughly disapproved of him and would almost have preferred Maggie to marry the Enderby son.

Bennet could not think of a stronger comparison; for the Enderby son, though no one had ever seen him, had been a recurrent source of maternal foreboding and anxiety. But that, in a way, was natural enough (except that Maggie had never showed any sign of being interested in the Enderby son), and this wasn't. Why on earth should Cecily disapprove of Maggie's marrying Thomas?

The door opened and Cecily glided in, wearing her winter dressing-gown and carrying a glass of milk. The milk was a placatory offering and the dressing-gown was to keep her warm while they talked. For talk they must; she could not keep her feelings bottled up any longer, and moreover she did not see why she should.

"Here's your go-to-bed milk," she said. "I've just hotted it up."

"I only have milk in the winter," Bennet replied ungratefully.

"Yes, I know, but it's quite a chilly evening and you have had a tiring day."

It was yesterday, not today, that had been tiring, but to Cecily it seemed all one day, going on interminably and likely to continue unless she could somehow put a stop to it.

"Drink your milk quickly, darling, before it gets a skin on it," she said, thrusting the glass into his hand. "Would you like a biscuit to go with it?"

"I've had one."

Cecily took no notice, she opened the biscuit tin and hunted for one of the favourites, the sugar-topped ones, and put it into his free hand as if he had been a baby.

"There you are," she said gently.

"Choo, choo," said Bennet, drinking his milk in quick gulps and clutching the biscuit like a mascot. He saw that he was being humoured, and he was humouring Cecily in return; only she did not see it, she was waiting for her own humouring to take effect and put him in a good mood. When he had finished the milk he dutifully began on the biscuit, while Cecily dutifully inspected the bedside table to make sure everything was in its right place. For a moment both of them felt a strange reluctance to depart from the nightly ritual—the wifely peck on the cheek, the placid exchange of goodnights—but then Bennet broke the spell by asking if Maggie had returned.

Yes, said Cecily, Maggie had come in and had said goodnight and was now on her way to bed. No, she hadn't been late, had she? Well, not really late; but it had been a long tiring day, all the same.

Glaring at the bedside table, she added that it was tiring to have to have Thomas here so often.

"I don't think we shall be seeing a lot of him," Bennet said cheerfully. "He and Maggie seem to prefer their own company. Natural enough, isn't it?"

Maggie and Thomas had not returned for supper. But Maggie had remembered to telephone; Cecily could not complain that she had been anxious, or even kept waiting for a meal. It was natural enough, Bennet repeated, and if Cecily found Thomas tiring she ought to be glad of it.

"If! It's all very well for you—when *you* feel tired you can just say so and go and lie down."

"Precisely. But why should I find him tiring? Why should you, come to that? Nice chap, Thomas. A Seamark, of course—a typical Seamark. He'll settle down to being a model landowner—making improvements, mechanised farming, that sort of thing. He doesn't care whether buildings are old and picturesque; if they aren't efficient, he'll pull them down. Not much sensibility about Thomas, but one can't have everything. Anyway, he'll suit Maggie admirably. Convinced of it. And she, the dear girl, will be just the right wife for him."

Bennet chirrupped in slow time, watching alertly to see what it was about Thomas that Cecily found so tiring. His typical Seamark qualities, his passion for improvements and his blind eye for the picturesque, his lack of sensibility, or perhaps some imagined fault of character that would make him an unsuitable mate for Maggie.

But no, she showed no reactions at all—until he reached the end of his speech and his little compliment to their daughter. And then, to his astonishment, she cried:

"Hester!"

"What?" said Bennet.

"Hester!"

He said nothing, because for a moment he was too surprised to speak. Then, finding his voice and at the same time the clue to the mystery, he began, "Surely you didn't think that those two—"

"Of course I did! It would have been perfect—they're made for each other—Hester would have been a wonderful wife for Thomas, and such a happy ending for her after all she's gone through. And she's so capable, so good at running things. The Priory, I mean. And then they've got that in common—the past —not the same experience but the same sadness and loss—they'd have helped each other to get over it! And Thomas *was* thinking of proposing to Hester, I'm sure he was, he sort of hinted at it and talked about being lonely. And that shows how fickle he is, doesn't it? And Maggie . . . I'm sure it's a dreadful mistake. Could she possibly have misunderstood him and he is too chivalrous to say so? Or could he—"

"Thomas is hardly likely to have proposed to Maggie under the impression that he was proposing to Hester," Bennet said loudly.

"Oh, I don't know—I can't believe it—we've got to stop it! I've been hoping for it and thinking how wonderful it would be —for Hester, I mean!"

He wished he had not drunk the milk; hot milk would have come in handy for soothing Cecily, he could have made her sit down and sip it slowly, with one of his sedative pills as an additional help. But before he could think of another remedy for hysteria she was off again.

"I *know* I was right about Hester and Thomas because I had an intuition about them—and ever since I've been thinking about it and doing what I could to help. And she likes him; she said so, that day we went to look at the fishponds. Of course I was careful not to talk too much about him, but—"

"I should hope so," Bennet interrupted. "Though in this case it wouldn't have mattered. But you might have done a great deal of harm."

"You don't understand."

"Yes, I do. And you're being very unfair to Maggie."

"But Maggie didn't come into it. It was Hester and Thomas—"

"But they're incompatible," said Bennet.

He couldn't imagine how any woman, even Cecily, could be so stupid and unobservant.

"They're incompatible," he repeated. "You only thought it would do because you wanted a happy ending for Hester. You would have liked to have her near at hand, but not too near—not here in this house, upsetting Mrs. P. and irritating you by her efficiency. And, of course, you wanted to go on being the fairy godmother, waving your wand and working miracles. So you looked round, and there was Thomas, and you said 'Hey, presto!' and called it an intuition."

Cecily remembered, just in time, that Bennet was an invalid to be humoured. She could not bring herself to feel his forehead (which was probably burning with fever), but the training of years enabled her to produce a wifely smile.

"You mustn't get over-excited," she said, "or you won't be able to sleep."

"I shall sleep. It's been a tiring day, remember."

"Are you quite settled? Then I'll put out the light."

"You don't have to worry about Hester," Bennet said, in a more amiable voice than she expected. "She won't stay here to plague you. She'll go back to London."

He yawned, and then added confidently, "She'll go back and marry her young man."

These words were meant to be comforting, but in fact they were just the reverse. Cecily could not bear to think that all her sympathy had been unnecessary; therefore she could not allow Hester to be anything less than broken-hearted.

"And then you'll say 'Hey, presto!'" she retorted, "and call it an intuition."

Omitting the rest of the ritual she turned out the light and walked swiftly to the door. Her torch was in her pocket but she did not use it. Only the opening of the door and the slam of its closing told Bennet—but how forcefully—that he had been left unkissed and ungoodnighted.

He could not remember its ever happening before.

# CHAPTER TWENTY-FOUR

"I'D FORGOTTEN you were starting your holiday," Hester said. "I thought everyone had overslept."

"Derek did oversleep," Maggie explained. "His alarm didn't go off and he's only just woken up. And I was later than usual, because I'm not going to work, so I didn't realise he wasn't up."

"I woke early," said Hester, "and I thought I heard you moving about. Then, when I came down and found no one here, I thought you'd both overslept—I was just coming up to wake you."

"Well, Derek's awake now, but he's only just gone to his bath. We'd better get his breakfast."

They were in the kitchen. Maggie laid the table and Hester started cooking breakfast. "Yours and mine as well," she said. "We might as well have it, now we're here. Though you needn't have got up so early, Maggie, as you're not going to the farm."

"I didn't know *you* were going to get up."

"I woke early."

"Two of us, both rising early to cook Derek's breakfast which he could quite well do for himself!"

"Not this morning," said Hester. "He won't even have time to eat it."

Maggie laughed. "But if he misses the bus, will it much matter? It's not as if he was going to the bank."

"Of course it matters. You think the antique shop is just another whim—a job that won't last—but you're wrong. Derek really has found his *métier*. He's going to make a success of it."

Hester had said this, and much more, in the antique shop on the day Maggie tried to buy the lustre jug. And Maggie had liked her for saying it, but had not really believed her. Derek had had so many new jobs; Hester did not know him as his family did. Still, it bad puzzled her that Hester should take Derek's new job seriously, and believe in his success, when she was so practical and clearsighted herself—the last person, surely, to indulge in wishful thinking.

Now, quite suddenly, the puzzle was solved. It was the sight of Hester with the frying-pan in her hand, beginning to cook Derek's breakfast, that made everything plain. For an instant Maggie felt resentment, as if Hester had wilfully deceived her; then, remembering their talk in the shop, she realised that it wasn't so at all. Hester was deceiving herself, if she was deceiving anyone— that was why her championship of Derek, and the reasons she gave for it, had seemed so silly, and yet so endearing.

She might even be right about Derek, Maggie thought; right for the wrong reasons. The real reason for his settling down to hard work would be Hester herself.

"So he must not miss that bus," Hester said earnestly. "But if the clock's right, he's hardly got time for breakfast."

Maggie, who would very much have minded Thomas going without breakfast for any reason whatever, knew just what Hester was feeling. "Why don't you drive him to Scorling yourself?" she suggested. "It will be quicker than the bus, so he'll have time for breakfast first. Father wouldn't let him take the car, but he won't mind you driving him."

"Good idea," Hester said casually. "Here's Derek coming now. He can start his breakfast while I go and ask Cousin Bennet."

Maggie perceived that her own breakfast (and Hester's) had been forgotten. Stepping into the role of elder sister which Hester had vacated, she commanded her to make some more toast and have a cup of tea, while she herself went to tell Bennet about taking the car to Scorling. She was sure he would not object, but it would be more tactful to consult him.

Derek, who had been prepared to make a dash for the bus, sat down to the excellent breakfast Hester had cooked for him. Hester began to make more toast, and Maggie left the kitchen to tell her father—or, more tactfully, to ask him—about taking the car.

She had expected he would still be in bed. But to her surprise he was just coming downstairs, brushed and shaving and wearing the dressing-gown and shawl in which he breakfasted. His coming down to breakfast was a fairly recent innovation; but his coming down at this hour was unprecedented. Although Derek was later than usual it was still much too early for the parents' breakfast, which they ate in the dining-room because it overlapped with the arrival of Mrs. Pilgrim. Maggie thought at first that she, Hester and Derek must be even later than they supposed, because that seemed less unlikely than her father's getting up too soon.

"Morning, Maggie," he said genially. "What's the matter?"

"Good morning, Father. Nothing, only I was so surprised to see you."

"I woke early," Bennet said, just like Hester. "Woke early, heard you all up and about, thought I'd come and see what was happening."

"We weren't up and about," said Maggie. "We were later than usual, because Derek overslept and I'm not going to the farm today. So—"

"Quite right. Go out with Thomas instead. My full approval."

She was glad that her father approved, but his unusual geniality —at this unusual hour—was a little strange. "Derek overslept," she repeated, "and so we wondered—Hester and I—we thought perhaps you would let Hester drive him to Scorling, because he has missed the bus."

"Quite right. Won't do for him to be late at the bank. So you weren't up and about? Must have been your mother."

It seemed to Maggie that her father was hardly listening to her; that he was so far from thinking about the precious car that he would almost have agreed to Derek driving it himself. But his next words contradicted this impression.

"I suppose it's still there?" he said.

"What? The *car*? Oh yes—I came up to ask you first."

Bennet turned back from the stair and walked to the window at the end of the landing. Maggie followed him, hoping Hester had not already got the car out and thus made nonsense of her tactful errand. But the carriage-house doors were still shut and the yard deserted. They stood side by side, looking down at the yard, and then Bennet said, "I thought your mother might have gone for a drive."

*"Mother!"* Maggie cried.

"Well, she must have got up early. If it wasn't you."

"But that's nonsense! You know Mother hates driving the car anyway—why on earth should she get up early and go for a drive before breakfast?"

"I don't know," Bennet said snappishly.

His genial morning face, which had been part of a cautious approach to an unusual and alarming situation, was now creased with anxiety. He didn't know. Since the moment when Cecily left him without completing the goodnight ritual he had felt blankly uncertain of her intentions; he had only felt that, having done that, she might do anything. It was this uncertainty which was so unusual and alarming, for a man who relied on his sixth sense to warn him of coming events.

"Mother is still in her bedroom," Maggie said confidently.

She went to look, and, as Bennet had expected, the bedroom was empty. But at least Cecily had not driven off to the Priory, he thought, groping in the darkness of not knowing.

"Perhaps she got up early and went to paint the sunrise," said Maggie. "Come downstairs and I'll get our breakfasts."

Everyone was behaving oddly. There were the parents, both getting up so early without telling each other, and Hester and Derek, who should have been starting for Scorling, still sitting at the kitchen table as if they had forgotten about going. Maggie noted the oddnesses without really worrying about them, because half her mind was filled with thoughts of Thomas whom she would be seeing quite soon. She would be seeing him today and tomorrow and probably every day this week; it was happiness enough to dim all worries.

"Yes, yes," said Bennet, as Hester and Derek began telling him all over again about missing the bus and taking the car. They stood up, he sat down; Derek said he would go and open the yard gates, and Hester said she would fetch a cardigan because the morning was quite chilly.

Before either of them had moved the door opened and Cecily made a dramatic entrance. (Even Maggie, thinking about Thomas, was startled into attention.) She came in with a rush and then stopped dead, looking at each of them in turn and most ominously not saying anything.

The tense silence was broken by Bennet, who wished her good morning in a voice that was resolutely genial.

"I woke early," he went on, not waiting for a response. "Fine morning—bit cold for August—still, I thought I'd get up."

"I got up early too," said Cecily. "I came down to make a telephone call. To catch him before he went out. He goes off so early."

"Who?" asked Maggie.

Cecily looked at Bennet, who was uttering warning chirrups and drumming with his fingers on the table. These were pleas for discretion, but she ignored them.

"Malcolm," she said. "I telephoned to Malcolm."

The chirrups and the drumming stopped at once. Bennet knew why she had telephoned to Malcolm—he was Maggie's godfather as well as her uncle, and he was Cecily's brother, and she had had the wild idea of briefing him to disapprove of Maggie's engagement. Ridiculous, of course, but harmless. What a relief to learn that she hadn't been telephoning to Thomas!

He sat back, savouring his relief, and remarked that it was a long time since they had heard from Malcolm.

"He thought we knew," said Cecily. "He was angry because I hadn't written to explain or apologise. Letting him down, he said! You see, he thought we knew. Well, naturally!"

Bennet couldn't imagine what she was talking about. "Knew what?" he demanded.

"That I'd left the bank," Derek said loudly.

He got it out first, though only just, and for a moment neither parent said anything. It was as though he was alone in the room.

"Have some tea, Cousin Bennet," said Hester. "It's a bit stewed, but it's still quite hot."

"Sit down, Mother," said Maggie. "Sit down while I get you some breakfast."

"I have a much better job," Derek said rapidly. "It's an antique shop. In Scorling. I didn't tell you about it, but I was going to—"

Cecily came to life. "The career Uncle Malcolm found for you!" she cried.

"—as soon as I was really settled. And I *am*!"

"Bennet, do you *realize*? Derek has left the bank. The bank Malcolm got him into!"

"Cousin Bennet, drink your tea," said Hester. "It's a bit stewed, but—"

Bennet came to life. "You knew about it," he said.

He looked at Hester, then at Maggie.

"You both knew about it."

"No, they didn't," said Derek.

"Yes, we did," said Maggie and Hester together.

"But Maggie didn't know!"

"I found out by accident. And Hester said it would be better for you not to know I knew."

"You see, Derek, I thought it would be awkward for you—"

"They were all in it together," said Bennet.

He spoke to Cecily, because there was no one else to speak to; Derek, Hester and Maggie were engaged in a heated argument. Cecily had been standing at the other end of the table, but now she walked round it and sat down beside him, the better to hear and be heard. They had no need to shout, now; their voices dropped to an agitated murmur, and presently grew warm with sympathy. There was no one else deserving of sympathy; they had to expend it on each other.

Hester and Maggie . . . helping Derek to deceive his parents, encouraging his irresponsibility. Hester, of all people. (Biting the hand that fed her, said the tone of the voices.) And Derek—throwing up a good career for a job that can't possibly last! And Maggie (who knows perfectly well how touchy Malcolm is), not warning us —putting us in this awkward position. (The reason for telephoning Malcolm could be ignored; it was no longer a point of dispute.)

What about *us*, said the voices; are we not parents, trying to do our best for our children? And look how they treat us!

"Oh, all right," Derek said to Hester. "You meant it for my good."

"Bossy of me, wasn't it?" said Hester; and Derek looked at her and laughed.

His laughter brought the argument to an end, and it also brought to an end the private lamentations at the other side of the kitchen table. Cecily and Bennet looked up indignantly, hearing the laughter as a new defiance of themselves.

"There is absolutely nothing to laugh about," Cecily protested.

"Will you ever learn to settle down?" Bennet asked rhetorically.

"Breakfast," Hester said to Maggie. "Breakfast for the parents. While I take Derek to Scorling."

She spoke in an undertone, but Bennet heard her.

"Not in my car," he declared.

"Why not?" said Hester. "You don't want Derek to be out of another job, do you?"

"I can go on the bus. The next one. Not long to wait for it, now."

Derek gave Hester a meaning glance as he spoke; a look that warned or begged her not to intervene. But she took no notice. She smiled sweetly and reasonably at Cousin Bennet, and said:

"Derek won't be out of a job, anyway. He has found the thing that suits him, and the owner of this shop wants him to go into partnership—which should show you that he's giving satisfaction. He didn't tell you about it because he knew you'd make an absurd fuss and say he was being irresponsible. I thought at first he was wrong not to tell you, but now I see he was right. Right, I mean, to prove to himself that he could make a success of it, before he told you about leaving the bank."

"It's a golden future," said Derek. "You see, I've already convinced Hester."

"It's an awfully nice shop," said Maggie. "In the little lane going to the station. It's called *Minnie Wildgoose*."

She burst out laughing, and Hester and Derek joined in. Luckily Bennet and Cecily did not realise that it was their expressions—confronted by the name of *Minnie Wildgoose*—that were so irresistibly comic.

"We must go," said Hester. "You don't mind our taking the car, do you?"

"I shall tell you all about it this evening," said Derek.

Mrs. Pilgrim, arriving in extra good time, found her employers sitting at the kitchen table, eating a scratch breakfast off the bare boards; a meal which they had got for themselves in the intervals between indignation, bewilderment and mutual sympathy. She knew why they were alone, of course (Derek and Miss Hester had gone off in the car, and Maggie had been opening the gates for them when Mr. Seamark drove up, and now she'd gone off with him), but she couldn't fathom why they were sitting here in the kitchen and looking so flabbergasted, and the beds not made or anything.

"The beds!" cried Cecily, seizing on this housewifely task as an escape from Mrs. P.'s searching eye.

"I'll come and give you a hand with them," Mrs. Pilgrim called after her.

But first she made another pot of tea; the kettle was simmering but they hadn't seemed to have noticed it, and the tea she poured away was cold dregs. "Did you have the end of *theirs*?" she asked, and the master said he supposed so. "Then you must have the start of mine to make up for it," she told him, forgetting about giving a hand with the beds and bringing her own tea-break forward by at least an hour. It wasn't like him to be so deflated; cross he could be, or inquisitive, or humorous, but not in her experience mute. He was sitting there as mute as her own husband.

Primed with hot, strong tea, and fired by an inquisitive spark from a kindred spirit, Bennet's sixth sense exploded into life. Not that it needed a sixth sense to see what lay in front of one's eyes and hear what was being practically shouted aloud; but the sixth sense analysed the evidence and without it he might as well have been blind and deaf. Now he was neither; nor, in the exuberance of recovery, was he dumb. Mrs. Pilgrim had always enjoyed her talks with the master, but never more so than today.

# CHAPTER TWENTY-FIVE

THE SPACE WHERE the attic window had been was now boarded up; a great nuisance for Mrs. Hyde-Ridley, who could no longer look up and down the village street from her own private eyrie. The lower windows did not give so extensive a view; and it was just good luck that she had been out of doors before breakfast that morning, hunting for one of the pussies who was due to become a mother any moment and who had been missing since the previous afternoon. Pussy and her kittens were subsequently found in the dark attic, happily settled in Mrs. Vandevint's hat-box; and that was her fault, for forgetting to close the lid when she put her hat away after the Fiesta. But before breakfast their whereabouts were still unknown and Mrs. Hyde-Ridley was worried in case Pussy had gone to have her kittens in the airing cupboard at the rectory, as had happened once before. A cat-loving Rector would not have minded, „ but neither Mr. Merlin nor his wife liked cats, and on the previous occasion they had not shown a Christian spirit towards Pussy, or towards her owner either.

That was why Mrs. Hyde-Ridley happened to be leaving the rectory at this unusually early hour. She was, of course, properly dressed and hatted, but she wasn't in her own opinion tidy enough to meet people. "Meeting people" did not apply to the

Rector's wife, who—as everyone knew—did the morning house-work in an old dressing-gown and a duster-cap, and therefore could be interviewed by someone who had not put the finishing touches to her own appearance without any feeling (on the side of the interviewer) of not being tidy enough. But it did apply to one's other friends and neighbours. Mrs. Hyde-Ridley had scuttled along the street to the rectory with her head well down, an ostrich-like manoeuvre which she believed would make her less visible; and afterwards, seeing the car drawn up outside The End House, she dodged behind the rectory gate-post and waited for it to go away. At the same time, naturally, she looked through the little chink between the gate-post and the wall, to see whose car it was.

"And Mr. Seamark was just getting out of it when Maggie Hutton opened the yard doors and saw him," she told Mrs. Van-devint. "And she called out that she was just coming as she was late, as he was saying he was too early. Then she came out in the street and went in at the front door as it was nearer I suppose as she was there by the car. And she was hardly a minute as I had just watched the car drive off when she was back again!"

"You mean he went away without waiting for her?" Mrs. Vandevint asked eagerly.

"No, no, Dulcie, the *other* car! Of course Mr. Seamark waited as I told you she was back in a minute."

"What other car?"

The hunt for Pussy had agitated Mrs. Hyde-Ridley and she was dimly conscious that she wasn't doing herself justice, not giving the news with her usual assurance and clarity. But really it was too stupid of Mrs. Vandevint, when she had *told* her about the yard gates being opened by Maggie before she came out to speak to Mr. Seamark.

"The Huttons' own car," she said angrily. "It came out of the yard and that was further away from where I was standing but I think it was Hester Clifford and Derek."

"Hester Clifford and Derek. Maggie and Mr. Seamark," said Mrs. Vandevint, thoughtfully.

"Oh, that would be just because Derek missed the bus," Mrs. Hyde-Ridley retorted. "He usually goes on the early bus to Scorling but he must have missed it. Hester Clifford would be taking him to Scorling as he's her cousin and cousins marrying is rather a mistake, isn't it?"

Mrs. Vandevint, who was less stupid than she looked and who was quite accustomed to Violet's swift transitions, followed her without much difficulty. She meant that Hester was taking Derek to Scorling because he was her cousin (cousinly goodwill) and that she would not think of marrying him because he was her cousin (cousinly caution). She nodded her agreement.

"My doctor says one can't be too careful," she said. "About first cousins marrying and that sort of thing. He says it always comes out in the children."

Mrs. Hyde-Ridley, slightly revived by burnt breakfast, suddenly remembered that Hester and Derek were not first cousins but only second ones. But she did not tell Dulcie because that would have meant admitting an error; she had certainly implied that they were cousins within the prohibited degree. Instead, she conjured up several doctors to dispute the opinion of the single oracle.

"Oh, but he's an old man," she said vigorously. "You ought to get a *younger* doctor—all the young ones say there's nothing in heredity! Why, all these modern doctors would tell you you could marry anybody! Still, I think it would be a mistake myself as he's a Hutton and I know they all die young."

Mrs. Vandevint lit a cigarette. It was on the tip of her tongue to say that Violet was behaving ridiculously—first saying cousins shouldn't marry and then saying they could; and still pretending Mr. Hutton was a dying man because he wore a shawl in the house; and rushing to open the window as if a whiff of cigarette smoke would suffocate her! The words were on the tip of her tongue, but they remained unspoken.

Poor old Violet. Getting up early, chasing after that wretched cat, had been a bit too much for her; she really looked quite shaky and it wasn't only because she had rouged one cheek and not the other. Staring at her old friend, Mrs. Vandevint had an instant's apprehension of a future when rouge and rachel pow-der and new hats weren't going to disguise the fact that she and Violet were getting on in years, and it caused her to swallow the words waiting on the tip of her tongue and to say instead that it looked like being a fine day.       .

"There's my woman!" shrieked Violet, jumping up as it the clatter of the pussies' tin plate had released some mechani-cal spring. Of course Mrs. Vandevint knew why she jumped up like a jack-in-the-box and rushed out of the room; it was to avoid, or at any rate postpone, the question of entertainment for today. It cheered her up at once, to see Violet acting as usu-al (how cunning she was, how ready to take advantage of one!), and she quickly began to make plans to counter Violet's plan (if she had one) of pretending that callers were due and staying quietly at home.

Thomas and Maggie intended to go to the sea; it was to be a pious pilgrimage to the place where they had gone on Maggie's tenth birthday, and it would also be a good excuse for starting early and escaping from Mingham for the whole day. Another day of avoiding congratulations and fuss.

Both of them realized that these would have to be faced, and that nothing could be kept private in Mingham where official announcements were always stale news. "Father is probably telling Mrs. Pilgrim about us this moment," said Maggie, "and she is probably telling him that she heard about us on Satur-day evening." And Thomas laughed and said that Mrs. Turle, his housekeeper, had congratulated him that morning at break-fast—in an oblique way, so that he could neither thank her nor take offence.

"How did she manage that?" Maggie asked.

"She gave me notice. Said she had been thinking of retiring and now the time had come—that she hadn't liked to leave me but now she knew I wouldn't miss her, and it was a great load off her mind to know she wouldn't be leaving me in the lurch."

"Oh, dear, you *will* be in the lurch without Mrs. Turle! As a housekeeper I shall be a poor substitute."

Thomas said, with truth, that he had been trying to part with Mrs. Turle for years, and that efficient housekeeping was the last thing he cared about.

Maggie's parents would have contradicted him, for they firmly believed that all Seamarks liked well-kept surroundings and preferred order to beauty. In a way this was true, but Maggie's shortcomings as a housekeeper were counterbalanced by the fact that she loved the Priory as much as Thomas did, and was as blind to its ugliness as the Seamark who built it. It was Thomas's home and therefore she loved it; not only the house but every object it contained. There would never be any arguments about getting rid of the trophies of the chase or re-papering the dining-room with something less funereal than dark grey stripes; there would never be any criticism of the Seamark ancestors or the artists who painted their portraits. Thomas and Maggie would live rather uncomfortably, without noticing it; for, in a house which so admirably suited both of them, comfort wasn't going to be missed.

But that was all in the future, a future so certain to be happy that it hardly needed to be discussed. Instead, they talked about the past, finding significance in trivial words and new meaning in perfectly ordinary encounters. And in the intervals between talking about themselves Maggie told Thomas about the parents and Derek and Hester, about the dramatic scene in the kitchen (which made him laugh), and the revealing moment when Hester had praised Derek while devotedly cooking his breakfast, and how everything was going to turn out all right for Derek after all, and for Hester as well.

"And for Mr. Frost?" he asked, after hearing as much about the antique shop as Maggie could remember.

"Well, of course it won't be his shop any longer, with Hester and Derek both running it."

"It won't even be there," said Thomas. "They'll move it to Salchester. Mr. Frost will wake up one morning to find that it's gone."

Maggie agreed that the country town, with its cathedral and other tourist attractions, would give Hester and Derek much more scope.

"They'll make their fortunes," she said.

"Your paragon of a Hester will make a fortune for both of them."

"Oh, darling, that's not fair! Hester really isn't as managing as all that."

Looking back, she could see Hester managing, or trying to manage, every situation that had occurred. But looking forward she could see a different Hester, happier and gentler and less scornful of other people's stupidity. Of course she would always be wonderfully efficient, but she wouldn't be so arrogantly self-confident as she had been in the past.

"She'll leave things to Derek, more than you think," she said. "Oh, look—look where we are! This is where we ran into the cow."

"A sacred memory," said Thomas. "I shall never forget how you screamed."

"You should have left this to me," said Derek.

He had waited to say it until Hester stopped the car outside the antique shop. But she knew he had been thinking it all the way to Scorling, behind his teasing about her fast driving and his prediction that old Frost would have rearranged the shop window and put up another card saying "Assistant wanted." She had known what he was thinking and she had had time to think of a reply: of convincing reasons for her intervention, and tangible evidence of its success. (Had not Bennet relented about the car?) But her actual reply was quite different.

"I'm very sorry I didn't," she said.

"It was my chance," said Derek. "My chance to speak up for myself and show Papa that I'd found the right job. It would have made a better impression if I'd said it myself, instead of letting someone else defend me."

"Yes, I realize it now."

"You would do better to point out to me that I'd had my chance and missed it," Derek remarked amiably. "I should have said my piece right at the beginning, firmly and loudly. I tried to, but I got side-tracked, bickering with you and Maggie about wheels within wheels. . . . No, I suppose I *let* myself get side-tracked, to stave off having to say my piece."

"Perhaps you did," said Hester. "But you would do better to point out to me that I was being frightfully interfering. That's what you were thinking, weren't you? And it's true. Instead of taking the blame yourself and apologising and being nice about it!"

"Now, now, Cousin Hester."

"Please stop calling me Cousin Hester. It's true. I—"

"I'll never call you Cousin again. Just Hester. Dear Hester."

"Dear goose—for goodness' sake stop thinking of me as another Raymond who will shy away from the slightest sign of bossiness because it's a threat to his ego. Unless, of course, you haven't really got over Raymond and are just looking for a good substitute. But I'm not like Raymond, am I?"

"No," said Hester. She tried again, but the words eluded her. "No," she said inadequately, "you are not."

And Scorling wasn't like London, and the antique shop wasn't in the least like the future she had once envisaged.

"Splendid," said Derek. "I don't want to be a substitute for anyone."

"You aren't going to be," she told him fondly.

The attic studio did not concern Mrs. Pilgrim; she had often made it clear that her ministrations stopped at the first floor, and if any dusting and sweeping was needed above that it must be done by Cecily herself. So her heavy tread on the uncarpeted attic stair was a plain warning of trouble to come.

"Of course," Cecily told herself. "Of course it *would* happen now. Troubles never come singly."

She left the studio and went to meet Mrs. Pilgrim on the dusty landing. "I've done the beds," she said allowing herself to speak quite sharply because tact no longer mattered. She knew, in her bones and everywhere else, that Mrs. P. had climbed the attic stair to give notice.

"So I saw," said Mrs. Pilgrim, speaking with equal sharpness. "If you'd only waited, I'd have helped you."

"I can't wait all morning, while you potter about down-stairs. And I suppose I shall have to get used to doing them by myself, now."

Cecily meant to rob Mrs. Pilgrim of her triumph; she meant to show her that it wasn't a bombshell, a bolt from the blue, or whatever Mrs. P. was counting on its being.

"I've been expecting this for some time," she added precipi-tately, staring her treasure full in the face.

"Have you really? That surprises me, I don't deny. And pot-ter I don't," said the treasure indignantly. "But this morning be-ing, as you might say, special . . ."

She broke off, as if false accusations were altogether unim-portant.

"I came up here to congratulate you," she said.

Cecily was standing at the top of the stair and it was as though she was standing on the edge of a precipice, over which her next step would have taken her. For the next step—or the next words—would have made it quite clear to Mrs. P. that her giving notice was neither a surprise nor a disaster; and would inevitably have produced the notice which she had not intended to give.

"Oh, thank you!" Cecily cried. Drawing back from the dread-ful precipice, she clutched at a hand for support. It was Mrs. Pil-grim's hand and she shook it effusively, accepting the congrat-ulations with all the joy that belonged to a very narrow escape.

"It'll seem strange though, won't it?" Mrs. Pilgrim said pres-ently. "This house is going to be much too big for you."

She was a treasure, privileged and esteemed. But sometimes she talked nonsense and Cecily had learned to ignore it.

"I don't think so," she answered lightly.

"Well—it'll seem kind of empty, won't it, if they all move out?"

"If they . . . ?"

"But you've still got me," said Mrs. Pilgrim, making a joke of it. Perversely, she added, "We shall be quite lost without Miss Hester and all her fancy cooking."

This was her parting shot, her little revenge for that nasty remark about her wasting her time pottering. She turned away and went stamping down the stairs, artfully muttering something about having to get on with her work.

Two minutes later, as she had forseen, Mrs. Hutton left the attic and came down to look for the master, calling his name and sounding all of a frenzy. Just what she had *not* "expected for some time," Mrs. Pilgrim thought scornfully. But there—she meant well enough and the master had brains for both of them.

"Mrs. Pilgrim's gone mad," said Cecily, bursting into the study where Bennet was taking a nap. "She thinks Hester—she said *Hester*—"

"Hester not Maggie?"

"But she's not leaving! But she said *they* were!"

"It'll seem kind of empty, won't it? That's what she said to me."

*"You've been talking to her," Cecily said disdainfully.

"I had to talk to someone. Sit down, and we'll discuss it as parents. I had to talk to *someone*!"

Cecily sat down. He had to talk to someone, and she had been up in the attic. He would never come up there to find her, because the attic was a studio and he had always been jealous of her painting. Of her "artistic temperament," which had made it impossible for her to live in the Midlands where their married life had begun. But if she hadn't come into that money they would have stayed in the Midlands, and he would have been the breadwinner and she would have been there to be talked to.

The painting craze was abating, Bennet thought. If it had not been on the wane Cecily would still be shut up in her attic, taking refuge in romantic landscapes and not worrying about anyone. Not rushing down to find him; not caring enough to reproach him for gossiping with Mrs. Pilgrim.

Still, it had been wrong of him to tell Mrs. P. what was happening before he told Cecily. Generously admitting his error, nobly admonishing himself for a failure in loyalty, Bennet almost managed to forget the genuine anxiety which had been with him since last night. But he could not quite forget it. The moment when Cecily walked out of the room had shown him how much he depended on her.

Already, this morning, surprise and dismay had drawn them together; they had sympathized with each other as parents, and it had been, so to speak, a rehearsal for the future. For it was as parents that they now settled down, to discuss the events of the morning and to shake their heads over the intransigence of the young. It was as parents that they presently found themselves in almost whole-hearted agreement, and it was as parents that they indulged themselves with sherry and cake, to make up for the miserable breakfast.

The End House had sheltered many generations, and its walls must have heard many repetitions of this scene, with abandoned, outdistanced parents finding unity in their grievances. As they were finding it now.

"I suppose I had better write to Malcolm," Cecily said.

"I'll do it if you like."

Bennet who never did anything he didn't wish to, whether other people liked it or not. And writing to Cecily's relations had been anathema to him for years.

"Derek should write, really," said Cecily. "Yes, why should we have the bother? It ought to be Derek."

Agreeing about this, they also agreed that Derek would never do it. Nor could he be made to, because he had somehow grown up while they weren't looking, and passed beyond their control.

Cecily fetched pencil and paper, and, with more sherry to inspire them, they sat down side by side to draft the letter.

"Parents have to do everything," they told each other, sadly and complacently.

THE END

# FURROWED MIDDLEBROW

Printed in Great Britain
by Amazon

61514842R00140